Climb to the Sky

CARAF Books
*Caribbean and African Literature
Translated from French*

Renée Larrier and
Mildred Mortimer, Editors

SUZANNE DRACIUS

Climb TO THE Sky

Translated by Jamie Davis

Afterword by Edwin C. Hill Jr.

University of Virginia Press
Charlottesville and London

Originally published in French as *Rue Monte au Ciel*,
© Éditions Desnel, 2003

University of Virginia Press
Translation and afterword © 2012 by the Rector and Visitors
of the University of Virginia
All rights reserved
Printed in the United States of America on acid-free paper

First published 2012

1 3 5 7 9 8 6 4 2

LIBRARY OF CONGRESS CATALOGING-IN-PUBLICATION DATA
Dracius-Pinalie, Suzanne.
[Rue Monte au ciel. English]
Climb to the sky / Suzanne Dracius ; translated by Jamie Davis ;
afterword by Edwin C. Hill Jr.
  p.   cm. — (CARAF books: Caribbean and African
literature translated from French)
  Includes bibliographical references.
  ISBN 978-0-8139-3319-1 (cloth : acid-free paper) — ISBN 978-0-8139-3320-7 (pbk. : acid-free paper) — ISBN 978-0-8139-3321-4 (e-book)
  I. Davis, Jamie, 1968– II. Title.
  PQ3949.2.D73R8413 2012
  843'.914—dc23
                                            2012009829

*To my son,
Germinal*

Great history is nourished by fables, do not forget it. . . . They call everything fabulous that is faraway, irrational, located in the past. . . . They do not understand that the fabulous is located in the future. Every future is fabulous.
—Alejo Carpentier, *Baroque Concert*

Contents

Her Destiny on Climb to the Sky Street
1

Sweat, Sugar, and Blood
79

The Three Musketeers Were Four
100

The Virago
119

Sister Soul
126

Chlorophyllian Creation
145

Oedipus on the Train
156

A Little Child Is Not a Speck of Rock
163

Written in Lime Juice
171

Afterword, by Edwin C. Hill Jr.
185

Bibliography
200

Her Destiny on Climb to the Sky Street

To Elmire, my Creole "ma"

Fire Mountain

In girum imus nocte et consumimur igni.
(We turn around in the night and are consumed by fire.)
—*Palindrome by Virgil*

"The Fire Mountain will avenge us!" the great Carib chief had yelled before giving himself up to death by throwing himself from the top of the gorge, baptized from that moment on as the "Tomb of the Caribs," rather than accepting servitude under the yoke of the conquistadors who had come from the other side of the seas. "Live free or die?" In the turbulent twilight of the fifteenth century, this man had made his choice.

Mount Pelée is not a spectacular volcano. It isn't a "red volcano," does not vomit those superb blushes of liquid lava flows that you can flee while watching them. When it explodes in anger, Pelée Mountain spits thousands of incandescent rocks that tear down its sides at a dizzying speed, and from which no one can escape.

"Ma Pelée isn't going to let them do it!" screamed the slave, rebellious against the slave drivers, when the twilight of the so-called century of "Enlightenment" fell and he saw vaguely dawning from afar a new revolutionary daybreak, without necessarily delivering him from the dark agonies of the *Black Code* or from the whip or from the "four pegs" or from croppings of the ears or from the brand of the hot iron or from barbaric mutilations.

2

Climb to the Sky

Far away, over there, on the Other Side of the ocean, one heroic Mirabeau had gone as far as to put the necessity of the colonies in doubt, affirming prophetically that France could prosper without this disgraceful system, fighting to set the revolutionary corps on a course for the abolition of slavery. He died on April 2nd, 1791.

But Leonard the slave knew nothing of this. The decree of the sixteenth of the fifth month of the French Republican calendar year III (February 4th, 1794) tried in vain to abolish slavery in the colonies; it was never applied, not in Saint-Pierre or elsewhere . . . The most influential members of the Society of Friends of Blacks, an ecclesiastic, a certain Abbot Grégoire, and a woman, a certain Olympe de Gouges, incited to the best of their ability in vain, but this decree was hastily repealed. A long time would have to pass, another revolution, then a Second Republic, all the persuasion of a Victor Schoelcher would be needed, all the sensitivity of a Lamartine, all the wisdom of an Arago, and even the prancing intervention of an Alexandre Dumas, so that in 1848, slavery was actually abolished. And still, with great difficulty, after hours and hours of stormy deliberations, with the intention of dealing carefully with the interests of the colonists, and leaving aftermaths! . . .

He would not live until then. For Leonard, the only remaining salvation was in escaping from his master. He had nothing left to lose, he, the slave from Saint-Pierre. Even if he knew with what tortures escape was punished . . . Even if he, Leonard, knew, through having experienced it in his flesh, that the escaped slave was chased like game, with huge dogs, nigger dogs, hunted up to the hills, with gunshots, and brought down without warning if he refused to give up. Give up? Why? So that the master would have the right, since the *Black Code* authorized it, to cut his hamstrings, to mark him with a red-hot iron on the other shoulder? . . . For he is a recidivist, Leonard the slave. The first time, when they got him back, he had his ears sliced, they marked him like a beast with a fleur-de-lys on his left shoulder. There will be no third time. He knows that the fugitive slave is punished by death. (It is written. Although he

3

Her Destiny on Climb to the Sky Street

does not know how to read, Leonard knows about it, because he has seen the hangings and other "warning executions," and because it's been told and repeated to him, bluntly, that for slaves, if you escape two times, the third time, you risk death!)

He already has death in his soul, his virtual and controversial nigger slave soul. He calls to death of his own will, since the woman he loved was sold in the South, in the outback of Vauclin, to a man from Souci. The master separated them. Their "mating" offended. The children they made together were too black, too rebellious. Escapee seeds, for whitey. Nothing but girls, however! . . . Just girls, as part of the bargain! That sold for a lot less than the pickaninny boys or girls. Especially escapee seeds with dark, ferocious looks like their own mother, Himitée, a tall, upright Negress who never accepted lowering her eyes, but burned with her live ember eye the eyes of any whitey.

Had she tried to rejoin him? The public rumor had rumbled, crossing Martinique from the South to the North, swelling from the Massy-Massy plantation to Saint-Pierre, reporting that, on the morning of the thirteenth, Himitée was flogged with twenty-nine strokes of the whip, bound to a ladder by her hands and feet, after having received from the overseer several punches in the face that broke three of her teeth, made her deaf in one ear and blind in her right eye. So that the blows would hurt more, the commander had added a fat, short block under her belly, on the express orders of Dispagne, the overseer of the plantation. She was four months pregnant. The next day, she had a miscarriage. ("No great loss! Damned breed! . . ." commented this devil of an overseer, as a funeral oration for this "dirty nigger bastard.")

Had they wanted to punish her for having chosen her companion, for not having accepted the stallion that the master was imposing on her? Would Himitée have turned down the advances of the commander, of the overseer, or, who knows, maybe the master himself, wanting to make little mulattos out of her, reputedly more docile, more amenable to "education," more decorative for serving at the White Man's table?

Climb to the Sky

Translated simply into correctional policy, Mr. Jules Dispagne has been condemned to fifteen days in prison, ladies and gentlemen!

"This is not gossip, alas!" the unfortunate Leonard lamented, in his flight, under a purifying, beneficial rain: he had his news from the mouths of the gendarmes themselves! These same mounted gendarmes who had been sent "to reestablish order" in Saint-Pierre at the time of the slave uprisings that were multiplying endlessly, burning the plantations and endangering the colonists who had mistreated "their niggers." He no longer believed in revolts, which were never anything other than riots, never revolutions, from which they ever only got beatings, if they managed to escape from them, then were put down in blood. He had had enough suffering. Enough giving his blood for nothing, enough undergoing tortures to end up going back to pour his sweat and his blood making that damn sugar. Of sweat, sugar, and blood . . . Enough of this perpetual recommencement, of this endless damnation weighing on his nigger head! And now, Himitée! . . . It was too much. Even if it means getting caught again, too bad!

He would walk, hiding himself by day, walking through trails and shrubbery at night, with opossums and manatees his only companions. He would go alone into the darkness—the darkness of his amputated body, of his tenebrous memories and the protective shadow of the night—lit up, as if by winks of an eye, by the elusive lights of fireflies. The stars in the sky would guide him. Leonard was heading toward a place unknown to him, a mythical place, a symbol of freedom for the black man: the hills of the North. A haven of wild peace, inaccessible to evil persons, where he had never gone, but where the beautiful air sang clandestinely to the sound of the *gros ka* drum, of which they spoke without having to spell things out at the time of the cassava vigil, the night of Saturday through Sunday. The next day was the Lord's Day: the slaves could drain and grind the cassava; they could spend sleepless nights there: the next day, they didn't work. It was God's will. Leonard would take advantage of it to slip away. On Sunday morning, the

Her Destiny on Climb to the Sky Street

mass would be a diversion; the alert would be given later. This would give him a head start to distance himself from his pursuers. This time, he would succeed. This time, he would not fail to pinch a share of pepper to sprinkle on his heels in the hope that it would aggravate the noses of the nigger dogs let loose in pursuit of him. Oh, those dirty beasts! If he got his hands on one, he would cut its throat. The scars from their bites still blistered his flesh. The marks of their fangs had become forever embedded in his body as in his memory. He would not forget his cutlass! He was ready to kill to live. It was perhaps not their fault, these huge dogs, that they had this ferocity. Their rage in tearing black flesh to shreds was not natural to them: the white man had given it to them, by feeding these brave beasts on nigger flesh. This wasn't a legend told at the cassava vigil. Leonard had seen it himself.

At that time, they didn't call him "Leonard": they had not baptized him yet. The man bore his name from Guinea, his title of being free: Noh-La-Har. They trampled him, Noh-La-Har. They denigrated him, maimed him. Disfigured him. Mutilated him. Rode roughshod over him, the dashing African warrior, dispossessed of himself. Noh-La-Har or Leonard, the man had really seen too much of it.

He had seen with his own eyes, on the slave ship that took him far from Africa, the beginning of the horror. They had left Gorée Island moons and moons ago, suffered terrible tempests, but the worst was yet to come. Without being able to make a timely stopover for provisions, the slave ship diverted, tossed about by bad winds, wracked by famine and fevers. The food shortage decimated the crew. The Negroes were dying like flies. A few of them threw themselves ahead of a certain death by swallowing their own tongues. Noh-La-Har still had the will to live.

Only the most robust young men and women survived. Lost at sea, with no resources left, the master on board ordered that the mastiffs be fed at all costs. A colonist from the Antilles was awaiting their delivery and they had not been paid for. But with what meat to feed those animals? How to keep them alive?

Climb to the Sky

The client would only pay for them upon receipt. Certainly, the cargo of living "ebony wood" was eminently precious, but hardly as precious as these "pedigree" dogs, a burdensome order from a marquis, one of those "Messieurs from Martinique." These expensive beasts had to be fed no matter what the cost! Dead, these dogs would be worth nothing. On the other hand, the bodies of the niggers, even deprived of life, could prove of some use . . .

Why not accustom these mastiffs to tasting their future game? After all, were these dogs not destined for nigger hunting? This would only be a sort of training! The industrious captain thus had the malicious idea of feeding the dogs with the nigger cadavers that were piling up in the steerage posing the risk of epidemics, instead of throwing them into the sea. He had more urgent things to do than feeding sharks! Too bad for them! The dogs first. Thus the happy man congratulated himself, for he was offering himself in this instance a double satisfaction, in the joy of doing his job well: not only was he ensuring "hygiene" on board, but he was fulfilling his contract by giving the dogs things to eat. A beautiful benefit in perspective! To have a clear conscience and to "keep things in order," the captain recorded in the very official ship's log the quantities and "portions" of dead Negroes served raw to the dogs. Why the choice of these crudités? To arouse their cruelty and perfect his beautiful business of canine training. He grew more enthusiastic, anticipating being richly compensated for it.

In the long run, the famine lasting without the cry of "Land Ho!" ever being heard, the captain's face darkened: the doctor on board seemed scarcely to have time to verify that the Africans dead from hunger or suicide were not afflicted by scurvy (if their teeth were not loose), so as not to run the risk of contaminating his precious big dogs. This negligence bothered him; it was his only source of worry. As for everything else, he was convinced that there had not been the slightest breach.

When they arrived in view of the coasts of Martinique, the captain of the slave ship could congratulate himself, all things considered: thanks to his brilliant rationing policy, there was

Her Destiny on Climb to the Sky Street

enough tafia rum left to practice mating. It was the tradition, the rule. It was the law of sea people, on slave ships. Hurricane or no hurricane, rationing or no rationing, they didn't break from the tradition. Obviously, thanks be to God, the conscientious captain would have fulfilled his mission to the end, up to the most minor details. The ship owner would be grateful. He was allocating Negresses to the white crewmen to make them pregnant, in order to make in advance, before the sales, low-cost people of mixed race. Here the operation proved doubly fruitful: it lifted the morale of the sailors and made "hybrids" who would bring in a lot of money at the sale. A pregnant Negress was worth twice as much. Impregnated by a white man, a young black girl could be sold for an even greater price. This would compensate for the losses. His boss would be pleased with him.

With jubilant haste, the captain broached barrels and Negresses. Although weakened and half-dead from hunger, the seamen then found in the drink the strength to mate, drunk with exhaustion and rum, with the surviving Negresses, half-dead from malnutrition and shame. Chained, petrified with horror, the few surviving African men could not help them. The captain was on cloud nine. The brave man rubbed his hands. He almost applauded. The crew members seemed to go wild more bestially than usual. The alcohol, in their famished bodies, produced more than the ordinary effect.

This is what they did to his women. This is what the white men did and continued to do to the women of his race. Noh-La-Har saw too much of it. He saw the splendid blue pickaninny who troubled his heart and his body brought down into the half-light of the steerage. The same one he liked to see, but whom he had respected, all throughout the crossing, the African man saw her brought down, blood between her two beautiful thigh quarters, when she stepped over the bodies to go back to sleep, slouched, aged by ten years, unrecognizable. Odds were that in the abomination of the mating, it was she who had had the greatest success . . . She was the most desirable. Woe unto her! She remained sublime, however; she came

Climb to the Sky

out more womanly and more steadfast from the disgrace of the mating.

Heroism was surviving. Through some unknown miracle, Noh-La-Har was one of the rare survivors of this slave ship.

Noh-La-Har or Leonard, the African had seen too much, suffered too much, in the blackness of his great body and his candid "good nigger," beautiful expensive "pièce d'Inde," magnificent "ebony wood" soul, greatly impressing his masters, and their fortune, when they sold him on the auction block at the Saint-Pierre slave market of Martinique. They would put no more shackles on him. He would no longer be a "good nigger." He would be a runaway Negro.

Even if he is hungry, even if he is sick, he will never be as hungry or as sick as during his captivity.

As if he needed it to justify his cruelty, the overseer chanted the *Black Code* while they were administering the punishments to him. The hoarse voice of an alcoholic flogged his cut ears. "Article 36: The thefts of sheep, goats, pigs, poultry, sugarcane, peas, millet, cassava, or other vegetables committed by the slaves will be punished according to the caliber of the theft, by judges, who will be able if required to sentence them to being beaten by switches by the executor of High Justice, and marked with a fleur-de-lys," the raspy drunkard voice recited in a drone, stumbling over the complicated words that, anyway, Leonard only half understood, words that, in Negro memory, no slave had ever understood and would never understand.

"Article 42: Only masters will be able, when they believe that their slaves have deserved it, to have them chained up and have them beaten by switches or ropes . . ." continued the harsh voice, mispronouncing words of more than three letters and flaying the slave caught eating a little bit of sugar during his work. They had to produce the sugar, but it was forbidden to eat it. They put a muzzle on him, on the famished sugar thief!

So, go let it be heard that this so-called *Black Code* is signed by the very hand of the king of France, Louis XIV, the Sun King, written by the most illustrious Mr. Colbert, oh righteous

Her Destiny on Climb to the Sky Street

minister! Go try to explain to him that this *Black Code* means him no harm—Leonard would refuse to believe it. This corrupt code regulated and legitimized his torture, gave a civilized appearance to the maneuvers of the lower ranks of the police and the other dirty tricks of the commander: this is all there was to understand. If they mentioned this *Black Code* to Noh-La-Har again, he saw red. They could treat him like a beast, but not take him for stupider than he is! The only sun king he knows is the one that climbs to heaven, very high, in the middle of each day, that ate his head, that tore his shoulders to pieces, and then gnawed his skin in the furnace of the sugarcane fields, when he sweated the sweat of his body to make the colonist fat.

After coming out of so many tortures, the African can suffer no longer. What he saw is no longer suffering; it is a challenge that he imposes on himself. The last, the sole, the only challenge of his own choosing, of his own guidance and of his own movement. If he triumphs, he will live. He will live free. If not, he will welcome death with great calm. His soul will return to Guinea.

The runaway takes a deep breath. In spite of the palpitations caused by anguish and the hard journey of an injured man, Leonard would manage very quickly to discipline his heart, without becoming afraid of its hastened beatings, without fearing these knocks on his temples. His ears, they cut them, but without taking away from him the power he has to listen to his heart. He would hear it beat strongly, not as a sign of trouble, but as the presence of a friend who will never cease being free. Finally, he would feel himself live.

He would run away, as far away as his strength and his cut hamstring would allow. Fleeing Saint-Pierre, infirm but firm and fierce, he would go back up more toward the North, up to the hills inaccessible to the nigger dogs, to the heights of Grand Anse. There, he would wait for Himitée. At every twilight, blowing his conch horn, then beating his drum, sitting

Climb to the Sky

astride his *gros ka* drum, relayed from the North all the way to the South, from hill to hill, by other brother conch-horn blowers and other young goatskins stretched over other empty tafia rum barrels, all the way down to the bottom of the Massy-Massy plantation, he would let Himitée, the upright Negress, know that Leonard, the runaway nigger, was waiting only for her in the heights of Grand Anse. She would join him there again one day. They would have their descendants there, delivered from all restrictions. Their own children, not the master's. Their own children. Free, at last. Under the protection of the *loas*. Children who would belong to them. Himitée would no longer be tortured. To spare her children the horror of servitude, she would no longer need to resort to abortions using medicinal herbs that put her life in danger.

Unless, tired of the solitude and the suffering of his memories, throughout the course of nights and days with the image of Himitée fading, one fine morning Leonard ventures to dispel the nostalgia for Himitée in the arms of that cheerful girl with high cheekbones, a descendant of the last Caribs who had fled to the North upon the arrival of the first European colonists. (For not all of them had thrown themselves into the void following their chief, into the Tomb of the Caribs, after putting out their eyes. Some, their eyes wide open, confronted with the destiny of their people, preferred life to collective suicide. They sought refuge more to the north, in the steep slopes of the solitary hills. Opting for a different form of courage than voluntary death, these Caribs chose a solution certainly less spectacular, but no less heroic: that of the fight for survival, simultaneously perilous and harsh, called back into question every morning, at every daybreak and every nightfall.)

In each clear twilight, the beautiful woman climbed up the narrow, craggy path singing. All of a sudden Leonard would hear her, and then suddenly her copper-colored body would make its appearance, emerging from among the arborescent ferns, balancing in casual turns her custard-apple basket crammed with appetizing victuals, putting water in his mouth.

Intrepid, playing with danger, the young Carib woman came

Her Destiny on Climb to the Sky Street

every day to bring fresh supplies of cassavas and country vegetables grown by her community to the runaways on the top of the hill. Her ancestors were part of that rare group of Caribs who, preferring flight to suicide, escaped genocide by hiding themselves in the mountains of the North in order not to be reduced to slavery by the pale, "long-eared" invaders.

Each day the luscious West Indian girl bartered the fruits from her Caribbean garden for the game hunted by the runaway Leonard or the beautiful living crawfish for which the man fished barehanded in the Saint-Jacques River. Everything suggested that from this constant trading would be born the mother of the child they would christen Leona.

"I am removing my feet from this city of debauchery," the furious bishop predicted pompously, leaving Saint-Pierre by shaking the dust off his sandals, a few decades earlier.

It must be admitted that, in the "Pearl of the Caribbean," this "Heaven of the Windward Islands," the most populous of the communes in Martinique, with the false airs of a capital, this "Little Paris of the Antilles," as it had been nicknamed, certain people lived the good life! ... Carnivals into bacchanalias and all-night sprees, not a very Catholic good life, in the eyes of the upstanding cleric, who saw only black masses, blasphemy, and fornication there. It smelled like sulfur and ash, to his irritated nostrils, amid the orgy-filled madness, in an ambiance of decadence, an atmosphere of fiendish end-of-century frenzy, this insolent, blazing, crepuscular colonial fever of the nineteenth century coming to an end. (At least for those who had the means to do it, within this Creole society, the few privileged people who could offer themselves final orgy-filled nights in Saint-Pierre.) The bishop saw witching hours there. The good apostle imagined only copulations at these parties, only lasciviousness in these dances. He heard only obscenities in this singing. For him, this flourishing city was Gomorrah in the Tropics. The prelate left without greeting these people who were going to die.

Climb to the Sky

Fast-living walking dead, those people of Saint-Pierre, taking everything into account! As usual, the Carnival season had opened in January, immediately after the Epiphany; they gave themselves over to it in full joy, to the "Great Casino balls" and to the "masked Balls of the Trocadéro." And the bacchanalias continued, in the political turmoil. The century was only one year old—even if some people, following the example of Victor Hugo, unleashed, in the local press, an impish polemic, like in the very serious Catholic newspaper *Les Antilles*, where the purist grandpa proclaimed, "No, poet, you are wrong; the century wasn't two years old, but just over one year, it was starting its second year." He attached a friendly carefreeness to Saint-Pierre.

"There's no way in this house!" the little servant girl exploded suddenly. "I'm going to leave. I'm gone. A very good morning to you, companions!"

In this muggy twilight of the dawn of a day meant to stand out in history and in this newborn century, the little servant girl has a premonition that her destiny is being strangely drawn.

At Climb to the Sky Street, in the rooms, things were really cooking! Especially in Leona's tiny little chamber. Although normally, at that time of the year, the sunrises are fresher, for there are hardly any fat clouds to keep back the diurnal heat, the temperature is unbearable on this morning of Thursday, May 8th, 1902. For some time, in her little room beneath the attic, she had put a lit candle out to burn even during the day, out of a good Christian woman's devotion, not as a church hypocrite, mind you! A pious little Catholic believer, just a good little convert, very diligent in her religious studies—a fierce soul, all the same, following the example of her ancestors, Negroes from Africa and proud Caribs.

The wax, in melting, formed a Virgin. That was a sign. Leona gathered her things, and then she closed up her old clothes in her Caribbean basket. The puny basket concealed all her treasures: her wax Virgin, a novel by Alexandre Dumas with the premonitory title *Twenty Years After*—her most recent petty theft—the pencil portrait of her mother, languid in

Her Destiny on Climb to the Sky Street

a rocking chair, nicely "sketched" in a rush by Paul Gauguin, and the solitary Totor earned at such a great cost.

Everything became so hard and so strange, from then on: birds no longer sang, no longer could the little nocturnal concert of the frog be heard. The milk of the cows was drying up, people were having nightmares, snakes had come all the way down from the Mountain up to the plantations . . . The Ancients had predicted the worst. The earth had even trembled, an underground detonation had rattled the city, a column of black smoke had escaped from the volcano. In Prêcheur, there was panic; it had become night in the middle of the day, the runaways were flocking to Saint-Pierre, convinced that they would be safer there. If only they had known, the poor souls! . . . Metamorphosed into a torrent, the White River had carted along a burning mud, buried the Guérin factory, killing all its workers. Pelée was only talking in misgivings: a bizarre brightness had emanated from its summit, dreadful falls of ashes and incandescent blocks hurtling down its slopes.

Decidedly less sulfurous but just as worrisome and just as unbearable as the brimstone emanations burped by Mount Pelée, the Mistress had become more and more cantankerous, more and more tyrannical, and Leona was shocked that she hadn't had her period in a good while.

Bizarre: since the end of April, this column of blackish vapors that rose from the Dry Pond, these rumbles that made themselves heard . . . It smelled like sulfur: "I've had enough of smelling this odor of rotten eggs!" Madam complained endlessly. And the flow of the White River that tripled in a few hours! Last week, when the morning pipiri bird sang, Leona was awakened by tremors, in an atmosphere of a boiler, a demonic uproar of detonations and sparks making grooves in the portion of the sky visible through the skylight in her attic room. That night, Leona was alone. No one to reassure her. Madam considers herself safe, between the cut-stone walls of her plush residence . . . But Leona did not feel sheltered anywhere, shut away in her garret, fleeing the electrical discharges only to find the Master in her sheets.

Climb to the Sky

When at dawn the firemen water the street, strewn with a sowing of ashes filtering the habitual sounds of a city awakening, Madam's bitter voice rises: "Go put out the volcano's fire instead, cowards!"

As for Leona, she had neither the heart nor the spirit for mockery. Even if the shaft of smoke has turned white, from then on, Leona feels oppressed. When the ashy cloud blurs, then comes back more bitter, lower, thicker than ever, her determination is clear. Coming out of an infernal night, pierced with the illuminations and stridencies of the storm, she had to confront the impudence, the false friendship, then the lightning of her Mistress! . . . It was too much.

It had not started badly, however, this year 1902, if the Master of the house's newspapers are to be believed, the ones he abandoned everywhere, in the four corners of his vast residence, to the great displeasure of his wife, allergic to this disorder and to what it represented, but to the greatest happiness of Leona, who, under the pretext of straightening up, hurried to glean the precious pages of *L'Opinion* or the *Colonies* that were dispersed here and there and took her mind off things without her Mistress knowing it. When the Master didn't come bother her in her attic room, the little woman treated herself in secret, scouring them from one end to the other, including the little advertisements that sometimes gave her joy or filled her with hope. Thus, on her pseudo-housewife investigations, she savored, often several weeks late, such and such enthusiastic editorial, incisive or inspired, cynical or deceptively naïve, like the one from the *Proletarian*, dated Saturday, December 23rd, 1901: "In a few days the year 1901 will take its place among its sisters that constitute centuries past. It will give its place to its young sister 1902. A new year is thus going to begin soon. What does it hold? Will it bring a little more well-being, more justice? . . . If 1902 should not be the year of deliverance, it can at least serve toward bringing us closer to the goal, to get us reforms capable of improving the Proletariat's lot." But who would worry about improving her own lot?

Her Destiny on Climb to the Sky Street

Without completely understanding what she was reading, Leona had plunged herself, over the course of months and years, in the twists and turns of political issues with lively delight, almost as exquisite as her dives in the waters of the Saint-Pierre harbor, and just as forbidden—with this remarkable pleasure of banned things, that, if she found out about them, would earn her Madam's lightning!

Tired of brooding over her bad premonitions and her immense resentments, the little servant girl from then on had only one desire: to leave Climb to the Sky Street, the hulking cut-stone "high and low" building, more and more topsy-turvy, yes, to leave Climb to the Sky Street, the cracker woman, her little crackers, and her cracker of a husband. To leave Climb to the Sky Street and its funerary atmosphere! To leave Saint-Pierre!

She loved this town, however. She loved it undeniably, to the point of adoration, fascinated by its magnificence, the opulence of its buildings, its hot springs, its cathedral, its Ursuline convent, its Palace of Independence, and especially its proud theater.

But she had no rights to the city, in that Theater of Comedy. She would never set foot there. She would never climb up its apotheotic flight of stairs, far from the apocalyptic attic room on Climb to the Sky Street. She would never escape to a magical firmament, never would she feel the vertigo of flying toward multiple lives, characters out of the ordinary, roles inspiring admiration and pity, unbelievable denouements, guile, misunderstandings, true and false admissions, dramatic turns of events, in ascending her two-revolution staircase. It would have been a revolution, in the Saint-Pierre microcosm, to see such a swarthy woman at the Comedy! What a farce! Through what scandalous mystery? For her, more than an emotion, more than a social evolution, a veritable miracle that would play out in her life . . .

May it be given to her, just one time, having the Revelation of a young handsome leading man as a god, even a *deus ex machina,* far from the eschatological loft!

She, a domestic pickaninny, could only imagine, from her clandestine readings by the light of a puny candle, these

Climb to the Sky

nocturnal illuminations, the sumptuousness of those decorations, the munificence of that gold, the splendor of the tragedies that they put on there. She, Leona, lived a drama, behind the hundred-year-old stones of a particular hotel. An odd and secret drama. A drama that was only too real, a drama whose somber reality she dreaded each nightfall. However, the young servant could not keep herself from dreaming wide awake about the vaudevilles and comedies that were given at the theater, representing marvels, being envious of Madam all dolled up, adorned with her fat gold beads, when she saw her getting dressed, putting on her best outfit, made up, powdered, curled. Then she realized. She considered bitterly to what point she, Leona, was a persona non grata in this world.

But nothing prevents her from dreaming that she is going up to the oneiric heaven of the Theater of Comedy. No one can desecrate her dreams.

In a hurry to taste another quality of pleasure, the Master, back at home, stumbled up each one of the seventy-four steps of this vertiginously steep street that is Climb to the Sky Street, which is only, all things considered, a colossal staircase of cut stone leading to the Seminary, after multiple zigzags between countless brothels. Located at the edge of the sea, in that alley called Hell Street, because it was the hottest of all the back streets where all the Saint-Pierre streetwalkers abounded, his favorite one was worthy of its original name of *Bordeau*. This whorehouse concealed the most diabolical temptresses, good for broadside sailors and to satisfy the most shameful fantasies of the bourgeois men whose wives barely even inspired them to reproduce. Good and drunk, the Master generally went down Hell Street, after a roundabout trip through the stuck-together-hold-her-tight Anchorage balls, to the Dionysian Crystal Palace, and a detour through the torrid sheets of some matador woman from the Saint Philomène neighborhood, to the house of "Baby Face," to the Casino or to the bottom of Bouillé Street, in the gambling circles or other houses of ill-repute where the guy was a good client, before getting back home.

Her Destiny on Climb to the Sky Street

At the end of his ascent, once back home, on Climb to the Sky Street, there were still three times six steps for the drunkard to take, in his tall stone house, to climb up to Leona's attic room. Staggering, he brought back some unpleasant odor from the Comedy, alas, polluted by the stenches of rum—of all ages and colors—and the heady perfumes of the whores that he was pawing afterward—they, too, of all ages and colors—coming out of the spectacle, before ending up, stinking and sweating, sometimes dripping with vomit, clothes disheveled, his zipper still open, in Leona's attic room. (This sloppiness earned him, in spite of his royalist ideas, the nickname "No-Pants.") Lecherousness at its extreme, not content with diligently frequenting the whorehouses of Climb to the Sky Street, No-Pants tried to ascend to seventh heaven in Leona's little room. However, the insatiable man agreed only grudgingly to tell her, in total haste, about the room seen not long ago, impatient to go on to something else. Misery! The essence of the plot, a dramatic or vaudevillian one, had already dissipated in the alcoholic vapors and courtesan plots. She only had a right to fripperies.

As for asking to go there! ... In the house on Climb to the Sky Street, Leona is no less shut away than the unhappy loose women from the brothels. "The THEATER? And what's worse than that? What comedy? That isn't a place for servants, after all, Leona, are you crazy? What would I look like if I dragged you along with me? And then, who would pay for your seat? One year of your wages would not suffice, my child! Are you not thinking? What exactly is this Negrohood? You're not going to play some nigger trick on me?" begged No-Pants.

As if by another sign from the Gods, a bizarre bankruptcy closed the Comedy, one year ago, fateful omen! First destroyed by a hurricane, then renovated time and time again, its restoration had needed, the previous year, a loan so Pharaonic that it never would have gotten out from under it. Anyway, therefore, even if they let her, through whatever miracle she did not know, Leona could not go there! Nothing else is keeping her within these walls!

Climb to the Sky

Of Saint-Pierre, this city of pleasures, sophistication, and ostentatious richness, the only meager delights that this "nigger child" knew, in spite of all its haughtiness, the only splendors that were offered to her, in order to flee the brutality and ancillary seductions, were diving into the sea.

Yes, that was her only luxury there, to wash the lust off herself. What's more, a forbidden luxury! But this time, she paid dearly for it.

"Worse than Sodom, a brothel of shit!" swore the priest. "The great Saint Pierre's hair must be standing up on his head! When they present themselves before him on the Day of Final Judgment, they will see what their vice is worth! If they believe that he will want them in Heaven! . . ." Leona caught only one side of it, and the worst, of this Saint-Pierre decadence, in her little room under the roof, at the end of Climb to the Sky Street.

Leona doesn't much feel like climbing up to the sky right away, nor does she feel like seeing Saint Pierre, even if it were for him to give her the key to Heaven, like the priest had said. "Yes, even if it were to go to look for the key in his hands, I am not in a hurry. I would even wait a little bit."

At any rate, she has nothing to lose: "The Mistress is so hard!" And everything was becoming so disturbing . . . Leona had seen a black column of cinders and vapors rise from the volcano, on the 24th of April.

She was seething in her attic room: "I've had enough! I can't stand staying here anymore. One day it's night in the middle of the day. One night, the earth trembles three times in a row . . . In the sky, not a single bird. And furthermore, I can no longer look at this black smoke. Impossible: I can't see the end of it! Housekeeping! I never finish cleaning all Madam's porcelain that she bought in the ritzy store at the seaside, her silverware set, her crystal . . . I'm not going to clean up everything for her like that until her tail screws in! And the thanks I get! My great big salary is a misfortune. As for the rest . . . I don't even want to think about it . . . not even dream about it."

Her irritation was such that she didn't even feel like reading

Her Destiny on Climb to the Sky Street

anymore, she who was so fond of reading. In her anger, Leona sent the pages of an old copy of the *Opinion* dated Tuesday, January 7th, 1902, fluttering, forgotten among the stack of newspapers regularly stolen from the Master, who really got everything from the press, including *Voice of the Mulatto and Masonic Party*. Ah! Saint-Pierre's newspapers! There were so many of them! Leona enjoyed them thoroughly. Each time she managed to pinch them from the Master to decipher them on the sly, wearing out her eyes in the dim light of the candle, Leona found mind-blowing things there.

The Master bought them all, every day: "Because of his politics! His damn politics!" grumbled Madam. All the daily newspapers landed on a daily basis in all corners of the house, even the voice of the French Masons, putting Madam his wife into fits all the time, who said with loathing again and again: "Will you burn these rags?" before taking it out on the little servant girl as soon as the Master had his back turned. "Don't stick your nose in there, vagabond! That's trash. I don't even want them to wipe my ass." On a regular basis Madam challenged her husband: "Go read that at the café! Those things will not come into my house!"

A big title caught her glance: in the "News and News in Brief" column, after a farcical story entitled "DRAMATIC DEATH," telling with humor and a hint of irreverence about the demise of the police officer Desanti, whose mare had bolted, they told about a theft of jewels where the "matadors" lived. And the gossip columnist pretended to be surprised, with the salacious tone of feigned admiration, that these women of easy virtue "earned some real treasures" . . . but what held her attention was the article headlined "THE HEALTH OF MISS CLÉMENT." Who was this illustrious unknown woman? Leona did not have the honor of knowing her . . . She was surely not from this world . . . What was she, to be worth the effort for them to publish her health report in a great daily newspaper of Saint-Pierre? Doubtlessly some Creole lady from local high society with a lily-white and rose complexion made pale by her illness, could it be consumption, phthisis? No, typhoid

Climb to the Sky

fever, the journalist specified, reassuring his readers: the precious health of the lady continued to improve, "according to the opinions of her doctors." Several doctors for her alone? The little offspring of a mulatto and a black would just like to see a single doctor, she who never saw one, from near or from afar! . . . She would really need the help of medicine! It would not be out of vanity, Leona started dreaming, if they took care of her in her state, more and more worrisome.

Is there, in this good city of Saint-Pierre, a single good soul interested in her fate? Sad, forsaken, far from her people, the little servant girl still does not know that an undreamt-of passion has already been gazing longingly at her for long months. If she dreams about protection, fervent Catholic that she is, it's toward Heaven that she turns, but she expects nothing from humans, especially those from Climb to the Sky Street. For the time being, Leona no longer believes in friendship, and does not yet believe in love. And yet, thus far, love has appeared to her only under one of its most unpleasant aspects and by coercion. What Madam's husband pompously calls "making love" seems meaningless to her, purely physical. Leona is disgusted by everything. From the bottom of her dark cubbyhole, the entire universe seems devoid of feelings, and the muffled threat rumbling on the sides of Pelée Mountain scares her less than the cataclysm that she sees descending on her life and about which she has premonitions, from the very depths of her belly.

Belly of Air

"More of your filth!" Madam yells out. "I thought I had already told you that I didn't want these obscenities in my house anymore! Out of my sight! Take that away from me immediately! Make that disappear, I tell you!" orders the Gorgon, pointing her plump right index finger at her innocent victim, the inoffensive *Voice of the Worker Party* that is hanging on the arm of an armchair. The unfortunate *Proletarian* risks ending up in the trash can, if Leona doesn't save it covertly, doesn't grip it under her smock, until this evening, taking advantage of Madam's plunge into an abyss of bewilderment.

Her Destiny on Climb to the Sky Street

"Really, he is stuck on it ... What in the world can interest him with these sorts of people, these 'Red' niggers? What is his idea spending his time and his money buying these rags? ..."

It is true that the Master is passionate about politics. The Master is subscribed to all the newspapers, without exception, even to the impertinent *Voice of Martinique Democracy*, even to *Freedom of the Colonies*, even to the *Republican Voice of Martinique*, so diametrically opposed to his monarchist ideas, even to this biweekly that is so boring but of the proper Catholic complexion, the *Antilles*, "Industrial, Commercial and Agricultural Newspaper of Martinique."

Leona reads them all on the sly. Even if she doesn't understand everything, she devours them, from the first to the last line. In her bulimia of reading, she is capable of gulping down the most insipid articles, of sacrificing her sleep time to stuff herself on the blandest, most insignificant news. She swallows everything. It matters little, as long as she is reading. She is always waiting for something. She knows that there will always be, somewhere, in the midst of a page, once she's gone past the platitudes and society life and the nonsense, a sudden illumination, a truth: the discovery, for example, in the *Opinion*, that "210,000 men of color live on this island, scorned and exploited by 7,000 white men." Or, in the *Proletarian*, in a not-so-old edition, by luck!, dated last February 22nd, that even if Roosevelt "is himself a bourgeois," ... however, "this conservative is a revolutionary, in the sense that he goes vehemently against one of the most entrenched and most violent prejudices of the nation over whose destiny he presides. Americans, be they bourgeois or proletarians, have a hatred of the Negro ... He (Roosevelt) set himself deliberately on the task ... The most odious of fanaticisms will have to bow before the energy of a man who makes himself look taller through his love for humanity." And Leona making a hero out of this unknown president of a far-off America, who "incurred the jibes of the entire press by receiving a black man at the presidential table, Washington, a man of great merit, to whom the damned race owes several schools and a university." All these words

Climb to the Sky

made her dream. She reread them a thousand times, looking in the dictionary for the ones she did not know. Even if the realities that they made her glimpse seemed dreamlike to her, they enthralled her much more than the sad reality of Climb to the Sky Street.

Besides these epiphanies, Leona learns, here and there, that "the city of Bristol, infested with rats, had 10,000 mongooses ordered to Jamaica to destroy them" and that "Mr. Turquet, the former undersecretary of state, entered the order of the R. P. Franciscans in Paris. Mr. Susini, the fiery former minister of Corsica, also entered the order of the R. P. Franciscans." A fat lot of good that will do her, but she travels far, Leona, she escapes, through this exoticism, far from Climb to the Sky Street, thanks to her newspapers and her books. Well, their books! Those of the Master and those of Madam . . . But she appropriates them for herself, with no guilt, since she loves them. She is the only one who appreciates them at their true value. Besides, she's the only one who really reads them. The Master only fishes for what concerns him, he only skims over them, on the lookout for the occasion to tap on the paper while ranting:

"Look here at these hoodlums, my dear! . . . Listen to this, Euryale: 'This time it was not a free thinker who got himself buried "like a dog," but an authentic white woman, a lady from the upper aristocracy. Refusing all prayers, all religious ceremonies, what a slap in the face given to the church, my friends!' And they rejoice about it in the mornings! Where are we headed, my tender friend? Decadence! Everything is going with the flow. And it offers opinion columns! Where are we going? Listen to this one! 'WORDS OF A PROLO!' What sort of title is that? 'War to the evil institutions, peace to men!' For whom do they take themselves? They take themselves for men, these monkeys?"

As for Madam's novels, they would have already been digested by cockroaches or winged ants or some book-eating mouse, if Leona hadn't saved them by stealing them. Let's not talk about poetry! Leona had never gotten to the end of *An Angel's Fall*, whose last pages had been, ages ago, the culinary

Her Destiny on Climb to the Sky Street

delight of some famished bug, as fond of literature and good books as Leona was.

"They saw you at the harbor fighting like a fishmonger-woman, Miz Leona! So, as soon as I have my back turned to go to mass, Missy dashes off to the Anchorage? I surely cannot drag you everywhere behind me like a little dog! Do you not know that you have tasks awaiting you at the house?"

God, how gossip flies! The Gorgon hardly out of church, they had hardly rung the morning bells, and she's already heard about it? Which one, among the servants, was able to denounce her to win Madam's favors? Leona saw hardly anything, she didn't recognize anyone, in the gathering that formed instantaneously, to the cries of "Isaiah! A fight! . . . Girls boxing it out! . . . The two *L*s!" The poor girl had been too stunned.

"Mixing with dockworkers! . . . What were you looking for, among the bargemen? A servant from a good house! It was pointless to send you to religious school! If all that was just so you could keep your bad nigger manners! You can't get them out of you, can you? They're stronger than you? Do you need to be put into slave quarters? You have that in your blood."

A fat bubble of air that spoke.

"When I think that I deprived myself of your services for hours and hours so that you could attend religious school! I who am even sweet enough to send you to church . . . But it's that it cost me money, what do you think of that? Hours of lost work. Days, weeks, in the end! For whom, for what? What for, I ask you? So that you end up scuffling in the streets, hollering like a fishwife? It's a sacrifice I make, you understand, don't you? You don't even realize that. A considerable sacrifice. And I'm not even obligated to do it. It's a gift I give you . . . A result of my goodness. And you, what do you do with my magnanimity? What do you do, you little ingrate, with everything that your Mistress gives you?"

The Mistress gave her gas.

". . . The abbot claims it's my Christian duty! . . . He has some good ones, that abbot! If he saw you all helter-skelter down at the harbor . . . You should hear him, with his little falsetto voice, that goddamn abbot! . . . 'She's bright, that little

one, it would be a shame not to teach her to read.' Oh that, she learns even faster than my big oaf of a son!"
A soft belly. An old, dry belly. With no stomach, with no pity. Without a heart, without love, speechless. Loves no one, not even her children, not even the fruit of her loins. But what does this woman have in her belly? A fat lump filled with air.

"But what do you have in your belly? . . . What's this knowing look? Lower your eyes, impertinent girl! Is Missy showing off? . . . Missy learns well, supposedly? . . . You think that authorizes you to square off your body in front of me? What do you know more than I do, huh, Leona?" shrieked the Gorgon with the protruding jaw, ragged from scolding her, shaking, to hit her better, her old, livid belly full of air.

"You don't dare tell me, huh? You don't dare! But on the subject of brawls, Missy knows about that too . . . After all, what do you have in your body? . . . The devil in your body! There's no other possible explanation. Have you seen what you've done to me, the condition in which you've put your linen, Leona? And who's going to pay for that? The priest, perhaps? And who's going to do your work while you go wasting your time sewing up all these tattered rags? And what's worse is that you're not going to do it for me at night, using up a whole lot of candles again and ruining your eyes for me. I forbid it. I find that you use up too many candles . . . What can you be doing with so many candles? . . . Huh? Answer me!"

Keep on talking . . . ! Talk and stop talking until you've had your fill. Talk into the void. I'm not going to shed any light on it for you!

"You will not set foot back in religious school, that I guarantee you. You already know enough as it is. And for what you get out of it . . ."

Hollowness, simple-mindedness, futility. A batch of useless words.

"Everything you learn there at religious school is monkey business! If it's for you to have fun emptying your inkwells in the holy water! . . . The other day I almost had a face blacker than yours while making the sign of the cross! . . . But now you've gone too far!"

Her Destiny on Climb to the Sky Street

No mischievous boy had a liking for this woman, and especially not Leona. Not even her own children. (But who did have a liking for her? Maybe not even herself? Seeing how this person had let her body go, they had a right to doubt.) The other woman can still keep talking up a storm, now she knows how to read and write, because she has it in her head, the little young black girl Leona. You don't have to believe it, she has it in her skull . . . There, she lets it be said, but it must be known that deep down, Leona thinks about it less.

It can always fill her head . . . It doesn't make her hot or cold. She watches, in the distance, the Mountain . . . Pelée, its head in the clouds.

"What's going through your head? . . . Go on, tell me! What is this story about fighting with Lusinia again? Go on, don't lie, they saw you. And your clothing speaks for you."

— . . .

"This childishness is over! Both of you are too big to go rolling around on the ground like that. Do you not see that you are ridiculous, two big perches tall like filao trees who roam around with a horde of kids? You are both almost women, Leona, do you not realize that?"

Madam doesn't realize how right she is . . . And how did she realize it? . . . People other than her, for a long time, have also noticed it, to the great displeasure of Leona.

"Do you not want to come out of childhood?"

Don't talk to her about her childhood! They stole her childhood from her. They stole it from her. Violated it.

"It was you who were screaming the loudest. They just told me everything. You're not going to tell me that it's not true? Lower your eyes, insolent child! Are you going to speak, yes or no?"

— . . .

"You damn little liar, Leona! You lie, goddamn little frog that you are! You little dishonest thing!"

Lie? She said nothing. She already knows that if she ever were to open her mouth, it would be worse: the simple sound of her voice would provoke a catastrophe.

She feels it. She recognizes all the telltale signs. It's like the

Climb to the Sky

Mountain, up there. It's going to explode, surely! She has a foreboding that it's going to turn out badly. There is catastrophe in the air. She hears it rumbling, rumbling . . . Do not provoke her, especially. It would take so little . . .

"One would say that the very sound of my voice has the gift of making her explode. I am not going to give her that pleasure," she said to herself while rejoicing on the inside. But her face remained marble, black marble like there was in the bathroom where I don't have the right to bathe because I'm black, and my blackness might rub off on the bathtub, which is white. (I only have a chipped pitcher, a ewer and a scaly washbasin, with which I clean myself like a cat in my loft.) However it's me who cleans it, the big upstairs bathroom, Madam's bathroom, completely made out of black marble, from top to bottom of its high walls. But I am also made out of marble, of black marble from head to toe and I will never gain her rank, this jellyfish of a Madam of my two asscheeks, this Gorgon, this Fury! . . . I have read your books, I have understood everything, I have placed my gaze about and black is my gaze as well. You don't know it, but I have done it and I have discovered so many things . . . Yes, I have learned some juicy things! . . . And I even know that your first name is the same as one of the Gorgons, Mrs. Euryale Fairschenne de Dendur! I'm sure that you don't even know it.

Yes, I have read your books. All your books. Even though now I get bored reading and rereading the same ones, always the same ones. I know them by heart, your books, better than you, and better than your oaf of a son, you've said it yourself! . . . Besides it's the only intelligent thing you've ever said! It's not so surprising that he's an idiot, they have a name for that: it's intermarriage. (I read it in one of your books; you don't even know what's inside them! You think you talk like a Parisian? . . . You don't even know these words. Yes, intermarriage!) Your husband, isn't he your cousin? . . . Your first cousin, furthermore. You are almost like brother and sister. It fixes nothing, making little folk together . . . A beautiful family of degenerates, whether you say "great white people" or

Her Destiny on Climb to the Sky Street

not! . . . (You would have done better to mix your blood . . . That might have prevented you from having this defective offspring . . . And you, you wouldn't have that goiter! . . . And you would not be such an idiot . . .) The only thing good in your house is your books.

But, since I have nothing left to read, I will leave, I'm gone. You don't have enough books. Besides, you haven't even read them. You don't even notice it when I take one of them into my attic room. You are absolutely unaware of what I have in my room!

Only the Master could know that. You, you never set foot in there, in my room under the attic. You don't go up there, no, you leave that to the Master. But it's certainly not he who's going to repeat it. I am not worried about that.

It's certainly not Master who's going to denounce me! . . . And I don't give a shit if you're not going to send me to religious school anymore. You're right: I've known it already for quite a while. Much more than I would like to know . . . "She learns well, that little one . . ." That's all the abbot knows how to say!

In fact, in order to learn, I have learned! I am perhaps a "persona non grata" in their beautiful brand-new Boarding School for Girls, I am perhaps not from their world, but I've gotten along rather well . . . It can be said that I've learned some beautiful things . . . I, the little black Negress, I've seen them in all colors, one can say! If you knew . . . All these things that I have discovered . . . All these things that I have had to do . . .

"You were doing those forbidden things, weren't you, Leona, I'm sure of it? Go on, fess up, little girl! You know very well that a sin confessed is half-forgiven. Go on, tell it, that you were diving to go looking in the bay for those little gold coins that those rascal tourists were throwing to you, to amuse themselves seeing you gesticulate like the macaques that you are, like all of you are, huh, wasn't that exactly what you were doing?" ("Macaque yourself, you fat slovenly thing!" Leona screams at her in her belly.)

Climb to the Sky

"Well, don't deny it, hey, you capuchin monkey, I know everything, you pay attention, huh? I know all about the stupid little acts that you do behind my back, you seed of a Calabrian bandit! Nothing escapes me in this house. I have the Master's eye, me, ha ha! I know everything, you hear, EVERYTHING. Bad seed, hey, are you going to confess or not? Are you going to ask for forgiveness and promise not to do it again? No! Don't swear. Especially not that. That makes the Holy Virgin cry."

The Mistress beat her, as if the poor unhappy soul hadn't already had enough blows of all sorts! She beat her like a conch.

"Never should I have taken that child into my house. I believe that the devil's in her body."

Madam farts from anger from it all. Her fat belly empties, what an odor! Leona pretends that she feels nothing. If she grimaces, it's not from suffering, but from a curious desire to laugh.

"Oh! You're making fun of me? Have pity! Give help to those in misery. Take their brats under your roof. You see how you're repaid?"

Leona still does not answer. She was suffering, she almost closed her eyes under the pain, but she didn't lower them. Nothing will ever make her lower them.

"Ain't you got everything you need here?"

This whore of a mistress doesn't even speak correctly.

"Answer when you're spoken to! . . . Lower your eyes, I tell you!"

No, it will not be said that those cracker eyes have burned her nigger eyes.

The blows fall, unpredictable. Wham! The horsewhip. The suffering, right there where she has bruises. She doesn't have the right to leave. She has to stay there, to put up with it. Pretend to be unaffected.

Wham! Wham! Not even the right to cry. She has forbidden herself that. Not in front of the old jellyfish. "In a little while, when I'm alone in my loft . . . the little bit of time that I have alone, I will cry stealthily. During my little drop of rest, my little time of respite, I will be able to cry, have a good cry, before the Master . . ."

Her Destiny on Climb to the Sky Street

But pain every moment! We are not there yet. In waiting, this dirty jellyfish is pounding her: "You need to go visit the riff-raff, you can't resist, huh? Birds of a feather flock together. You find it necessary to associate with those people? Those animals! Those nasty, vulgar, violent beasts, that smell bad, that whole band of sweat-stinkers, barefoot bums, the unemployed, thieves? Everything about them is just bestiality, immediate satisfaction of the most primary needs, without the least refinement, without anything. All a nigger needs is a hot place to go shit. Everything they do, they do like beasts, like they had just disembarked from Africa the night before. They eat like beasts, mate like animals, in front of everyone! Even their dances are beastlike and lascivious. Look at them dance their calendas and their laghias! They have the gall to call that dancing? I've never seen anything more obscene. Aren't you better off with us? Answer, Leona my girl! Aren't you well off with us? Are you bored with us? People of quality don't entertain you? Distinguished people, they are too stiff for you, you find us too high-collar, do we make you itch? Do you need to mix with the riff-raff?"

— . . .

Madam is full of herself; her puffs are going to stink up the room, already laden with the heavy atmosphere that the volcanic ashes bring. Leona plugged up her nose. She would like to plug up her ears, shut her up, to withdraw . . . But the only thing she can close is her mouth. Leona will not answer. She will not give her this honor.

"Oh! I understand. Try as we might to do everything we can to give you nice pleats, the Master and I, nothing to do about it, it's lost effort, it's pissing in a violin. Jam to the pigs, everything we do for you, the Master and I. The natural ways return at a gallop. When I think about how the Master is so indulgent with you . . . Isn't he good to you, the Master? You're not going to dare to tell me that the Master isn't good to you? What's this look you're getting on your face?"

— . . .

"He who is always the first one to defend you . . . you dirty little monster of ingratitude! Not even basic loyalty!"

Really, she doesn't know how right she is, the woman with the goiter with a belly inflated with gas . . .

"She's going to see what I have in my belly . . . This piece of work loses nothing by waiting," Leona threatens tacitly, reckless and unruffled under the torture.

"He who does everything to convince me to keep you, even when you do the stupidest things. Hey, do you remember, dirty ingrate, do you remember, you destructive child, the day when you broke one of my beautiful crystal glasses that I reserve for Christmas, in order to drink champagne from France? Hey, Leona, tell me something, who prevented me from slapping off your linnet head, to teach you, and from chucking you out? Hey, is it not the Master, maybe? The Master who always comes to put himself between my anger and you? But hey, today there's no Master to hold me back. The Master's not here today to protect you. The Master's too busy with his politics. He and his elections! . . . During that time, his house can collapse. The Master has better things to do than fool with a little insignificant thing like you! Have you not seen how ugly and black you are? Your face resembles the shit from all beasts! So, Leona, my girl, are you going to fess up or not? If not, I'll tear your head off. I'll twist your neck all the way around so that you'll walk with your head backwards. Even that won't change you a lot, you filthy brainless thing! . . ."

She runs out of breath from hitting her. Madam wears herself out. She's going to end up bursting open! Her soft lump is going to fart! Her flabby flesh is going to implode! The Gorgon is going to disintegrate! . . . Her immaculate marble walls will be full of her putrid, fragmented, pulverized guts! Vile projections everywhere! The sumptuous white marble soiled with spatter from the woman with the goiter, with a gigantic gurgle and sprays of stinking puke, dripping with miasmas from the sewer. Madam is going to empty the cesspit that serves as her belly on her marble.

Leona would not like to be there to see that. Even less to clean it up afterwards . . . However the spectacle delights her, even if it is the stuff of vomit. This furtive but strong fantasy

Her Destiny on Climb to the Sky Street

makes her forget her pain. She would smile about it to some extent. A stranger to all charity, the space of a very brief moment, the time that the matron is getting back her breath, she offers herself an ephemeral balm to her suffering, a fanciful comfort. Then, horrified, she thinks better of it, she crosses herself, like a good little Christian. Her face clenched, her stare fixed, she watches out for the blows to begin again. It is not an ironic smile that her lips outline painfully; it's a trismus of distress that twists her mouth cruelly.

She needs to stop imagining that, she's going to end up throwing up! The other woman would be only too happy about it, and would only hit harder. Do not supply any pretext for her above all! . . . Alas, Madam does not need one:

"I would be very curious to know what's going through your head! Enough looking at me like that with your eyes . . ."

With what does she want her to look at her?

"Lower your eyes, insolent girl! Lower your eyes, I tell you! So, you can swear to my face that you are not mixed up in all that at all? . . . Look at me when I talk to you!"

She should make up her mind.

"You think you're impressing me, giving me that big face? Where do you think I can be tricked? . . . Go on, fess up! Are you going to speak, you little pest? Or do you prefer that I cut you open? You are going to see if you are going to be able to taunt me like that. I'm going to toss your guts into the air! . . ."

What Leona prefers? Leona prefers not to talk about the Master and the way Master treats her. As for the rest! . . . But she is boiling on the inside.

"And I, Leona my girl, am I not good to you? You little heartless thing! The Master finds me too hard on the servants! . . ."

And full speed ahead for the hypocritical couplet "good masters" to whom gratitude is owed for being willing to take us under their roofs, we, the niggers, "fed, lodged, whitened!" What is she talking about? Is the old gargoyle clowning around? Fed, Leona? So little. Lodged? So badly! In the most abject attic room, where her privacy is violated . . . But certainly not whitened. And beaten, as part of the bargain. Madam can have

Climb to the Sky

her carnival . . . In looking at her, Leona has the impression of watching masks pass in a Mardi Gras parade.

Ash Wednesday, rather . . . Blows rain down and rain down again, like the ashes are raining down on the city.

The shrew displaces a lot of air. To a small extent, she would almost manage to dispel the feeling of oppression that this unbreathable atmosphere causes, this strange jinx that is suffocating you. But she imposes another one, more frightening, more insidious than the volcanic cloud. Madam is boiling as much as the Mountain. She ordered wet sheets to be tacked onto the windows, but it did little good, the ashes insinuate themselves everywhere. However, the day starts off well. Leona plunges her eyes desperately into the corner of blue sky that subsists, over the cloth and the roofs. A nocturnal storm washed off the cobblestones and the facades, but what power could calm the troubled vernacular spouts that swell the entrails of the monster?

The mountain of flesh flies into a rage, seethes but totters under the weight of her furor. In moving, her massive side collides with the hip of the plump demijohn from Aubagne that sits enthroned in the vestibule, as in any self-respecting residence. The pottery breaks. She gloats. Throws herself on her scapegoat: "Was it you who put that in the passage to make me break my neck? . . . "

Twist it, her ugly goiter neck, strangle it until she expires . . .

Husky with cinders and rage, the hoarse voice thunders again:

"Oh! I know. You can't get your blackness out of you, can you? From the moment I send you to get something for me in town, you take advantage of it to go throwing yourself shamelessly half-nude on the pier, corrupt child! You don't think you're too scandalous? You dare to do that to me? But what do you have in your body? Missy has the nerve to go around bare-chested, and still in pants! And who gave them to you, those pretty hardly worn lace pants, huh? Wasn't it I? . . . in what a state have you put them? Look at that for me! Tatters. To think that I had worn them only two or three years. Cute,

Her Destiny on Climb to the Sky Street

almost-new pants, with English embroidery, beautiful piping on the knees . . . Pretty ladies' pants, that I had hardly torn, and that little whore there is going to show that to everyone? But you don't walk around all nude in pants like that, Leona, my girl! Where is your head? Are you not ashamed? Do you think that these are manners for a servant of a big house?"

Ah, yes. With important people, everything is big. So she must be big, too, to be in the service of important crackers? A lot of good that does her.

But what is she getting at, the great cracker lady? Leona is no longer standing . . .

"You have a rank to maintain, my girl. You are not at the home of just anybody! . . ."

That they are "important whites" is well known! Madam has already drummed it into her, taking on her Parisian accent:

"You understand, my dear, the rest of us, we are important true white people, without a drop of mixed blood. Ah, we do not have that, "the drop," neither the Master nor I, you can believe me!"

The Master sees to "the drop." He may not have it himself, but it is quite possible that he gets mixed up in spreading it around here. If she only knew, the goiter woman! . . . If she could suspect . . . But no, she is much too proud, too busy recalling that her prestigious family has flattering origins, and too bad if it comes at the price of an intermarriage that makes defective goiter children:

"You have to carry yourself as is necessary! You must never forget that you are in the service of quality people. You are not at a commoner's house, descendents from 'gobs of months,' like those arrogant Dubucs! . . ."

Leona hardly sees the difference: whities for whities, small or big! What does that change? Arrogant people for arrogant people! The advantage is that praising herself and demeaning others temporarily appeases Madam. The gargoyle takes so much pleasure in it that she suspends her rain of blows.

". . . They have nothing about which to be proud: their ancestor was an 'enlisted man' who fled royal justice after some unknown crime! Those people are just upstarts. They can try hard to invent, to show off, any sort of legend for the tourists! Ah, that's like them! A girl captured by pirates, that they would have brought to Algiers, delivered like a slave to the great Turk..."

"Well done! To each his own." That must have had a strange effect on her, to Missy Whitey This And That, to find herself in a slave's skin, as white as she was!" Leona could not stop herself from saying to herself secretly.

"According to them, this famous Aimée Dubuc de Rivery was so beautiful that she became the favorite of the harem. It even seemed that she would be the mother of a sultan, Mahmoud something... Tall tales, to restore their reputation! Whereas for us, it is historical, our ancestors were important whites from Saint-Domingue..."

Grr... Grr... the gargoyle was reveling in these important whites! Whether they had come out of Saint-Domingue or Jupiter's thigh, what good can that do Leona? As if the blows were not enough? No, on top of that, she has to be subjected, for the millionth time, to the genealogy of the Fairschennes de Dendur:

"And on my mother's side, we go back to the first colonists of Martinique, my dear, the ones who had a sailor's soul..." mocked the gorgon, puffing out her breast. "You know nothing of that! But my great-uncle explained to me. Can you imagine that his ancestors set themselves up on the Under-the-Wind side, in the Saint-Pierre anchorage, well sheltered. The first to arrive had a royal concession of two hundred paces wide and several thousand paces long, toward the interior, a band of land perpendicular to the Caribbean Sea. They called it the 'seaside layer.' So, you understand, you can recognize by their name the last-minute inhabitants! Because, when all the seaside layers were distributed, they went to the upper layers. When you see these people who are named 'des Etages,' it means that their concession was not 'on the coast.'"

The only thing of interest in the story is that during the time she is telling it, Madam stops hitting.

Her Destiny on Climb to the Sky Street

"But, in all that, you are still not telling me what you were going to look for in the harbor without my authorization? Aside from a fight and disobedience..."

— ...

"So that's what you've found to bring me?" the gargoyle yelled. "Ugly shameless little black girl! Do you think that I don't already have enough worries with you?"

— ...

"So, it's in front of everyone who knows you and who knows my house and even worse who knows my name that you're going to exhibit your body and make a spectacle of yourself, half-nude, like a wild child, to soil my reputation, to make people talk about me and insinuate that I don't give you enough to eat and that I haven't given you an education, that they all can see you all skinny like that, with all your little body hanging out, that you need to be the first one to go throw yourself headfirst in that old nasty water, at the risk of getting hot or cold and going there to die for me. Why, Holy Virgin, I ask you? For the love of gold. To fish up two or three Totors! What a shame! Is that not sad? A girl that I cover in lace and send to school!"

However, Madam loves gold. She does not spit on gold when she wears her big jewels around her hideous goiter in the morning, to go parading off to the five-thirty mass at the cathedral.

They shine so much, her gold chains, her lion-claw clasp bracelets, her cameo earrings, that the timid rays of the just-risen sun never gleam as much as her specks of gold and her pearls.

Would gold be good for her, and not for Leona? Two weights, two measures. So much injustice flooded her, so much more than the waters of the bay, so sweet, so refreshing, so delicious, almost maternal, for this motherless child when she went to these waters looking for treasure.

The treasure was tiny, but what does it matter? Something with which to buy a little something, two inches of new lace all her own? A pink satin ribbon, some sweetmeats, two or three fruits, a macaroon, a cassava, to improve the routine? Never

Climb to the Sky

enough for a book, unfortunately . . . Nor for a ticket to the theater. Books were too expensive. The shows were inaccessible. She had to be happy with Madam's antediluvian library, with her three antique dictionaries, one for common nouns and one for proper nouns, with her incomplete encyclopedia of three and a half volumes, and her mushy or swashbuckler novels. Between the *Illustrated Petit Larousse* and the *Etymological Dictionary*, she didn't know what to think. As for the encyclopedia, sometimes she submerged herself in it. Leona emerged from it haggard, coming out of her nights of clandestine reading. She had the hardest time tearing herself away from it: one page called to another, one section led to another, through an intoxicating frustration, and, suddenly, dawn was coming.

But her happiness was total when she threw herself into the bay headfirst. Oh, diving, good diving, plop! into the belly of the sea.

She dove well, Leona, plop! . . . Now she swam even better, a fine crawl, long, nimble power. Badly nourished but well muscled. A true fishgirl, the little lioness.

"All that for some gold! What misery! . . ." ruminated the enormous sea cow, paradoxical, impermeable to all forms of understanding, unable to let herself be taken away by any wave of empathy. She who hated to swim! . . . She, the great lady, who, in the morning, went reluctantly to surrender to cold ablutions, without even taking off her fetid nightshirt, for, according to her, disrobing the whole body was not Catholic! (That's what Madam repeated, to hide from herself that she had trouble accepting her own body, looking at herself in the mirror, except to mask herself maniacally under thick layers of makeup.) She who dragged herself clumsily to the imperial bathroom of white marble where she hardly touched the water, doing a brief "eye washing" followed by an elliptical cat's bath, under the fallacious pretext of having to rush to mass at full speed, proving herself powerless to catch a glimpse of aspects other than risks and vice, in this smooth insubordination to her sacrosanct authority. As for the upstairs bathroom, the most spacious one, the one made out of black marble, Madam

Her Destiny on Climb to the Sky Street

never set foot in here. She felt like a stranger in her own house there. It had become "the bathroom for friends," adjacent to the friends' room, but Madam considered herself in enemy territory there. Friends hardly ever came . . . (It must be said that she had very few of them.) The place was frequented only by Leona, for housekeeping, not for her personal hygiene, the servant girl didn't have a right to that, a washbowl and pitcher should suffice for her . . . What was she going to look for in the sea? Had she not forbidden these swims in the sea that she hated so much? Like showering under the rain! . . . All these savage manners! Must she think of herself as something dirty, this naughty child Leona, to have such a great need to wash? On all fronts, this vagabond had a soul as black as her body.

"Disobey me in such a way?! How dare you, Leona, huh? What are you doing there like that? . . . Missy thinks she's protected, huh? By the Master, huh? Through what devilry I don't know? . . . By virtue of what?! . . . Your pranks? . . . The evil spells that you cast? . . . All your politeness? . . . What does he see in this female monkey? . . . You're going to see! . . . Little vicious whore! . . . Wow! I'm choking. You have put a hex on me!"

She pronounced "hesk" and pounced on Leona. "Devil woman! Devil woman! . . . Sorceress!" howled the harpy out of breath, on the verge of mental asphyxia, moving her hands first to her apoplectic goiter, then onto her whipping girl.

"But what have I done to the Good Lord to provide a home for *that* under my roof?"

In her home, it was not at all the custom to plunge into such abysses of perplexity. Drowned, in her own defense, in a torrent of reflections that threatened to make her skull explode, Euryale de Dendur the Gorgon struggled as best she could with her intestinal demons and her bad conjugal aftertaste. Then, weary of war, Madam tried to avenge herself of her own humiliations, of her own frustrations and her domestic torments by tormenting the little servant girl, trying to make explode through violence—the weapon of the weak in spirit—this pretty head of an overly intelligent Negress.

Leona would have wanted to cut herself away from the

Climb to the Sky

world, to see no longer, to escape from the teratological and revolting vision of this less than human mountain of flabby flesh, worse than the Sphinxes, the Cyclops, or the Gryphons encountered in the encyclopedia in the "Mythology" article.

Full delirium reigned. The monstress no longer felt rage, accused her sharply of triggering the anger of all the evil powers. To believe her, it was Leona who attracted, to this city, to this residence on Climb to the Sky Street, and to all its inhabitants, the ire of the hellish gods grumbling at the center of the earth. They were far from the paternosters and the affected ways of the high mass! In full pagan frenzy, forgetful of her religious souvenirs, Madam would have willingly offered the little woman as a sacrifice if she had the power.

". . . And they want me to give an education to that? . . . Tchip! Pearls before swine! That doesn't even know what to do with gold! . . ." Madam continued bellowing at her while shaking her overripe skin on her. "Pearls before swine, I tell you . . . Diving to look for Totors? . . . Diving to look for death, yes!"

Ah, diving into the belly of the sea! Coming out of each immersion, emerging from it, triumphant. Playing with death each time, enjoying this dangerous delight, shooting out splashing from this painful happiness.

BELLY OF THE SEA

Leona felt just a little less nimble these days. It was because of this that Lusinia was able to steal her coin from her. Well, the coin. The Totor! The one that she had seen first, she, Leona.

For it is also she who can see the best, normally, her big eyes wide open underwater, at ease, happy, as if she were in her ma's hut.

An ordinary person isn't faster than Leona at finding the gold coins, sweeping down on them, boom! seizing them and bringing them back up triumphantly to the surface in no time at all.

Normally she is, she, a girl, the commander of the Totor

Her Destiny on Climb to the Sky Street

fishing in the waters of the Saint-Pierre bay. "Normally, nobody beats me. But then, Lusinia . . ."

But then, she didn't know what vertigo grabbed hold of her, what nausea came up to her throat with a taste of curdled milk. (Since Pelée Mountain had started awakening and overheating the atmosphere, milk turned before your eyes!)

She felt queasy all of a sudden. Very queasy. Like she wanted to throw up. Might the morning tchololo have gone down the wrong way? . . .

Not surprising. Baark, this old overly clear coffee water—where clouds of creamy milk slithered in a suspension of fat, without agreeing, in spite of energetic stirrings with the spoon, to mix itself with the tchololo that the Mistress had the infinite goodness to deign to leave to her servants, after having drunk her own coffee. Real coffee, that Leona has to bring in person, no matter how she spent the night, no matter whether she slept well or poorly, all the way inside her high canopy bed at 5:00 a.m. sharp, if you please (but without the least thanks).

It's not a matter of lazing around in her attic room, when the day begins to break! She hardly has time to stretch. No staying in bed for Leona. Neither on Sundays nor on holidays. The little servant girl works every day: getting up at dawn, the Mistress's service forces her to do it; no question of lazing around in bed. Moreover, who would feel like it? It's a furnace, a kiln, that you desert, that in a rush, on the sly, that in a nimble stampede reduces the bedroom where she is supposed to sleep, supposed to get some rest, to something unsanitary . . . Finally, it is a deliverance, before the day begins, for Leona, to spring out of the scraps of sheets torn, smudged, dirtied, stinking with unhealthy sweat, soaked in countless humors, that scatter across her terrible bed . . .

First thing after getting out of her sickening bed, at the latest on the fifth strike of the bell ringing at the cathedral, in order to avoid the blows, every good morning that the Good Lord makes, "so strong, so tight, so spicy," whispers Madam while sipping it in little delightful swallows, her mouth pursed like a chicken's asshole, baark! Baark! Leona carries her coffee to the chubby Gorgon still bleary from sleep. She has to wait for the other woman to sample it slowly, her damn strong coffee, in her metal goblet engraved with her initials or in "her Limoges china," on Sundays. She has to ensure that the Gorgon is satisfied, that her coffee is very hot, to avoid her morning crisis, to duck the early-morning flicks of her finger, to escape as soon as possible, because the other woman is in a bad mood as soon as she wakes up. In a mood as bad as her breath, when she leans over to harass or admonish Leona:

"What are you dragging in the bed like that for? You little pervert! What keeps you in bed like that, huh? . . . You're going to make me late for mass!" Every day Leona, nauseated, hears this damn coffee gurgle in that fat gullet. Every morning that the Good Lord makes, she sees this fat slimy jellyfish get up angry and go off to mass without washing, after splashing herself with perfume, the disgusting thing. It could make you vomit.

Then, grudgingly, Leona dips her lips in her tchololo.

Baark! This third coffee water! Because the second batch, a little less clear, is reserved for the children of the Mistress. Leona only has a right to the third, if there's any left, when she goes back down to the kitchen. But all the other servants have already gone through there. They have already gulped everything down, band of voracious wolves, dirty gluttons, baark and rebaaark! . . .

Baark! This old tepid tchololo, too sugary, too insipid, that has a taste of dishwater because it hasn't even been reheated. Everything costs too much, grumbles the goitered Gorgon: the coal for the stove, the matches, not to mention the coffee! "Let's not even talk about it!" simpers Madam, who has the temperament of a Spanish woman, baark! baark! A black temperament like her coffee. Coffee costs you the eyes out of your head, on the other hand, sugar, we walk on top of it, according to her. Nothing left to do but think again of her throaty voice saying those words, baark of baark!

Coffee and sugar remain for Leona symbols of suffering and subjugation, like they were for her people, during the cursed time of slavery.

Her Destiny on Climb to the Sky Street

"Sugar, I hardly ever consume it," coos Madame. Baark! She only has disdain for sugar, the plump mistress. She prefers leaving it to the niggers, this sweetness that makes her fat, transforming her into a sea cow, baark! baark! She doesn't need that! She savors her black coffee, boiling, without cream or sugar. The only additive to her delight is to take her coffee in bed. The truth is that this is the only pleasure given to her in bed. She blows delicately on top of it, her eyes rolled, holding her porcelain cup ornate with a coat of arms with her little finger in the air, all ruddy, all podgy, baark! around the fatty bulges formed by her fat signet ring, supposedly marking her pseudo-aristocratic ancestry. Although it was not really a feminine piece of jewelry, Madam wore it night and day, on her right pinky finger, the garish signet ring inherited from her dead father, a grotesque outgrowth of 18-carat gold from French Guyana, adorned with a fanciful coat of arms, coming out directly from the fantasies of display from her ancestor the bidet salesman, where you could see the threat of some sort of aggressive tooth like a mammoth would use for defense, presumably intended to create the illusion that the origins of these people went back to the dawn of time.

Madam relishes it while making faces that no one can admire, because the Master turns his back to her, baark! The august and legitimate husband is still sleeping, snoring or pretending to. He doesn't appreciate either the coffee or Madam his wife, besides. Baark!

Those aren't his morning lips pinched on the edge of the cup, baark! ("Watch out, Leona! That's precious! That's fragile! Don't clack my Sevres porcelain like the lout that you are!") It was neither her goiter nor her profile with the protruding jaw nor her podgy pinky finger nor her tangled hair nor her pestilential breath nor her face the color of a cheese from France, baark! that the Master married. What led him to the church was her Papa's money. And especially her Dendur name, baark! so well known on the spot, that he attached it to his own, baark! As well as the aristocratic name of nobility that goes with it, baark de baark! so that nobody makes a mistake and the prestige splashes completely all over him, baark! Even

Climb to the Sky

if it means he has to put up with sharing the bed of one of the least lovable wives, baark! with an escutcheon with the hard tooth of a mammoth, perhaps, but, in truth, one of the ugliest pachyderms of the city, baark! One of the best matches in Martinique, notwithstanding, a rich heiress, still young . . . (Well, a girl who wasn't too old, suitable for procreation, probably coming up to her marriage a virgin: who would dream of deflowering such a monster, baark! if it weren't to make himself some legitimate children Baark? Pure Baark of Baark, if you please!) Her lips on fine porcelain? A trait traced to the jaw of a swordfish, sharp like her meanness. As for the rest? . . . Let us not talk about it! Just thinking about it . . . it's baark. Leona is nauseated by it.

"As for the Master . . ." Is it his fault, if he hardly had any choice? If it hadn't been she, the rich cantankerous heiress, it would have been the devious hunchback from Saint-Fouay rums, or the hypocrite progeny from the Great Adolphe de Quarrequant Warehouses, who has one eye at noon and the other at twilight, baark of chez baark! From the "good matches" of Saint-Pierre, the Master took the least awful . . .

For his pleasure, however, the Master prefers other flesh; the Master tastes only lips that are fuller, thicker, fleshier, more sensual to kiss him, baark, than those of his gargoyle wife who swallows her coffee in her goiter in the cherished bed of the pipiret bird.

The Master values finer fingers, longer hands to caress his body, baark!

The Master chooses mops of hair of steel wool, little frizzy zeroes to stimulate the hair of his crotch, bark and rebaaaark!

The Master likes blacker skin to stand out against his own—whiter than the sinks newly imported from France by the Denys Le Tirran Corporation bought at the price of gold by Madam his wife, installed with great pomp in the downstairs bathroom reserved for the Master's personal use but where he never washes, baark! baark! baark! "What a waste of time! Feminine perversion! Hell and damnation! You waste all that time masturbating in the bathroom, Euryale?"

Her Destiny on Climb to the Sky Street

The Master hates his well-born wife, but is crazy about darker skin (the skins they call ill-born, around here, but the Master finds they match the whiteness of his skin well), to create, with his own skin, white of white of baark of baark, a contrast that drives him mad.

Mischievously, upon examining Madam's mug when she woke up, with her skin prematurely afflicted by Methuselah Syndrome, the girl amused herself imagining that all these age spots that sprinkle her puffiness all of a sudden gather together, to form a single one: she would be brown! Madam would be a "woman of color!" The idea had made her laugh, but the sight was one to vomit over.

When Leona had finished vomiting up her tchololo, Madam her boss, the Master her boss, and the little bosses, bark! Just think about it, she wasn't very strong. Lusinia took advantage of it.

"Where is my second Totor? . . . Holy Mother, where the devil did it go?" Leona asked herself, snapping out of it, kneeling on the dock. "It seems to me that there were two of them. I dove, picked up two. Afterwards, I came back up. I had time to get dressed again from head to toe . . . I can still see myself, yes . . . my underwear soaked, my dress clinging down there, so I had trouble slipping into it . . . I sneeze, I'm queasy . . . I'm starting to give up . . . Then, I was so dizzy . . . No way for me to remember. In my apron pocket maybe? Would I have already squeezed it out? . . . When? . . . But no, Good Lord!"

Of the two Totors that Leona remembered having fished up (she saw them again, gold shining at the bottom of the bay, she saw herself taking them, she, Leona, the fastest, the best), there was only one left. In vain, she dug into herself, searched herself, rubbed her eyes . . . Near her, Lusinia, mocking. This is how she figured it out: standing on her muscled legs, her hamstrings tensed like two bows.

In her right hand, quite shiny, standing out like her big teeth, the missing Totor was glowing.

Climb to the Sky

Through the water in her eyes, tears and sea salt mingled, stinging her, preventing her from seeing well, Leona could only make out this: those rows of gleaming teeth, bursting with hostile whiteness, that stolen gold.

Carnivorous incisors and canines laid out in battle order, the Totor almost within her reach, in an evident challenge.

Lusinia seemed enraged. Her mouth foamed: "Look at this! It's mine, this Totor. I found it there, on the ground."

Lie, a cheeky lie. Lusinia lies like she breathes. Her whole body oozes hatred, dishonesty, aggression. Everyone knows that no piece of gold dawdles there on the ground, at Saint-Pierre; that if the gold Totors walked around like that, all alone, on the Saint-Pierre pier, it would have been noticed ever since the times of the Marquis d'Antin! There would not be so many barefoot Negroes and half-starved Negresses!

The gold is in the safes of the crackers, in the pockets of the tourists, and around Madam's fat neck, when it's not sleeping in her precious porcelain jewel box, in the style of a Louis XV chest of drawers, adorned with the same fantastical herald as her signet ring with its pachyderm escutcheon. "I still feel like I want to throw up, just thinking about Madam, bark! . . . With the mammoth escutcheon! . . . Baark of baark! . . . I don't need to start vomiting again . . . I've seen what that cost me!" Furthermore, she had already thrown up her thin breakfast, the tchololo, the sour milk, and the stale bread. She no longer had anything more to puke up. Other than bile.

"On the ground! I found it myself! Who's going to say otherwise, huh? . . . Huh? Who, huh?" Lusinia dared to bark, squared off in an aggressive pose.

Without taking time to answer—would she have the strength?—Leona gives a hint of a feeble movement while still staring at her treasure, hypnotized by that eye of gold shining in the already high sun.

Between her vicious teeth, Lusinia spit: "Go on! . . . Go on, come on, my dear! Come and get it! Whop! My pretty! Go on, come on, I'm going to give it to you . . . I've been dying to do it for so long!"

Her Destiny on Climb to the Sky Street

Lusinia, her best friend, Lusinia, her alter ego, her double, so much so that they were inseparable! So much so that they called them "*L* and *L*," or "Elles" for short. (Around here, people like nicknames: for these two, an overall nickname: no Leona without Lusinia. At least, until further notice . . .)

Stuck to her like snuff, she followed her everywhere like a little doggie . . . Lusinia, her best friend! Well, her ex–best friend! . . . Lusinia, her best enemy, who for forever always imitated her, admired her, adored her, envied her secretly. Idolized her. Fawned upon her. Hated her. Applauded her, complimented her: "Hooray! There you are finally, dear Leona! I've been waiting for you there for a century." Loathed her. Congratulated her, deified her, raised her onto a pedestal . . . Damned her. Cuddled her, cherished her, praised her to the skies . . . Exposed her to public scorn. Liked to be seen with her, to strut at her side, liked to slide into her shadows to light up in her sun, with the secret hope that some of the sparkles of Leona's success would splash back onto Lusinia, that Leona's aura, the little lioness, would project a little light on Lusinia, the obnoxious one, who had nothing brilliant about her other than her teeth—and if that, because of the contrast, because she had skin black like last night.

Leona had said to her that in one of her Mistress's books she had gathered that her name meant "Lioness." What crime has she not committed there? What an idea, also, to reveal that to Lusinia, who still hasn't succeeded in remembering the alphabet!

"The lion, the king of animals?" Lusinia moaned pensively. "That fits well: you have the sign of Leo, born on August 15th."

"The Day of the Assumption . . . found under the double sign of Virgo and Leo."

"High society . . . That's normal: everything is big in the big houses! And what about me? And my name? What does it mean?"

"Hmm . . . All I can do for you, my dear, is not going to please you . . ."

Climb to the Sky

"Yes, it will! Go on!"

"Hmm . . . I don't know too much . . . I could in a pinch compare it to a Greek word, from old Greek before Jesus Christ . . ."

"Which means what, that old word there?"

"You really want me to? You probably want it. The only word that I see that resembles Lusinia is the one that means . . ."

"Well? What suspense! Enough showing off! Just because you have your Holy Virgin and your Lion doesn't mean I can't have anything . . ."

"The word that means "destruction." So that surely isn't the right word. I am not so knowledgeable, you know. I didn't really learn Greek, I just look at it, like that . . . Out of curiosity."

"So that's all you have to pull out for me, Leona?" said Lusinia, getting impatient.

". . . And worse for me, if they named me Leona, it wasn't because of the king of animals. It was only in homage to my grandfather, Leonard," Leona had answered, too modest and too charitable.

Always "too much," she is always "too much," no matter what she says or does. The other girl swiftly jumps on the chance:

"Tchip! Leonard? A runaway nigger? Scum! Could you not have found anything better?! . . . My dear, that's nothing to be proud of . . ." Lusinia gloats, enjoying this unexpected condescension.

Leona managed to sit up, with difficulty, all mournful, panting for breath, almost crying, flesh quivering like a body that's just been killed. All doleful, she extended a hand to get her Totor back.

Lusinia was waiting for just that: she bit it on the inside. The outcome followed naturally. Reply: yells, scratches, tears to shreds. Slashes. Pummels at random, squashes with the flat of your good hand. *L* pulls hair, yank! The ears, the nose, anything that is sticking out. Shakes like a mango tree, strangles.

Her Destiny on Climb to the Sky Street

L insults, bombards, boom! Decapitates. "Watch out, I'll kill you!" Punches, kicks, head-butts, pow! Gouges out eyes, whore! Massacres. The other *L* tears apart. Bumps. Decimates, exterminates, "Dirty vermin! . . ." Slap, wham! Blinds, stuns: a knife springs out from who knows where, a flash of a dazzling blade perforating the air. Bleeds, hits, cuts throats. "Elles" roll on the ground, boom boom kaboom, bam! A galaxy of stars takes on a red glow in full sunlight. Countless vessels whirl, docked in the Saint-Pierre anchorage—never as numerous as today, this day is not like others, Leona has time to predict, in a flash. The high masts whirl, the yards, the big bodies that load and unload, in a gush of strong smells, of sweat, of sugar and blood, of rum, of stained wood, of cacao, of orange wine, in a tornado of blended indigo, manioc, and skin. All memory of friendship dies. The felon girl consummates the crime; the pineapples are preserved, Leona's heart is disgusted. Nausea unsettles her; she vomits on the blackness of her ex-friend. A spray of sharper scents makes her collect herself, then comes a nightmarish aggression of bare feet and shoes, a dizzy spell of calves and screeches: "Isaiah!" People like watching two girls fight. A crowd gathered: "A fight! The two *L*s are tussling!" The two *L*s are attacking each other violently. No one tries to separate them; on the contrary, the screams stir them up. Pride galvanizes Leona.

Free yourself, get back up, kapow! "Ha, I'll show you! Daughter of a whore! I'll teach you, bitch child!" . . . Hit again, hit harder: Bam! Bang! She loses her breath, staggers, wham! Collapses.

Crowning Lusinia, haughty, her long silhouette standing against the azure of an intense blue, a high plume of steam rises straight ahead, triumphant.

Her "best friend" tramples her, dislocates her, knocks her out . . . Leona gets up, then loses her footing. She slumps. The other *L* almost finishes her off.

Climb to the Sky

Belly of the Earth

The little marble carver from Climb to the Sky Street, who saw Leona pass by every morning the Good Lord makes and who liked to see her, but who had never dared to speak to her, had come down very early to the harbor to haggle over a delivery of white marble for the luxurious tombstones of the bourgeois buried like princes in the middle of the proud chessboard with black and white tiles of the superb Anchorage cemetery. (He would never have the chance to use it, this white marble from Carrara, neither to make one of those chapel replicas housing white virgins, nor to decorate the walls of some patrician bathroom with it: the people of Saint-Pierre who were soon going to die would hardly have need for his services; but he still didn't know it.)

The wholesaler was in the process of yelling at him: "My money is in peril, Massa Homer! Where will I go with that?" because he was begging for a discount and some terms of payment, when suddenly his apprentice, who had heard him confess aloud, from the bottom of his workshop, the pleasure he felt watching Leona pass by each morning, ran up all out of breath.

He felt a great wind go by that overturned his heart, and understood at that same moment that it was, that it could only be, his little marble lioness who found herself in mortal danger.

"She hit, pow! Pow! A bloodbath! The other girl kicked her butt to the ground, zoom! A bloodbath! A FIGHT! Men, it's a FIGHT! . . ."

Suddenly the tufts of his spiky hair bristled with sweat. He paled, becoming paler than the whitest of his Carrara marble tiles, the little marble carver from Climb to the Sky Street, a little wealthy low-class white that a certain Euryale de Dendur wouldn't have wanted for anything in the world, not even to wax her ankle boots, "An artisan! a manual laborer! A penniless, nameless, luckless man! A zero before a number! . . . You think there's anything white about that? What whiteness there is in him is polluted by his servant blood! And on top of everything else, a tombstone merchant!"

Her Destiny on Climb to the Sky Street

Her "great whitey" grandfather had been a bidet salesman. Bidet salesmen from father to son, the Dendurs, so keen on heraldry! But she concealed that. Madam said "Importer of Sanitary Material" with an uppercase accent when they said "bidet salesman" mundanely, the evil forked tongues of the ladies her friends from Saint-Foray and Quarrequant that never took off Sundays or any holidays, abominable old girls he wouldn't have wanted for anything in the world, he, the pauper.

He was overcome with love for Leona, the little black marble lioness, made of a black more beautiful than ophite and deeper than onyx, more precious than cipolin marble, blazing more than the red marble from Numidia, the yellow marble from Sienna, more shimmering than breccia marble, similar to mosaics, from afar more resplendent than variegated Pentelic marble, more graceful than blue turquin marble, more vivid than serpentine, without those macabre greenish reflections, more iridescent than lumachelle marble, with its veins encrusted with shells.

His apprentice was still stuttering, "And what's worse she f-f-f-fell, boom! She wasn't m-m-moving anymore, master Homer! The other *L* was still b-b-b-beating her!" and he was already flying to the aid of his little marble lioness to deliver her from the claws of her noxious ex-friend, was separating *L* and *L* forever with a broad, peaceful hand, with a gentle, calming look.

Between elles, there was not much left . . . Of their false friendship, nothing more.

When she got herself together, Leona in turn gave him a long grateful wink that, far from turning him into marble, put him beside himself.

He almost had a stroke, became redder than the blood that was pouring from Leona's numerous wounds. Although one was white like the bidets of the Dendur father and the other black like last night, their respective blood seemed to be exactly of the same red. Of the same color, yes! Hard to tell apart.

The little low-class white man from Martinique was seized with a terrible trembling, but Leona knew nothing of it, because she began to tremble herself when she saw the state of her clothes.

Climb to the Sky

Her impeccable servant's dress was no more. Nothing left of her spruce white apron that, in her haste to run toward the boat of tourists, potential suppliers of Totors, she had forgotten to take off (yet another act of disobedience!), there only remained a memory of it, in the form of a blackish rag, even more blackish than the one she used to polish the silverware of Madam Fairschenne de Dendur, that was getting abnormally blacker these days.

Oh, since last month, maintaining the silverware had become a true wife beater! Beautiful brand-new silverware, though? Since April, it was incomprehensible: it needed to be cleaned every day, and even several times a day, recently ... But it got black again. It blackened in plain sight. It could be said that the more a person worked away at making it gleam, the blacker it became, on purpose!

As for the rest of her clothes, let us not speak of them! What Lusinia's rage had not been able to tear up became irreversibly soiled when vanquished Leona collapsed, bloodied, half-dead, in mud mixed with volcanic ash.

There was catastrophe in the air. Indeed, without any possible doubt. How could she dare to present herself before Madam in this state? She was risking more than her position there ...

"You don't belong here, Miss Leona ..." the marble carver was able to murmur still. His thoughts were already far away.

"I know. I know that only too well. I'm not from here, furthermore."

"Where are you from?" insisted Homer, after introducing himself.

"I come from far away, from Grande Anse. From Lorrain, if you prefer; my ma is from Marigot. And I am not going to be long for this world in this Saint-Pierre, believe me!"

She stood up in front of him in all her stature of a lioness, impressive, beautiful with her head of hair as if it were woven with bamboo foliage, beautiful with the slits of her eyes shining like mice in a seed broom. More sparkling than mica, her pupils threw sparks onto the scalded-rabbit complexion of the

Her Destiny on Climb to the Sky Street

enamored marble carver. Then, suddenly, she shot off, beautiful with her long freed muscles like rivers running under her brown skin.

The goiter woman was still growling in her aching ears: "But I don't care which one of the two of you started it! Lusinia doesn't work for me . . . A big girl like you, who has already thrown away at least twelve or thirteen calendars for me! If not longer! A child who is only a "born around . . ." They don't know either where it was born or on what date, in truth. Thank God you're baptized! And what are you doing with it, your baptism certificate? Aren't you ashamed? Savage manners, quite simply!" Madam was able to shout.

No, Leona is not a "born around," unless her mother lied, which doesn't even graze her spirit. Her ma always told her that she had given birth to her—a little runt so minuscule that they believed she would not survive the night and that they would have thrown her to the pigs if she hadn't cried louder than any newborn here below, which impressed everyone—in a panic, right at noon on the blessed day of the Assumption. Her ma remembered the year well, the year when there were so many mangoes that they stepped on top of them everywhere and made love on top of them, after the memorable year when the white man with the hooked nose who was in love with colors, resembling the offspring of an Indian and a black or an Arawak "zindian," had descended upon Saint-Pierre, then had gone back, and then, just before disappearing for good, had visited her. (A biblical visit, all in all, from which Leona would remain the living memory.) Regarding the calendars, Leona would soon count fifteen of them. But how could Euryale de Dendur have known it?

Madam had to know that in 1887—this year and no other— a Frenchman by the name of Paul Gauguin had stayed five months in Martinique, at Anse Turin, a time to fertilize a dozen sublime works of art and a young woman from Martinique no less sublime, the future ma of Leona, destined and predestined to come into the world, a superb lioness of dark marble veined with white and colored with Inca blood, through her paternal ancestor Flora Tristan, the great militant feminist. Madam could boast well about having a gallery of portraits of aristocratic ancestors with faces of stale bread displayed with indulgence into the ears of whoever wanted to hear it (and even those who didn't want to hear it!); the secret genealogy of swarthy Leona had no reason to envy it at all. It was no less prestigious, and, even being clandestine, it was no less noble, while still being not noble. As mixed-blood as she was, Leona did not have to blush about her ancestry at all. Not only was she a little proud of her runaway Negro grandfather, even if runaways had a very bad reputation, but she also didn't hate dreaming to the image of this mysterious artist father whom she had never met. Often, in her daydreams, Leona combed into her imagination a portrait of this bizarre father who had sketched, at the time a rough draft, the portrait of her mother.

Let us suppose that this colossus Paul, who wasn't yet the great Gauguin, but, at the dawn of his early forties, an "iron man" eager "to live in the wild," "to flee Paris, which is a desert for a poor man," could no more resist the charm of Creole flesh than he could Mallarmé's "Sea Breeze" call, inciting him to "Flee! Flee far away! There where the birds are drunk . . . ," committing during his passage sultry unfaithfulness to his northern wife, whom he had left behind in Paris.

Born, oh prodigious symbol! in 1848, the year of the abolition of slavery, the ex-stockbroker, emancipated from the servitude of business, chose to leave, for, he wrote to his wife Mette, "life in the Antilles (Martinique, etc . . .) is exquisite like ease and amenities." (There are no coincidences; there are only *Correspondences,* in the Baudelairian sense of the term, all the more so in the birth of a symbolist.) "A beautiful country with an easy, cheap life, that's Martinique!" he wrote from Panama, where, "while working on the canal," he is going "to save a little money for two months to leave for Martinique." Not content with drawing countless sketches of monkeys, Gauguin unintentionally completed his Antilles bestiary and took pleasure in perfecting, in the arms of a black girlfriend from a

Her Destiny on Climb to the Sky Street

house of ill-repute in Saint-Pierre, an unusual emergence from his animal symbolism, in making himself the creator of a little lioness of black marble that they named Leona. To the pictorial exaltation of Martinique nature, the artist, aspiring from then on for a spiritual dimension, added in fact a work of art of flesh, from which came to him a natural daughter of a beauty more than human.

In fact, in April 1887, Gauguin wrote to his Danish wife: "I'm taking my colors and my paintbrushes and I will dip myself into a place far from all men." He did not say "far from all women," the grandson of Flora Tristan...

So, without knowing it, Leona had feminism in her blood—without even knowing the term—with color in her heart, in the manner of her painter father. As a father, this great man was only one in spirit for Leona: she never called him "Papa," other than in the space of her dreams. The white man with the curious hooked nose had already left again toward unknown Breton fogs and a faraway Tahiti when she was born, according to the time-honored expression, to an unknown father. A known painter, then still unrecognized, Gauguin was only her sire. (Furthermore he never knew it, that he had a daughter in the Antilles. The young illiterate ma would have been incapable of sending him an announcement!) However, through him she gained a little something extra, this surplus of pre-Columbian blood that haunted Gauguin suddenly, as soon as he met Martinique, pushing him to detach himself from Parisian impressionism, strong with the Indian heritage he held from his grandmother, Flora Tristan-Morosco, of Hispano-Peruvian descent through her father, and a friend of George Sand, that other "upstanding woman" from France, according to what her ma had understood, for whom things from France were quite far away.

Before a hurricane carried her to the shores of death and, alas, she went to Heaven, her ma combed her hair, oily, iridescent, dripping more than the Roxelane River, humming: "He said—What? Your grandmother is named Floraona? My grandmother's first name is Flora: we were made for each other! ... And then he started laughing kra-kra-kra. That's

Climb to the Sky

how he set about sketching me ... Girlfriend, I am going to sketch you ... Beautiful girlfriend, let me sketch you!..." And she laughed also, with her three teeth.

Leona starts laughing in her own way, in front of the portraits of the Dendurs, in front of the enraged Fairschenne. A sovereign contempt makes the wings of her hooked nose, the same one as Gauguin's, quiver.

Thus Leona assumed her *métissage,* confidently, standing strong and facing the universe in the profusion of all her bloods.

"Lower your eyes, you little nothing! Are you not ashamed?"

No, she didn't have to blush, neither about her actions nor about her birth. (First of all, black people do not blush.) All her brief history, her young life unwound in that moment, that morning, as if it were the last. Conceived, on the night before Paul Gauguin's departure from Saint-Pierre, in a brothel on Hell Street, coming into the world amid so much suffering that it was a miracle if she lived, Leona lived in hell on Climb to the Sky Street. But her entire life was nothing but signs: was it not the Holy Virgin in person who, on the day of her Assumption, on this 15th of August in the year of our Lord 1888, presided over Himitée's apocalyptic childbirth? (This woman, with a "boo boo" in her big heart from when she was slapped on the bottom at birth at the hospital, had received from her father, the holy slave Leonard, the first name of the first great love of the runaway nigger, the name of the beautiful captive Himitée, so cruelly martyred, full of the taint of the mating.) Once having come down to Saint-Pierre, fleeing the misery of the North and the hills of Marigot, hardly fifteen years old, this Himitée's only resource was the vivacious spring of her body, which gushed so strongly, between her two beautiful thigh quarters, so much so that she became proverbial because of it. Arched, her calves shaped by the cut-stone staircase with high steps of *"la calle"* coming down from the Center to the seaside, Himitée was a fecund spring. From a single ephemeral and, all things considered, prodigious embrace with a painter about to leave should be born our Leona.

Her Destiny on Climb to the Sky Street

When the funny white man left Martinique, five full moons after his return from Panama, Himitée couldn't have looked big, but she had not had her period since he had visited her the first time—and didn't have it again for a long time. She never opened up to him about it. What good would it do? He was too poor to be of any help to her. He hardly had enough to live on, in the back of his miserable hut in Anse Turin, selling off a few paintings or two or three engravings cheaply to the wealthy bourgeois of Saint-Pierre, who were averse to untying their purses for "art." He had said that he was coming back from the hell of Panama, where he had worked hard, where there were people who died "in three days." According to him, he had "so much to suffer that it almost goes beyond human limits."

"Evidently, he was white, but he was a little unhappy fellow, worse off than the rest of us!" Himitée said in her singsong voice.

He was a good man, the colorist, but he didn't eat his fill; what good would it do to talk to him about the child that was growing deep in her belly?

But through what miracle could Madam have known all that? Leona only reported it deep down inside, and, until she went to heaven, her ma Himitée had talked about it only to her only daughter. Even the gossipy washwomen from the Roxelane River didn't know. For them, Gauguin did not exist. However, while rinsing the dresses of the rich women and the precious linen from Milan thoroughly, no malicious gossip escaped them, so much so that these laundresses set themselves up, over the years, as experienced takers of "rumors." (The expression even spread from Saint-Pierre to Fort-de-France, with the same speed as gossip, and has remained to this day.)

". . . When I hear what they're spreading about you! . . . What am I going to do with that child? Holy Virgin, have pity on me!"

Suddenly Madam has something to complain about, now? She's the one hitting, and now, she's the one whimpering?

"It must be said that you're such bandits! . . . Always up to some trouble! Leona and, even worse, Lusinia. The last time, on All Saints' Day, they didn't have to look far: these two were at the head of the mob of wild children who were bombarding poor people with candle drippings in the cemetery! Can you tell me big girls behave like that? And hidden where, I ask you? Behind my family's tombs! Beautiful gravestones of fine white marble that they had just finished cleaning! Carrara marble, if you please! . . . So do you have no respect for anything? Do you have no pity for our dead?"

What does Leona have in common with these dead people?

"No way to deny it! They caught you, both of you, with your pockets full of wax pellets. It was you, Missy Leona, and your damned soul, Lusinia . . ."

Echoes of misfortune! The screams knock inside her head. Diatribes and sobs still clink under her skull. Leona is bewildered.

"You know, you can confide in me . . . I have always been your ally . . . I am your best friend. Not that rascal Lusinia. You know, I have also had my problems . . . The Master is not always nice . . . He doesn't even hear when I talk to him . . . He doesn't see me . . . You'd think that I were transparent . . ."

Certainly she is transparent, this old cunning devil of a jellyfish!

The blows, over. But the jeremiads! The false affection, the flattery . . . The semblance of a bond . . . It's what Leona loathes. The other woman has really tried everything. She's pulling out anything. With disgusting smoothness, the jellyfish finally murmurs:

"I who love you so much! . . ."

What a comedy!

The insults and the sarcasm still resonate in her ears. She sees the affected mannerisms alternating with the threats, sparking the cataclysm . . .

She left. She didn't wait for nightfall, or Sunday, the day of the Lord, a day off, a day of freedom, a rare day when she could

Her Destiny on Climb to the Sky Street

come and go so to speak as she wanted, or the festival of the Holy Virgin, her protector, or even for the celebration of the Ascension, and yet she is a good Christian. But there, the cup is full, really. Leona drank the chalice down to the dregs. Nothing will make her stay. Nothing is keeping her here. Leona will not remain in this city one day longer. Not one night longer!

Madam did not give her pay to her, but too bad. In exchange for all salaries, Leona has taken blows. The little servant girl is no longer a slave, but it's just like it! That fat stingy woman covered in jewels bought on account at full price on Petit Versailles Street, there where they're most expensive, pays her a meager sum whenever she feels like it. And now is not really the moment to ask for what is owed to her! . . . Yesterday was a day of goodness, in anticipation of the Ascension. Madam royally gave a single bead of gold to her nurse, who was in her nineties but nonetheless faithful, Ma Sonson. But Leona, too rebellious, too mocking, too aggressive, will never receive the generosities of her boss lady, who endows generously, at each special occasion, the most devoted of her servants. Besides, the special occasions were held so infrequently, and Madam was so stingy, that the poor unfortunate soul would never string together the entire necklace before the hour of her death tolled, brave Ma Sonson! In her parsimonious extravagance, Madam having started by making a present to her of the smallest ones; she would always be missing the five big gold beads in front and the spring.

But to the devil with avarice! Too bad if she is penniless. She will manage. She has her two feet, her whole head, she knows what to do with her ten fingers, unlike that fat useless woman . . . She will find a way to earn her bread.

As for the elections, Leona cares nothing for them. That doesn't concern her. It's not that she's losing interest in them, but, even if she had wanted, she would not have been able to vote. Leona does not have the right to vote, any more than any woman in this country, even the mulatto women, even the white women, even the civil servants who came from France, even the great whities, not a single woman! Not even the hatted women from mythic France. On this 7th day of May, 1902, Leona recalls the words of Olympe de Gouges, read in the "Woman" entry from Madam's encyclopedia. Adding to the *Declaration of the Rights of Man and the Citizen* the *Declaration of the Rights of Woman and the Female Citizen,* Leona keeps in her memory that the fierce candidate for the seat of representative said in substance, at the time of the French Revolution: "A woman has the right to climb up to the guillotine; she must also have the right to climb up to the rostrum." In vain. Try as Leona might to open her eyes, there were no more *Rights of Woman* than there were *Rights of Negroes* anywhere. The *Declaration* might be "Universal," but not for everyone! So, *Rights of Negresses*! . . . She has nightmares, but she is not dreaming. Leona does not dream standing straight up!

Even if the poor child had been able to vote, she hardly would have known how to do it . . . For, on the other hand, Leona, without being completely ignorant, is a complete stranger to the mysteries of politics. It is not the trifles of news grumbled by the Master that would have been enough to inform her. As for the recent newspapers, it was difficult for her to have direct access to them: it was the Master's exclusive territory. If Leona wanted one, she had to go through him. And that she preferred to avoid . . . The Master would have been only too happy to take advantage of it to fondle Leona under the pretext of helping her with her reading and to perfect her initiation into it, under the guise of an education of a special nature . . .

No more than the rest of them, the pickaninny would not vote on the 11th of May. There would be no second round of legislative elections in this good city of Saint-Pierre, not for her, not for anyone else.

His Excellency the Governor in person will have come in vain, with weapons and luggage, wife and children, to throw himself into the mouth of the volcano to "give an example of duty" and persuade the people of Saint-Pierre to stay and vote

Her Destiny on Climb to the Sky Street

... "Sleep, good people, nothing to fear, you can sleep, the volcano too! ..." Leona will not sleep one night more in her attic room under that roof.

"A woman has the right to climb up to the guillotine; she must also have the right to climb up to the rostrum"! ... She must have the right to leave. (Since she became a woman, Madam has repeated it enough! Since she is more and more a woman, through the Master's good care.)

The little lioness paid one franc and took the boat.

BELLY OF FIRE

> As for the flesh, that we have fed too well,
> it has long since been devoured or rotted.
> And we bones become ash and dust.
> May no one laugh at our pain
> But pray God will absolve us all!
> —*François Villon, "The Ballad of the Hanged Men"*

Huddled on the hard wood bench, aboard the *Rubis,* which is leaving the Saint-Pierre harbor splitting foam, Leona does not even spare a glance at this place that she is leaving without regret.

The salty air of the sea whips and heals the wounds and scars on her body at the same time. One cupped palm on her belly, the other gripping the ship's rail, she calmly turns her back on the dozing Mountain for a few moments more, and on bad memories. The fire of the sun cauterizes cuts and scars on her body.

Her eyes lower toward the sea waters. This time, she's the one on board; for the time being, she will not dive into the entrails of the sea. She is no one's amusement. The times when the wealthy tourists amused themselves watching her dive, risking her life, to fish back up the Totors have passed! The times when her body was used for enjoyment have passed. She is no longer anyone's toy. It is she who, henceforth, has taken her destiny

Climb to the Sky

into her hands. She is fleeing the stains on her honor, the rapes. She is fleeing Climb to the Sky Street. She has set sail, she is leaving.

She doesn't even feel like throwing up anymore. The healing sprays dress the sores and wounds in her body.

How everything rushed by! Leona had just enough time to catch the *Rubis;* her run, normally so quick, was slowed down by her injuries, her bruises, and her state of mind. This was one of the last boats to leave the Saint-Pierre bay, at 6:30 a.m., May 8th, 1902, but Leona didn't know it. The young woman was simply in a hurry to leave. Thinking herself protected by her devotion to the Virgin Mary, she feared nothing or no one, neither the Fire Mountain nor the devil. She turned her back to hell.

"Let's go! Let's go! Let's hurry up! I'm in a hurry to leave here!" the captain of the boat from Italy was yelling while contemplating, worriedly, the black smoke that was rising from Mount Pelée.

"Your Mountain is smoking; and it's coughing! Your Pelée doesn't know how to smoke! Watch out, if it ends up spitting! . . . I prefer not to be here to see that . . ."

All the boats of Saint-Pierre and even the smallest rowboats were loaded to the brim. However, no later than yesterday, the Master was reading while griping in his newspaper: "A commission of scientists wrote a typical reassuring note. The volcano poses no danger. Any Saint-Pierre civil servant leaving the city is dismissed by order of the governor, who is coming to Saint-Pierre today . . ." Only Leona does not give a hoot: the little servant girl is neither a civil servant nor a resident of Saint-Pierre.

She moves one hand to her heart. The run made her lose her breath, but neither its palpitations nor the emotions linked to recent events interfered with her serenity. Leona learned to tame her heart a long time ago by diving into the belly of the sea. She knows how to control herself. She does not fear the beats, even if they accelerate, like now, even if they become

Her Destiny on Climb to the Sky Street

chaotic, lively, and strong. She feels herself living. She has the same zest for life as her ancestor Leonard, the runaway Negro. Leona breathes in deeply, faraway, to the innermost depths of her belly, swollen to the point of bursting, draws vital strength there. She exhales, lengthily, sweetly . . . She feels the life that is in her.

Once in Fort-de-France, she hears all the people yelling, "Saint-Pierre is burning! Good Lord! Saint-Pierre is burning! "The Guérin factory has started coming down! The factory actually went back into the sea!" yelped an old woman, dumbfounded. "I took the steamboat just in time! It's the end! I'm telling you, it's the end!" the hysterical old lady shrieked.

From Fort-de-France, a glare could be seen. They couldn't see the flames, but everyone was talking about them, everyone was howling about them.

Leona already knew it, that the Guérin factory had been buried by a terrific flow of mud that had caused an extraordinary tidal wave on the Caribbean side, two or three days before. It couldn't be said that important news doesn't travel fast! They would've said that it was done on purpose, as if to keep the people from leaving! . . . For all that time they felt the tremors, that the earth shook in Saint-Pierre and in Prêcheur! . . . For all that time that the animals were in a panic! As for the thick rain of ashes, it dated back so long that they had almost become accustomed to it, except that they needed to clean more . . . For nearly a week, the White River had been flooding. Unheard of. No later than yesterday, the intense flow of mud coming out of the Pères River had bothered the inhabitants of the neighboring villages so much that they had sought refuge in Saint-Pierre in great numbers. What had they done there, the poor souls! . . .

As for Leona, she made a good decision. Stoic, lonely but serene, she lets the people talk. She is going away.

To learn finally to say no. Just as she had, some time ago, and through her own movements, assumed the right to learn to read, she grants herself the right to speech and the right to silence, as she pleases.

Climb to the Sky

More and more persuaded to tackle henceforth the good side of her destiny, Leona went back to her route, through ravines, hills, and savannahs, through depths, through trails and sugarcane fields, on foot this time. Otherwise the cost would be too great. She would have to break the Totor, and she didn't want that. This Totor would never leave her.

Unperturbed, her head high under her Caribbean basket, in spite of her fatigue and the load, she went back up toward the North: Le Lamentin, La Trinité, Sainte-Marie, Le Marigot . . .

Clenched tightly in her madras cotton, she kept it as a charm, her only surviving Totor, with which she disembarked in Fort-de-France. No one stole it from her on her way.

On the head of the illustrious unknown man named "Vittorio Emmanuel II, Re d'Italia, 1863," according to what she deciphered on the worn face of the Totor (who knows how these bizarre kinds of money had ended up there, arriving in Martinique heaven knows when, through some unknown mystery, engraved in a strange language that resembled the Latin chanted by the priest during the Sunday high mass—the rest of the time, outside his functions as officiant, immediately after coming out of his sacraments, the priestly officer leaves like all the poor fishers and sinners of Saint-Pierre and Miquelon: every day of the holy week that the Good Lord makes, the minister of the Heavenly Father swears in dragon Creole, cusses God in France French or in the patois of his province, delivers swear words, good swear words, as it is written, sends to his flock, to niggers as well as crackers, a delivery of impious bad words, and then atones on the Day of the Lord, praises be to God, the Seventh Day, yes, thank God, hallelujah! "Gloria in excelsis Deo!" Leona is so afraid for him, for the salvation of his soul, the pious child, some preacher he is)—she had made a secret wish, a wild, obscure wish, almost subconsciously, partially unspoken, at the same time she made her devotions to the Blessed Virgin.

On the heaven-sent gold coin, the symbol of this new turn that her destiny would take, she had dedicated Climb to the Sky Street to the Black Angel of Mercy, with a brief prayer for

Her Destiny on Climb to the Sky Street

the foul-mouthed ecclesiastic, the only human being she loved in this good city of Saint-Pierre, at least to her knowledge. (Or so she thought.)

He would stay until the end in his parish, at the foot of the Fire Mountain, to celebrate the Ascension, even if it meant blaspheming under the ashes spit by "that goddamn volcano," that "damn Pelée Mountain," during his preaching. She vaguely feels him very near having to account for his sins before the Creator.

She removed her feet from there.

Arriving after several days, she found everyone in mourning in Lorrain: two brothers had left to go to look for her with two horses. But they passed by Morne Rouge along the way, and they never came back.

One single being in Lorrain had a festive heart: the little marble carver from Climb to the Sky Street. The little poor white man from Martinique wasn't there by chance, but by the combined graces of the Totor and the Virgin who deigned to fulfill Leona's secret wish.

And yet had he come there because he had a good memory and still heard, and would always hear, the little beloved voice that said, "I am from Grande Anse," and he loved to see the little black marble lioness from Grande Anse? He would've done anything to see her again, even leaving the village of his birth, its white marble from Carrara, from Pentelique or elsewhere, all the marbles from Italy and Greece, all the most beautiful white marbles, crossing Martinique on the back of a mule, to find her again, black marble, upright Negress.

He left everything behind him, in order to help, chivalrous, his marble ladylove, immediately after his apprentice ran up stuttering: "M-m-miss Leona l-l-left! M-m-miss t-t-took so m-m-many blows! I don't think that Miss is g-g-going to return . . . Her boss lady beat her, beat her good! They heard her screaming from the top of Climb to the Sky Street to the bottom! How did you not hear her? Ah, that's right, you were

Climb to the Sky

at the harbor . . . Her boss lady set off a DISASTER! . . . It's a miracle that Leona came out of it alive. The other woman set off some GOSSIP! . . . And what's worse is that I saw her with her satchel."

Dropping his marble and family there, Homer rushed off. He didn't think twice, the little marble carver. He tore along to Grand Anse.

Little Leona did not remain marble for long, in front of him, when she saw him, fiery, exhausted from his romantic ride, his tall body proudly mounted on his frothing steed . . . He appeared to her, quivering in the flamboyance of the sun at its zenith and his golden spikes sticking up making a halo around his blond head. This valiant man came straight out of a book.

Without thinking about it any longer, the young black girl delivered to him instantaneously the sparkle of her smile.

For him Leona gave birth to the child that, in secret and by force, Madam's husband had made in her, on Christmas night, if you please, oh great sacrilege! And not through an act of the Holy Ghost, she would swear, if that didn't make the Holy Virgin cry. There is nothing holy about him, the sick spirit who came to visit her ever since her tits pushed through, ever since she reddened her ragged sheets, in her insipid little room. She puts on black panties in vain, the Master comes back, an incubus. But he is not an incubus! That, that proves that it wasn't an incubus that visited her at night and comes back, even today, in her nightmares, the sadist, to do to her, with her candle of a good little Christian Negress lit for the Blessed Virgin—who got angry, the day of her son's Festival, because of what they were doing to her, because of that, yes! not because of the last perverted carnival, for she had seen others—things she would not want. Things that she would never dare to say, and especially not to Madam! . . . All sorts of unscrupulous things . . . Things far more forbidden, she would put her hand into fire, even down into the belly of the volcano, than the perilous pleasure of diving half-naked to look for gold Totors at the bottom of the belly of the sea. Because he does all those things completely naked, those things, yes! He does them to her in her

Her Destiny on Climb to the Sky Street

belly. He gets naked all over and he makes her naked as well, even if the Holy Virgin does not like for them to get naked. He makes her get completely nude, even if the Holy Virgin is protecting her because she was born on August 15th, the day of Her Assumption. The Master doesn't give a shit. The Master sits down on top. Stories of virgins with or without capital letters, large or small, the Master does his business on top! The Master does his business in her body and after that, she feels like swimming, like washing herself with bitter foam, like diving down to the bottom of the bay and sometimes no longer coming up, staying there, in those good waters that are so maternal, feeling seized by the madness of the waters, and she knows well that Madam wouldn't like those things. She would swear it! But she won't do it: it makes the Blessed Virgin cry, if you swear.

Furthermore, the letch, the Master, who isn't even close to being one, the miscreant, the barbarian, swore to her on his head and on his children's heads that he would take off her head, with a blow from a cutlass, a single blow, if she ever said a word to anyone.

"So keep your head on your neck! And bury that deep inside you; do you see your mirror? Look: you see your mouth? Your mouth is pretty, huh? Incredibly luscious . . . Mmm . . . A treat! . . ." he whispered, twisting her lips to hurt her, in the grip improvised by his thumb and his threatening index finger. "Look at your mouth well! If you ever open it one day, you won't have the time to say 'hack!' So keep your head on your neck, do not forget what I am telling you here, if you want to keep it in place . . ."

No, she didn't tell anyone, not even her ex–best friend. (A lot of good it did her!) Not even at confession. She tried, however, encouraged by the quiet shadows of the confessional, but she was so ashamed! How to answer the overly specific questions of the abbot, who requires details from her? How to describe how it happens, when the Master shoves her, in her minuscule attic room where you can hardly even stand up, then straddles her, plays leapfrog, stupid and sick games where Leona closes her eyes, wondering what he can possibly need to come to look for in her body? To whom could she confess how the Master shoves her, throws himself on her and in her, so deeply that she's curious to know what he's seeking all the way down at the bottom of her belly?

What need does the Master have to skewer her like that? Leona isn't very learned: they pulled her out of school as soon as she was old enough to understand and participate in the sacraments to "place" her. The rest she learned all by herself, a little in Madam's service, a lot in Madam's books, and the abominable unnecessary things, at the Master's pleasure. (Rather *for* his pleasure, all in all!) She is not well informed, the little self-taught girl, but there are things that she knows. Leona must know that they are in a republic, even faraway in the sea of the Antilles, and that try as she might to be a Negress, she is a human being. She repeats it to herself in these terms. And yet vaguely she feels, because she read it between the lines somewhere, that no law of the republic or any human law obliges her to put up with that. No need to be well educated to guess that! No law can allow it, neither what Madam does to her, nor what the Master does to her in her minuscule attic room . . .

But all that is only nightmares. All that is just delirium. A load of bad memories. She is no longer at Climb to the Sky Street, in her miserable garret, but at her own home, in Marigot, in her big canopy bed. Leona wakes up in a sweat, stifles under the full mosquito net, runs to serve herself, from the terra-cotta carafe that will keep water cool until dawn, a good invigorating glass, rushes to the window, her cheeks on fire, to draw soothing from the night air. Hands cupped on her belly, she contemplates the stars in the sky. Homer is breathing peacefully. She is safe like she has never been before. Without fear, she can go back to sleep with this man.

In spite of everything she had suffered, the Blessed Virgin did not want Leona to miscarry. The child was born a mulatto, of course. To top it off, he was born with a full head of hair, a

Her Destiny on Climb to the Sky Street

little prematurely, on August 15th, like his ma. But the people didn't even notice, since the papa was white: wasn't it the little poor white man from Martinique who went to announce her at the Marigot town hall? Was it not he who married his little black marble lioness in a legitimate wedding?

His parents were entombed under the rubble of Saint-Pierre. They had vehemently refused to leave their city and their marble. An orphan since the massacre of that fateful May 8th, 1902, Homer no longer had to worry about getting the paternal blessing for his marriage. Lucky for him, in his unhappiness and mourning, for otherwise he would have never received the consent of his cracker father to marry a Negress, be he a poor white man from Martinique, be she made of the most beautiful black marble! He would have been rejected by the clan. But the clan no longer existed.

"You don't marry Negresses! You know what they're called? They're called 'girlfriends'! Take that to bed with you, to warm you up at night. That's what Negresses are for: to give pleasure and pretty little mulattos; not so long ago, you could sell them for a higher price than the ebony wood niggers, if those republicans from Paris, those Schoelchers and those Lamartines, hadn't imposed that 'Abolition' trash on us! . . . 'Abolition' my ass! . . . You can go to bed with her, but don't you give her your name! I forbid you to soil our name, my son!"

This is what Homer had heard not long ago, when, at the family table, he braved the paternal lightning bolts by talking about Leona. He saw the bald head again all enraged with fury . . . A short time after the eruption of Mount Pelée, the little marble carver returned alone to Saint-Pierre to gather, on Climb to the Sky Street, in the ruins of his house, what remained of his decimated family.

He erected a mausoleum of black marble for them with his own hands, in the permanent family burial plot, then went back to Marigot to rejoin his black marble lioness, whom he would love for life. He had found out how to tame her. He knew to overcome her with sweetness, the little lioness, to take her through sweetness . . . He gave his name to her, willingly, to the great displeasure of the paternal Spirits!

Climb to the Sky

They had united their destinies far from the Fire Mountain. Hate for one, love for the other, had made them just barely escape death, making them leave Saint-Pierre the day before the catastrophe. What, "the day before?" At dawn! On the very morning of the catastrophe! Some two hours before a terrible detonation jarred Saint-Pierre suddenly, and before an immense cloud of ashes and flames escaped from the volcano. Right before this burning cloud rushed onto the city, covered it, stifled it in less than two minutes, before reaching the sea.

When they fled Climb to the Sky Street, one after the other, she, in her haste, he in search of her, he had her image in him, she had a child in her belly.

It was a son. She named him "Dartagnan," like in the novel that she had read on Climb to the Sky Street behind her boss lady's back, her favorite one, the Dumas novel, the one she had taken away in her satchel in leaving Climb to the Sky Street. Little Leona was not aware of how marvelously this first name suited her mixed-blood son: the author of *The Three Musketeers*, who had made her dream so much, was he not the grandson of a black slave from Saint-Domingue, the future Haiti? The famous French novelist known all over the vast world, with mixed blood, like her own child, from a modest woman from Martinique? A quadroon, as they say, the great Alexandre Dumas? . . . Leona knew nothing of it. That wasn't mentioned in Madam's books. They would've been very careful not to speak of it! . . . That black blood ran in the veins of the Clarissimus—the most renowned of all French writers, the father of the best-known characters from the novel worldwide along with Don Quixote, they carefully avoided giving an account of it! What good would come of soiling the prestige of French literature with the stench of Negro blood and the miasmas of the shameful memory of slavery that ended with the defeat of Napoleon's troops? . . . How could she have known, Leona, in spite of her thirst for knowledge and her sharp spirit? She knew only what the books agreed to teach her, while suspecting only slightly how much they hid from her . . .

What Leona did not know was that Cessette's blood also

Her Destiny on Climb to the Sky Street

ran in her veins. For the aristocrat Davy de la Pailleterie had tasted many times the musky body of the Negress from Saint-Domingue who, from her earliest age, at the end of her first frolics, had a bad taste for giving birth, but produced only one girl child before giving him a son. As much as this man would rejoice, twenty years after, from the arrival of a "child with balls," mixed-blood, certainly, but with light skin, who would make a good officer—the general Alexandre Davy Dumas, the future father of the writer of the same name, the birth of this daughter would leave him indifferent. Especially as the unfortunate girl did not have "saved skin": this little female, according to what they said, "came out black like last night." Recognizing her as his daughter would have been greatly embarrassing, even indecent. So her natural father, who was also her young master, neglected to emancipate this offspring, but so little for nothing! How would that have served his interests? Impossible to raise this black girl as a young girl from a good family! Also difficult to assign the least domestic task, like serving at the table or sewing, to this unpresentable fleabag with enormous coal-woman's hands. The Creole squire ignored her, then forgot her. Turned over to herself, dispensed, by her special status, for jobs in the "workshops" imposed on the other slaves, but ignored by her mother—completely assigned to her favorite slave task, bed slave—the young girl grew up with disheveled clothing and hair, until the day when a black Hercules, noticing her existence, took advantage of her disinheritance, having sex with her in the ti baume shrubs. He pushed a son into her belly.

From Alexandrine, which was her baptismal first name, the young coal-woman ma had, through gibes, become Cendrine. (Such is the spelling that will appear on the baptismal certificate of her child.) Born from a slave mother, this boy proved to be of a recalcitrant nature and an impish temperament. Sometimes he nailed down a miserly frog on the door of the sugar refinery, making everyone break into a cold sweat, sometime he played zombies or disguised his voice to scare the gallery, dressing himself up as Baron Saturday or as horned Iron Ogoun, disguised in various rags or hats from his master

Climb to the Sky

or grandfather yet . . . One night during Lent this scamp Alexandrin was bold enough to go pee in the tub reserved for the mistress's monthly bath. It was no longer a question of impunity there. He had gone too far. This quarter hour of fun caused him to be reported cruelly once again: denounced by the ones who had laughed the loudest—the mistress's own offspring—the little boy discovered that a little boy's clowning, for a slave child, amounts to grave sins, for which one could be condemned to hard punishment. Without being in the least bit educated about the world, the quadroon had the ipso facto revelation that there exist two weights and two measures in this lowly world. As a result, this lighthearted capuchin monkey freed himself of his own accord in his head.

That was his last childhood trick. The scalawag became a man with a single blow. The mischievous brat understood that he was a man at the same time that he realized bitterly that he was only a slave, when they tore him away from his mother, to sell him separately. They got rid of him by sending him to Saint-Pierre, where slavery was in full swing and where those "Messieurs from Martinique" had an agreement with each other to put down troublemakers of that sort. After a pathetic auction, an examination of his set of teeth and a feel of his muscles, the unruly "pièce d'Inde" ended up in the outback of the Anse Céron plantation, above Prêcheur, far from any preacher or any sanctimonious person. He made it very quickly to the hills, running away like you regain your breath. He fell in love with Floraona there, the Carib woman with high cheekbones who brought Alexa into the world, coming out looking like a red creeper vine.

A tall formidable warrior, Floraona guided him, in the company of his brothers, into the vertiginous descents down into the plantations, where they took everything their bodies could carry: food, weapons, tools, pieces of cloth . . . Hardly risen from the bed in which she had given birth—which was hardly even worth mentioning, because the majority of the time the work had been done while she was standing, gripping the fork of a blown-down fig tree: the Carib woman stretched herself

Her Destiny on Climb to the Sky Street

out right on the ground only after having severed the umbilical cord with her teeth, and after having buried it at the foot of a giant kapok tree, so that the spirit of the tree would spread its protection over her progeny—Floraona taught him Martinique and the virtues of its flora, the benefits of certain plants and the dangers of its savage fauna. He told and told his memories of Hispaniola, chiming out confessions and threnodies, tales of farce and romantic cooings, in that language rolling like specks of rock in the river that Floraona did not understand. But they communicated by signs, and their bodies knew how to speak.

Their daughter received no baptism other than the stimulating ablutions under the waterfall. Driven by an unknown pressing desire, amused by this sublime grotesqueness, Alexandrin decided to name her Alexa. In spite of the rigors of his former master and ancestor, and although definitively excluded from his favors, Alexandrin passed on, through some unknown incitement, known by him alone, the ultimate tradition of the transmission of this august white first name, "Alexandre," colored with inventive variants, like his blood was colored, throughout his lineage. Obscure, but essential for his transcendence, this was his supreme prank, the paroxysmal childish behavior of a man, his way of affirming to himself finally his status as a human being and free individual. (He who had only ever received three syllables and reproaches from Alexandre. It was amply sufficient, given the little that this overly "dignified" grandfather had deigned to grant him.) Far from being his umpteenth practical joke, this choice crowned his scorned mother's revenge and his own. To rebuked Alexandrine, reduced to the rank of being called "Cul-Cendron" (Ash Ass), no longer being just "Cendrine" (Ash Girl), he restored the lost letters. Who knows if he was conscious of it? He rendered a faraway homage to his ma Alexandrine, demeaned, denied, consumed with abjection and grief, who was moping, cut off from her son, on the great island of Saint-Domingue.

Not so long ago his mother had issued the same challenge. For him, his mother snatched these four syllables, "Alexandrin," at the same time as four pralines were pinched from

Climb to the Sky

the silver platter brought by a mulatto woman light-skinned enough to serve white people, at the time of a poetic discussion in the marquis's salon, enraged by the blinds forbidding her access. Half-dead from envy and fear, but drunk with jubilation, Cendrine brought them back to her hut, in order to offer to her bastard child whom no one would dream of baptizing, even though he was already standing on his own two feet—a sturdy Negro boy, with a straight back—the pralines and the four syllables stolen from behind some precious sonnet whose warrior hyperboles put her in a bellicose mood, from some jumble of prosodic commentary where she only seized this word at random: "ALEXANDRIN." Alexandrin! This is what made her happy, for that would not fail to cause displeasure to Mister Alexandre, the master, without his being able to admit the cause of it! Tired of calling her son "azougoun," which means "treasure" in Creole, in order to ward off her destitution, Cendrine rushed off immediately to the presbytery yelling like a woman possessed: "Massa abbot! I told you to baptize my young one for me!" At the height of the excitement, she took the priest by the collar, shaking him like a hog plum tree: "Well, Good Lord! Why are you waiting to baptize Alexandrin, my son, the one there? Are you waiting for his tail to unscrew?" A holy force of nature, this illegitimate girl, to tell the truth. The abbot did not touch the ground until he had acquiesced by promising to grant the giant woman's request. The priest complied religiously, although stammering like hell, with chants and holy water, helped by his acolytes and flanked by two choirboys "who pooped in their albs," if Alexandrine is to be believed, delighted with this solemn reappropriation of her entire first time, and no less proud of having granted herself by force a semblance of legitimacy, to thumb her nose at her Alexandre of a father. However, since she did not know how to read, Alexandrine never knew that a hypocritical betrayal had unduly had "Alexandrin, a Negro male, born of the Negress Cendrine" written down in the baptismal register.

In turn, lacking letters of nobility, Alexandrin's only gift to his first-born daughter was these stolen letters: *A L E X A*.

Her Destiny on Climb to the Sky Street

Out of this hereditary fancy for the crossbreeding of first names as much as from the mixing of blood comes Leona's first name, mixed with that first name of Leonard—the runaway Negro who would unite with Alexa—with a suffix just like the one at the end of the name Floraona, in homage to the Carib ancestor. But never was Grandma Alexa able to talk to her granddaughter about the impertinent origin of her own first name. A storyteller following in her father's boots, never, in the stories that she pulled and stretched repeatedly to put the little girl to sleep, could the old woman go back to the events from Saint-Domingue. There was a break, maintained by paternal will. In fact, in his golden years, Alexandrin no longer wanted to hear the contemptuous name of the great island, rebaptized Haiti long ago. Handling admirably a good embroidered French from France learned with his half brothers and his young white uncles, with whom he had shared childhood games and, as a clandestine auditor, lessons from a preceptor who came from Touraine, in his grandfather's plantation, until the final betrayal that came at the cost of his being sold like a beast and chased like Candide from this earthly paradise, this strict joker had talked and stopped talking about Saint-Domingue for so long that he was sure that he was not understood by anyone, neither his companion Floraona nor his Carib brothers. But as soon as Alexa was old enough to master language, Alexandrin suddenly dried up the spring of Haitian stories. He erased forever all traces of his colonist grandfather, rejecting those who had rejected him, burying obstinately at the bottom of his memory the audacious Alexandrine etymology. He now only spoke in Creole. His stories were peopled with mongooses, manatees, cunning rats that could not be caught, an old horse with three legs, and unusual tiger accomplices appearing suddenly from an unknown Africa. From then on only the double Carib and runaway etiology of Leona's first name triumphed.

For all that, little did it matter whether Leona knew that she was a relative of the author of *The Three Musketeers*. For she had loved it, that book, read feverishly in the brightness of her candle that had transformed into a Virgin on the morning of May 7th, in order to tell her to leave Saint-Pierre before it was too late, to go far away from that town where the men drank so much rum and even worse engaged in such debauchery at the Carnival and even in the middle of Lent, what a sacrilege! What blasphemy! This tropical Sodom where the handsome men did so many disgusting things in all the streets and especially Climb to the Sky Street and even in the little rooms of little lionesses, who became black marble by those things that were done to them. Who would remain black marble, while those things were done to them. Who would stay black marble for life, the little lionesses. By things that were done to them.

Even once she became a big lioness—finally a grown woman—she had all those things present in her mind and in her body.

Thanks be to God, the young marble worker, gifted, in this new melting process, with an impassioned panache, learned how to handle iron and a blowtorch with a brilliant craftsmanship, previously unknown to him, that this beautiful body had taught him instantaneously. He put his entire soul into it. In addition to his mastery of marble and its engraving application, he acquired, from the first kiss, the dexterity of a bookbinder. Making his conjugal duty a work of art, finding himself, in the twinkling of an eye, a sculptor, a stringed-instrument maker, a glass founder, and even a gold-leaf gilder, he made, from this raped flesh, his radiant wife emerge. With all the delicacy of an engraver of fine stones, all the zealous refinement of a maker of coats of arms, he marked his marble lioness with the seal of fullness, conjuring up his wife from the rough material.

He put his heart into it! Intaglio carvings, cut champlevés, after the castoffs and bevels from the very first intertwinings, putting the finishing touches on casts and castings on their wedding night, he enameled their banal life with illuminations, outside the daily grind and the ashy memories of faraway Climb to the Sky Street.

Her Destiny on Climb to the Sky Street

It's that he didn't make do with tormenting and gnawing like that lout of a Master. But he chiseled out, pierced, filed down, bored into, pulled strings softly, handling crankshafts and drill chucks alternately with a master's hand, not without preliminary sandpaperings, complicated mixings, sizings of haut- and bas-reliefs, and various preliminary expert kneadings, making waves, etchings, and streams flow from so much beauty exalted.

Never was marble moved more strongly than this brown femininity with coral depths. Although he had become a marble worker out of a calling, he embraced, for the love of her, all the other professions of labor, for the rest of his days and nights. No marmoreal splendor ever inflamed him as much as the moving musky heat of Leona. No form inspired him more than those dark curves, that roundness full from then on . . .

Leona found herself filled with happiness from it. Forgotten, the false friendship and the servile humiliations, in the discovery of pleasure. So much joy made her black sun shine.

Then, the black marble lioness made for her poor white man from Martinique—who had as his vocation and job knowing how to work marble and who worked it wonderfully; he was crazy about marble, black marble especially—a café au lait eldest daughter, kindly named Clémence. Only her own mother knew why she called her "Mademoiselle Clément," laughing. "You have a little hot body. Do you have a fever, Mademoiselle Clément? You shouldn't stuff your lil' body with chocolate: Ma is swiftly going to call all YOUR DOCTORS for you! Don't worry, everyone here is going to watch over MADEMOISELLE CLÉMENT'S HEALTH!" teased Leona tenderly, which lightened her maternal concern gaily. Then Leona gave birth to two milky tchololo twins, named Roosevelt and Washington, a set of black coffee younger sisters (Jamaica, Floraona, Lamartine, Olympe, Georgia, and Himitée), then a swarm of coffee-colored boys, with a little more or a little less milk: Bristol, Grégoire, Homer, Schoelcher, Cromwell, Tristan, and Alexis.

Climb to the Sky

Finally, she brought to the world a magnificent youngest child, a tchololo boy without milk: Nolaha buckled the belt.

Leona threw up a lot, during her twenty-one pregnancies. She vomited up merrily the rancid memory of Madame Baaark de Baaark, the smell of death of Monsieur Baaaark de Baaaaaark, an odor of dead rabbit, yes! . . . That stench that she smelled even in her sleep, when the Master entered her little room under the attic, when the Master came in . . . Bark! She had to chase away those thoughts. (Three times, from thinking about it too much, the waters turned in her lump and Leona threw up the fetus through her mouth.)

Between each childbirth, her belly flat, she dove into the belly of the sea. Homer had a "fashionable bathing suit" sent to her from France. Livelier than the waters of Saint-Pierre, the tides of Anse Charpentier broke, ceding under the strength of her loose-limbed body emancipated from all condemnation.

He had very golden skin, her firstborn Dartagnan, from running in the sun. A golden yellow, like the Totor. He rightfully had a big baptism, as soon as the finances were in good shape. The sunny morning when they brought him in great pomp under the baptismal font wells, under the gold of the vast nave, only Leona knew why he was named "Dartagnan Victor Emmanuel." Sometimes, smiling, she nicknamed him "little Totor" affectionately, in Creole. No one was surprised by that. They are so frequent, in Martinique, the nicknames coming out of nowhere, from some family secret, from some memory buried under the rubble of some unmentioned catastrophe . . . Secrets that they had to keep themselves from revealing, even doing it in secret, oh eternal paradox! Like King Midas's secret, that his barber had great difficulty keeping. No longer able to hold it back, he yells it into a hole in the ground: "King Midas has the ears of a donkey!" Our "little Totor" was luckier! Like the reeds of Phrygia, only the bamboos of Martinique murmured in rustling, accomplices, the secret of his birth . . . Humans never knew anything about it.

Even though Dartagnan was not of black marble, the child was completely beautiful. The marble carver loved him and

Her Destiny on Climb to the Sky Street

raised him as his own son. Thumbing his nose at the ancestral spirits of his father, Homer gave him his name as well as all the honors owed to his firstborn rank.

Twenty years after, Dartagnan would come back to the place of the drama, among the collapsed walls and the charred trees. On the piles of rubble, the young mulatto would erect a branch office of the family's marble business, helping the resurrection of the martyred city. One day, he would be mayor in this city that had finally become a town again, on March 23rd, 1923, after having been wiped off the map of the municipalities of France and Martinique by the law of February 15th, 1910... There would be a place for his name, and maybe even a statue.

Until then, he would charge around, free, on the beaches of Marigot, enthusiastically breaking through the tides, following the example of his very young mother. As hideous as were the circumstances of his birth, the child felt a joie de vivre, like his parents.

The alley where they lived, sloping gently toward the church, had, thank God, nothing in common with Climb to the Sky Street. Leona renamed it lovingly "Seventh Heaven Street." In time, everything seemed predestined to her, under the auspices of the Virgin and literature, Climb to the Sky Street... And even Homer's name, a vibrant homage to the poet of *The Iliad* and *The Odyssey*!... Would she have had the same quivers, would she have looked at him with the same eye, if he had not sparked off in her, in introducing himself, at the end of her epic tribulations, these Homeric emotions? Would she have received him thus, disturbed by such shudders, overwhelmed by reminiscences? Would she have given him her hand?

On her husband Homer's arm, she could go to the theater, adorned with all the jewels he offered her for each pregnancy. (She had more particularly received the gift of the gold bead necklace all at once, like a lady, and not gold bead by gold bead, like a servant.) But alas, that was the end of it, the Comedy. Of its splendor of not so long ago, that made Leona dream so much, only its colossal ceremonial staircase remained. Never, having become a "Madam," would the black lioness climb up the rich spiral steps of this staircase of honor, powdered and bedecked in jewels, bathed in "L'Étoile" eau de cologne, in joy and brash pride, on the arm of her legitimate husband.

On the other hand, she bought herself books, dozens, hundreds of books, that she devoured at night, all throughout her existence, as if her life depended on it.

If Leona had returned to Saint-Pierre (something that she never did, she abhorred that town too much, even decimated) after the eruption of Pelée, the little black marble lioness would have been perhaps moved to discover, in the rubble of Climb to the Sky Street, among the charred cadavers, the stiff body of Lusinia. She would have doubtlessly liked to see, attached to her neck by a vulgar iron chain, the pierced gold coin that her false friend had stolen from her and which was not, all things considered, even made of gold, as it turns out! . . .

In seeing them all, the blacks, the whites, the people from India, the redskins, the light-skinned freckled blacks, the Asians, and the mulattos, all of them, the white descendants from the colonists, the French whites, the poor whites from Martinique, the high-class whites, the low-class whites, the capres, the black mulattos, the dark-skinned blacks, the light-skinned mulattos, the arrogant, racist, very light-skinned mulattos, the offspring of blacks and people from India, the blond-haired chabines, the redheaded chabines, everyone, the Chinese, the Syrians, the Jews, the Christians coming out of communion from the cathedral, everyone, the rich and the less rich and the poor and the miserable, all equally blackened by the same fire, she would have certainly thought that this Fire Mountain, the Pelée prototype of a "new race of volcanoes," had settled in a single blow, most expeditiously, although very provisionally, the problems of differences in color, class, race, and ethnocentrism.

Paris, July 1998, and Fort-de-France,
January–December 2002

Sweat, Sugar, and Blood

To my father

I don't know if Emma loves Emile. But that's not the question. The mulatress is sixteen years old. Creamy like the fruit of the soursop tree, tender like the heart of a palm kernel, two days have to pass for her to become, in a legitimate marriage, my great-aunt Emma B.

Emma has to marry Master Emile B., the day after tomorrow, a notable man, a notary in Fort-de-France. Everything is ready: the lilies, the organdy, the heavy damask and the tulle, and the breathtaking muslin, and even the royal orchids that they've had brought from Balata, still beating with the humidity of the tropical forest, everything all white, immaculate. Around her they talk only about her trousseau, her hairdo, her veil and fitting, her train, her behavior, and her grooming again.

Emma is capsizing in this marriage as if she were in a white whirlwind.

The third day after her marriage, Master Emile B. placed a brief kiss on her lips, then recommended to her, while leaving, that she was especially not to venture off toward the distillery.

In addition to his notary office located on Perrinon Street, downtown, Master Emile inherited an old, little distillery that stubbornly clings to struggling along, up there, on the Didier plateau. The property being vast, he had the former plantation house restored completely with old stones and wood from French Guyana. It is in this harsh dwelling with walls covered in portraits of ancestors that Emma now lives, before her husband, new only to her, but who has already been quite busy . . . For there are a good number of chabines from Morne Coco who can claim from now on to be B.'s bastards! But Emma

Climb to the Sky

never encounters any of these children made outside of marriage. The young married woman never goes to Morne Coco, even though it's on the other side of the road. It's not a place for her, if the plump Sonson lady is to be believed.

Every day the Lord makes, on the other hand, Master Emile goes down to his study by car, leaving her alone in Upper Didier with the women of the house: Mammy Sonson, the cook, and the little servant girl, Sirisia. Emma didn't think it useful to take on more servants. She gets bored enough as it is! So, morning after morning, the same evasive embrace, the same wish of "good morning," and the same recommendation: "Don't go walking toward the distillery."

"What is he thinking?" reflects Emma, protesting on the inside. (She dares not dream of coming out and saying it openly . . .) "But who does he think I am? Is he afraid I'm going to go get drunk on rum? I'm not a baby anymore! Besides, the small carafes of alcohol are all within my reach on the pedestal table in the living room, not even locked up. If I needed to get drunk, I would just have to extend my arm . . ."

Maybe Master Emile fears the powerful erotic burden emanating from those big, supple bodies with long, bulging muscles, with skin iridescent from sweat? Emma caught only a glimpse of the workers from the distillery when they came to present their congratulations to the newlyweds, on Sunday, the day after the wedding, their hair all curled, coated in Vaseline, wearing ties, smelling good with extra-high-quality "L'Étoile" eau de cologne with which they had drowned themselves, fiddling with, intimidated, the edge of their Panama hats, their eyes riveted to the floor. But they slipped away as quickly as they had come.

They weren't at the party. No one had invited them.

Thus passed the first part of her marriage. Night after night, on the threshold of each daybreak, Emma stands up, in a turmoil from the nagging clamors of the dawn. Who opened the day

Sweat, Sugar, and Blood

with these cries? Was it the roosters? The cayali birds? Eyes wide open to the shadows blurred by the mosquito net, Emma wonders what promises this new day might hold. Drenched in sweat, Emma jumps out of bed. Quivering, she rushes forward, in a haste to scan the garden.

On the morning of the eighth day, while Emile was absorbed in his daily grooming, always as long as a day without bread—Emma had verified, with a glance of her eyes into the bathroom, that her husband was quite busy passing the straight razor over his bluish mulatto beard, still stubbornly visible through the pallor of his very light skin, in spite of maniacal shaving, lovingly setting straight the contour of this goatee that she caught herself finding "a little" ridiculous, at that precise moment—the young married woman, half-awake, flew as if in a dream to the end of the veranda, in the opposite direction from the bathroom, to the place where, protected by the foliage of the poinsettias and the scarlet curtain of hibiscus from Barbados, she was able to look as much as she wanted at two or three bends in the long route leading to the distillery. She could never embrace the entire path with a single look, she knew: tufts of giant bamboos masked the greater part of it. But at the places where the frizzy heads agreed to open, a hole of light sprung forth exposing an end of the path. Emma needed nothing more.

The veils of the newborn day had lifted in silence. The birds, in the filao trees, had started their fuss: chirps into chitter-chatter, then quiddities into niggling, gluttonous turns into sultry coos, blackbirds and sissi birds had enough to do until the next twilight, squabbling with the bananaquit birds.

Noisy and swathed with tranquility, the calm of the dawn gave back beating life to the trees shaken up by a swaying of turtle doves, chasing the greedy beating of wings of humming-birds defying all laws of gravity, to the roosters in a hurry to be the first to crow to claim their supremacy among the male fowl, getting ahead of the chickens' cackling, to the acrobatic anole lizards already on the hunt, spread out on a leaf of a

Climb to the Sky

dwarf date palm, and to Emma, arisen with a leap from her nuptial bed, barefoot on the humid flagstones, one hand bringing back to her chest the lace of her negligee.

"How cool it is when the pipiri bird sings!" murmurs Emma, shivering. From cold? From fear? From a feeling of having nothing to do there?

Suddenly, sharply, tearing the air, rises the voice of a fellow that Emma, alas! cannot see.

Emma closes her eyes, listens:

"I pé ké ni siklon, man di'w! Pa fè lafèt épi mwen! Asé bétizé, ou ka plen tèt mwen épi tout sé kouyonnard-la."

(There ain't gonna be no hurricane, I'm telling you! Don't tell me stories! Stop with your baloney. My head's already full enough of your bullshit.)

A second voice loses patience, keeps on chiming out:

"Fé sa ou lé! Mwen, man za paré. Zalimèt, luil, petrol, bouji, man za fè tout provizyon mwen. Kité Misyé Siklon vini! . . ."

(Do what you want! I have already prepared. Matches, oil, gas, candles, I've already gotten my provisions together. Mister Hurricane just has to come! . . .)

"Gadé'y! I pa ka menm kouté. Yen ki chonjé toubonman, dépi jou-a I wè fanm-tala, lasumèn pasé . . . Yo sé di Misyé ni an gwo pwèl? . . . Piès siklon pé pa tjerbolizé'y!"

(Look at him! He isn't even listening. He's just daydreaming, daydreaming . . . Since he saw that woman last week . . . You'd say he's disappointed in love . . . Is the boy in love or what? . . . No hurricane can weaken him!)

This voice is new, it's trying to cover up the other one. It will succeed without difficulty. It's a third man who's talking. Emma recognizes neither the timbre nor the language of the previous ones. This man is talking a thick Creole all spiked with loose stones. So, a man from the North! she says to herself, without wondering why too much. (What he suggested bothered her.)

"Sa ou ni an ka-kabèch ou, nèg? Asé dépotjolé ko-ko'w! Ou ka sanm an t-toupi mabyal."

(But what have you got in your sk-skull, my old fellow! Stop

Sweat, Sugar, and Blood

th-thinking about it so much. You look like a spinning t-top), sniggers a higher-pitched voice.

Which one of them just spoke? She's getting lost. Not the first man, she's sure of it. She would recognize that voice out of a thousand others, now that she's heard it, piercing the mugginess of the dawn.

The humidity creeps in, takes possession of her bit by bit. She shivers. From fever this time? What else could it be? A redness stings her face. Ah! She wishes that they would get to the opening so that she can see them!

But when they get there, Emma can no longer hear them. Their voices are already dissolving; their words are lost in the air. She no longer makes out what they're saying. Now only a flurry of hammered syllables reaches her, the same ones, incoherent—"té-té-ké-ké-ka-pou-pouki"—the practiced barking of the one who stutters and articulates louder than the others. To make up for something, she says to herself.

The air in Upper Didier is healthy, but now, you also need to fear the invasions of spiders, linen-eating moths, and cockroaches that are there to shit or lay all sorts of eggs in the hems of your linen, the little servant girl explains to Emma.

Emma jumps with a start, promptly leaves her secret observation post. Here she is sitting down at the table like a good girl, anticipating the morning maxims of Mammy Sonson concerning her great theories about alimentary hygiene—full of good sense, in fact—enjoining her to eat copiously in the morning, with a laudable intuition of etymology:

"You just came out of fasting—you need to eat breakfast, little Madam!"

And Mammy Sonson adds:

"If you pack your linens in the wardrobe for an eternity, you are not going to find that time again! . . . But Sirisia, my girl, enough fidgeting like a big useless girl! You ain't going to be able to do your ironing, my dear, my God! Are you trying to catch a fever for me, huh? . . . So you think you can handle the

Climb to the Sky

hot iron with your clothes all wet and even worse with all that sweat cooled everywhere all over your body?"

For an answer, insolent, a little female anole lizard jumps promptly from a papyrus tree onto the sacred breakfast table, comes to lick the little drops of honey abandoned on a silver plate, voluptuously.

Today, for the third time, this phenomenon takes place. Emma feels moved by the original idea of having a little tamed lizard, of some sort (a little girl lizard, rather). She enjoys a keen emotion in discovering, so close to her, two fingers of her own hand away, the miniature tongue that pops up, quickly, out of the mischievous face, a vivid pink on a tender green, in the sun. Even better! It will swallow mosquitoes whole, when there's no more honey left. It's a useful animal—Emma learned that in class; she wishes it no harm, and the animal feels it. (But she does not want under any circumstances for that beast to touch her! Not it or any other beast. The contact would be unbearable; she shivers just thinking about it . . .) It's nonetheless bizarre, a lizard that ventures so close to her, at the risk of getting caught . . .

"If the anole lizard had good meat, it wouldn't have scurried on the fence!" popular wisdom puts forward, through Mammy Sonson.

Such animal turmoil lately! It moved from downtown and from Isambert Street, this rustic bestiary of Upper Didier. Last night, it was a scatterbrained bat that got caught in her mosquito net, just when she was going to bed . . . No magnificent husband in sight! Emile was not there, of course, kept away by some "business," some unknown "obligation" . . . No valiant knight coming to deliver her from the monster . . . Lacking a white battle steed, a Latania broomstick ridden by the eternal Sonson chased away the nasty animal—useful also, but so ugly!—courageously mounted by the servant, heaven-sent, to Emma's screams of horror. What would she be without her old nurse, a fearless knight-woman above reproach? . . .

And, for three days, this lizard, so familiar, almost friendly, that doesn't even flee when Emma gives a hint of a gesture in

Sweat, Sugar, and Blood

its direction, that approaches and comes even closer. What are these signs? . . . Witchcraft? She doesn't dare open up about it to Sonson, who claims to know all about oracles and omens.

The animal observes her carefully, with its curious oblique look, with its funny tilted appearance. Emma is surprised, ecstatic that the anole lizard can stay for such a long time in the same place, without moving, except for its little pointed face that pivots in impish rotations, and its shining eyes that blink, but imperceptibly. How not to marvel at so much animal agility, so much graceful impetuosity, combined with such a capacity for immobility on the watch? She knows she's also condemned to long phases of static inaction, on the lookout for something as well . . .

What is taking place in that little skull? The anole lizard is still licking and lapping with calm delight; since Emma loves getting these delicacies for it, she gently adds another drop of honey to the plate. The lizard turned its fine head with grace and alacrity. Its orb turns, cautious, toward this generous giant, with a knowing blink of its protruding eye. The two young females enjoy this shared intense pleasure.

Emma leans forward, although that scares it, to scrutinize from close up the prominent eyes gleaming with satisfaction, pleasure, and recognition, the end of its nimble tongue, its pretty bright-green shine . . . But she cannot stop herself from trembling when that skin, that she imagines to be cold and slimy and who knows what else, gets close to touching her. She cannot hold back a spasm.

Jealous about its hunting territory, a big male with a yellow craw came to join them, its dewlap puffed out: the female anole lizard fled. Bold but not foolhardy . . .

Master Emile must have finished his endless grooming. Standing straight, his goatee triumphant, he is going to come to give himself up to the daily ceremonial: good morning, a good kiss, and good advice, my little housewife! . . . In hugging him, the "little housewife" passes her hand along his ear, behind his

Climb to the Sky

back, pats its damp rounded sides. If he saw her, she would be entitled to the reprimand of the century! . . . That's it, now he's gone at the steering wheel of his Excalibur with curves watered in dew. Driving! She would like to drive! . . .

"You need to carry yourself like a woman, know how to hold things in," comments Sonson.

Up there, in the big house, Emma gets bored. With domestic noise and gossip as her only intellectual stimulation, the young wife mopes. What attracts her is what's outside.

Like an impertinent caress, a hot smell of caramel and sugarcane alcohol coming up from the distillery comes to taunt her nostrils. The young woman takes pleasure in sniffing, stronger than the aroma of punch, much more intoxicating than a Planteur drink or that "tropical cocktail" that they serve at the Annual Grand Officers' Ball, the disconcerting fragrance, a mystery to her, of rum being made.

While awaiting Madam's first childbirth, the little servant girl does her utmost to fuss fancifully over the future firstborn's hope chest. They don't get hope chests out much anymore. After the bride's outfit, they've been drowning Emma in baby clothes. They're preparing for her childbirth prematurely, as if that were all that was expected from her, as if she were only good for that: bringing into the world a horde of B. kids . . . legitimate ones.

The young maid Sirisia never finished washing, rinsing, ironing, and cleaning diapers, bibs, baby clothes, romper suits, and other trifles, the little sheets with English embroidery and the tiny mosquito net. No way to preserve in mothballs anything that will touch the newborn up close or from afar! "That would have ripped off his skin, the poor little devil, and even worse the smell is going to suffocate him," assures Mammy Sonson, pompous. Now the little servant girl makes it a point to watch enviously over the B. heir to come, even if he is not yet conceived, even if Emma's head is more inhabited than her belly, at the moment. Whether Madam wants it or not, he will be born and he will be a male, the child that she will make for Master B. There's no going back on that. "Ain't no wriggling out of it," Mammy Sonson would emphasize if anyone

Sweat, Sugar, and Blood

doubted it. (It's what's in the order of things: Madam will be a good wife and an excellent "mother to her children.")

Furthermore, a boy's name is already reserved—without even consulting Emma—for the hypothetical oldest child of her probable progeny. They will only have to add an *e* on the end of it if, through bad luck, she makes a girl instead of giving a son to her lord and master. If the Master had chosen Arsène instead of Henri, it would've been even easier; there would be nothing to change at all. Such is Mammy Sonson's opinion: although Arsène means "virile," the old servant sees nothing inconvenient in saddling a girl with it, for she will always have enough femininity and attributes of the "weaker sex," the unfortunate girl! Anyway, Mammy Sonson doesn't know Greek. It's really the least of her worries.

On the other hand, it will pose a real problem for the baptism, for the godfather, chosen in advance, is going to refuse to be a godfather for the first time in his life to a representative of womankind: evidently, "that brings misfortune . . ." If he gave his consent, it was for a boy! For a girl, it's another affair: he would not even think of this possibility, this dear Doctor P., he didn't even envision this sinister alternative of gender, the good doctor that he is, when he proudly said yes. As much as he was honored to be a godfather to a little male, not as much so for a "little fish" . . .

Certainly, Emma has the pleasure of being frightened by the jeremiads of self-righteous Mammy Sonson who tells her beads of miseries, past, present, and future, unfurls the agonies of childbirth while scaling fish, casts to her horrified eyes the pains of delivery while bursting the milt out of a male coulirou fish, terrifies her while prophesying the suffering that the laborious arrival of the fruit of her entrails will cause her, while tearing out the viscera and eggs from a fat full kingfish. Work is no sinecure! "It's not a ride on a wooden horse on a merry-go-round! Especially the first time, I can only tell you that. Afterwards, you wake up a woman. Only afterwards."

But the mystery of these men!

Climb to the Sky

Today Master Emile B. announced while he was leaving that he would not come back up at noon. As often happens with him, he has a business lunch that is keeping him in Fort-de-France. Tjip! Sometimes he even mixes until lunch, at the market, having a blaff stew reminiscent of wood from India or a stock spiced up with red pepper "as hot as Mammy Jacques's ass" or cacao pepper, served by impressive capre women, from trays or the crude wood platters resting on trestle tables.

Master Emile never spoke of taking Emma there one day.

She supposes it won't happen.

"You little tafia rum lush, so you're sipping your punch without even waiting for me?"

It's Aunt Herminie, who has just arrived with great pomp.

It's true, Godmother is having lunch here today, evidently! Every time Master Emile has a so-called "need" to have lunch in town, he appoints "Cousin Herminie"—"Godmother," for Emma, who's her aunt as well as the woman who will carry her child to the baptismal fonts—and serves as the occasional chaperone to his young wife ("guardian of her pussy" in other words), a thankless role that old Miss B. (a B. from Saint-Pierre, not a B. from Fort-de-France, quite a difference) plays with good grace, Master B.'s table being among the best in Martinique.

The B.s from Saint-Pierre affix a certain paternalism tinged with condescension with respect to the B.s from Fort-de-France, whereas these B.s from Fort-de-France despise them. There's nothing to be understood there. The Saint-Pierre B.s have a square named for them right in the middle of Saint-Pierre, in honor of one of their own, who was a great man in that town (Emma forgot why), but the Fort-de-France B.s have more money.

"What are you saying?" yells Godmother, her hand in a bag of peanuts. "You're irritating me, talking with the end of your lips, your mouth pursed like a chicken's ass, you pious hypocrite! ... Ar-ti-cu-late! You little pretender, with your good workroom ways and your so-called manners that rot your existence . . ."

Here she goes again! Aunt Herminie has started off on her recriminations against the residents of Fort-de-France, finding

Sweat, Sugar, and Blood

herself in "comparison" with these nouveau-riche ectoplasmic people. She's one to talk! ... "Why do you see the speck in your brother's eye, but do not notice the log in your own?!" Emma says to herself silently for fun.

The only remaining woman of the B.s from Saint-Pierre, after the eruption of Mount Pelée, the sole survivor explodes, keeps on trying to outdo herself complaining of daily catastrophes, ever since the volcano forced her to live in Fort-de-France—more or less sponging off her Fort-de-France cousins from Upper Didier, where she found a "change of air" on May 8, 1902, in their vacation house, which she never left again, her upstairs and downstairs residence in Saint-Pierre having been burned at the time of the burning cloud. Neurotically urban, Aunt Herminie pined for the bustle of the city; she hates these Creole villas, these broad single-story verandas "cluttered up with vegetation" where you're "outside when you're inside," around which nothing moves, except the beasts that she detests, the anole lizards, the centipedes, in front of which no one passes ... Desperately she longs for the masses of people from Saint-Pierre, the swarming, the noisy life of the "little Paris of the Antilles."

"Of the people who don't dare to yell, who don't speak their minds, but who take the liberty of saying to you: 'Enough raising your voice! We're not in Saint-Pierre here!' We, the people of Saint-Pierre, do you take us for a band of bumpkins? Wait a minute! ... Let me tell you what the B. family represented during the time of Saint-Pierre's splendor! ..."

Her nostalgia doesn't prevent her from having a voracious appetite, regardless of whether she's eating with a gold and silver fork or not. Aunt Herminie serves herself christophenes again gleefully, goes through the upper crust and her melancholy thanks to a good swallow of rum. The meal isn't even over before Godmother is already having her after-dinner drink.

The historic yet penniless mulatto woman revels in affirming that the B. family is a great family, but Emma repeats it in a burst of laughter:

"You shouldn't confuse coconut with apricot, great family and large family!"

Climb to the Sky

Great or not, the B. family never fascinated Emma.

Godmother cleans her receding gums with the point of her cheese knife. The ivory of the silver-banded handle shows cruelly the greenish yellow of her hideously long canines. Emma turns away her eyes . . . Is this all to which she has a right, as a show, in her new life?

"Eat, Emma! You're not eating anything. You're just skin and bones: they'd say you were a little poor girl . . . How do you intend to have children with that?" . . . screeches Godmother, pointing a menacing, podgy, accusing index finger at the young wife.

But she's blacklisted, condemned for some unknown mistake, in the most summary of judgments! (Perhaps her greatest crime, in this summary injustice, is not having as her only worry and primary pleasure stuffing herself like a goose, with her only project in life making beautiful B. babies?)

"Tchip! Can you tell me what you resemble, with that Paris fashion, that so-called 'urchin cut' hairdo, with no form or anything? . . . You look like a little shrimp, my poor girl!"

Better to be a shrimp than an old goat! Emma does not deign to reply. With the pepper and the punch helping, Emma feels sweatiness rising, feverish from the splattering of bursts of light, here and there. Fascinated by the dazzle of the features of the sun already high in the sky, she ventures a furtive glance in the direction of the bamboos, the faraway tufts, there, and beyond them . . .

The lunch is dragging on. The dusty old maid is talking to herself without knowing it: Emma is no longer with her. Emma is in her thoughts. Emma is outside the house.

The heat has reached its height. The austere room is in the shadows in vain, Emma is all damp, under the ardor of the sun now at its zenith. Aunt Herminie exasperates her. A hair's breadth away from suffocation, Emma is sweating from excitement. She peels away from her sweating throat the sensible dress whose silk oppresses her, unbuttons the top of her blouse, spreads the tails while sighing, oh deliverance! opens wide

Sweat, Sugar, and Blood

the clasp of the brooch that was locking up her collar, undoes the expensive "black stone" that was imprisoning her chest, throws it furiously on the table.

"Ugh! Like an oven! . . . I'm going to die in there! Air!" Emma murmurs, fanning herself with the insides of her liberated neckline.

"There you are all bare-chested, young lady! What sort of manner of dress is this?" shrieks Godmother, suddenly getting up from her plate.

The prim old lady is suffocating, almost choking, on the verge of having an apoplectic fit, grabs her eyeglasses, then plunges into Emma's neckline. For once, Aunt Herminie is breathless.

"But!? . . . But you're half-nude! Both of your titties are out!? My Lord and God! What is this shamelessness? Are these the manners of a young lady from a good family? Luckily we're alone! . . . How cheeky you are! . . . My dear, you don't marry someone to embarrass the person! What would your husband say if he saw you in this state?"

What would her august husband do if he saw her in this state? . . .

Emma just shrugs her bare shoulders.

If there's indeed anything that irritates her, it's not being able to know anything, being there to put up with Godmother and her old-fashioned snobbery, her obsolete prejudices and her limited microcosm. Only knowing one side of life.

"And what are you doing with your jewels? You don't let gold drag like that, well, my God! Or else the gold takes vengeance; it leaves you! Do you not have respect for anything?"

For nothing. Emma can see nothing, discover nothing. At least learn nothing by herself. Everything is retransmitted, distilled. From the outside world only echoes deformed by the twittering of servants or the drivel of an old girl reach her. As for Emile, he never tells anything about what he lives in Fort-de-France, in his man's life. Monsieur is always too exhausted. Because she is a woman, Emma would be condemned to molder all day long in this unattractive house, with books as her only friends? (And what books! That has to be seen! Just romance novels, those handpicked "little novels from France," all sorts of "acceptable" readings that Master Emile deigns to buy her in town: "Here, Emma, your little novels! They just arrived from Paris! This very day! . . . Lucky that I had ordered them for you and they were marked *Reserved for Master B.* because Madam Fairschenne de Dendur already wanted to snap up everything! But since the saleswoman likes to see me . . ." he levels like a provocation, when he comes back up to Upper Didier, at the end of his days without her.) Finally she collects more of them coming from the Other Shore than from her own island . . .

Look, for example, under the pretext that she is the "mulatto's wife," "the boss's wife, "the young lady," a Creole light-skinned woman herself, Emma does not have the right to go see what's happening down below, what they're doing over there, inside, in the interior of this mysterious distillery. Emma can just steal some snippets of conversation, when the gigantic black men are arriving in the early morning or when they're coming back, in the evening, their long day of work over. Between the two, a great void. A long day that drags on. Then, as soon as they leave, at twilight, an endless night where she can't stop waiting for the dawn to bring them back finally. For the rising day to return them to her . . . But in such a frustrating way! If the young woman sees them, they're still invisible to her, and as soon as she sees them, she can no longer hear them, they are too far away.

Then they enter the distillery.

That isn't what Emma sees, it's something that she imagines, that must happen afterwards, past the last meander of the path that tears them away from her, where she has a final vision of the group of tall black bodies walking with free steps, still big in spite of the distance: she has never set foot there, in that damn distillery! It is for her an unknown world, the interior of the distillery.

She would like to go inside, to see what they do there, in that den, learn how they go about it, these giants of whom she catches partial sight every day, whom she observes furtively,

Sweat, Sugar, and Blood

yes, discover how those big men manage to metamorphose sugarcane juice into rum. Emma has drunk rum: "straw" rum, old rum, amber rum, white country rum too, with a "little bit" of cane syrup flavored with vanilla or native red currants, at Christmas, a "flick" of brown sugar or a sweetening of honey and a lot of lime.

She's tasted sugarcane. Even raw. But this forbidden alchemy!...

Oh! They taught her a lot of things at the Colonial Boarding School on Ernest Renan Street where all the girls from the Fort-de-France "good families" "by comparison" go, prissy and resolutely secular indeed, which allows them to escape from the convent. But everything came to a stop so quickly! Emma remained hungry for knowledge. She would have continued, would've remained at the boarding school two or three years more with her classmates, would've gotten her diploma to become a teacher, instead of having to sacrifice herself at the altar of bourgeois conventions, to "make a match" chosen by others, to create a so-called "beautiful marriage" just to please her caste and to cloister herself up in Upper Didier for the rest of her days.

Miss B. was not a bad student before becoming Madam B. by marrying one of her cousins, a distant cousin perhaps, but a B. (her family wanted it like that). Emma gulped down entire chapters of the History of France and Navarre and Marignan 1515 and 842, the Sermon of Strasbourg, the first text in the Frankish or "Françoise" language (she no longer remembers very well...), which was not Latin anymore and was almost already French, "Pro Deo amor..." For the love of God, why does Emma get her knuckles rapped if by chance she speaks Creole?

In class, at the first word in "patois," they punished you with a black "square" coupled with a punishment. At the bell, the student who still held the square of infamy "took" a "checked zero." With your third checked zero, you were expelled. Emma

Climb to the Sky

and her unhappy fellow students (there were only girls, no coeducation, what a scandal!) thus had an interest in keeping an eye on each other, watching for the least verbal slip, looking out for who would get a "square," who would commit a "Creolism," any crime of syntax error whatsoever, in order to clear themselves at the expense of the guilty party and foist the square of disgrace onto her. Oh, French, what crimes they commit in your name! Under the pretense of your promotion and education, they stamped out the Creole language, while still cultivating, among the Creoles, the pettiest tattling, mockery, miasmas of scorn.

Up until now little Emma remembers. A few happy memories are still left in her, solid bases of grammar, and she hasn't lost her Latin!

Emma knows perfectly well who broke the Soissons vase, she knows everything about the auricles and the other ventricles of the heart, but only has a very watered-down, vague idea about "affairs of the heart." She knows well all her syllabi for Natural Sciences and Physics and Life Lessons, the départements of France, the main towns and prefectures, she knows that the Loire, the "savage river," has its source on Mount Gerbier-du-Jonc, but does not know where the river that flows in her own garden goes. Emma has the list of chemical symbols and even the geography of the vast world at the tip of her fingers; however, she knows nothing about the manufacturing of rum that takes place there, a few strides from her.

Today nothing seems more mysterious to her than what is there, so close to her, within the reach of her hands, but forbidden, so close to the touch but yet so far away, this distillery where tall men with blue-black bodies that she just sees go by shut themselves up.

Now that here she is married off, having become a woman, the "mistress" of her house, a submissive wife at the same time—a potential mother, moreover—nothing is more strange to her than that world that is nevertheless so close to her, that world that Emma brushes by every day without really comprehending it, this side of humanity to which she does not have access.

Sweat, Sugar, and Blood

They put up a fence between Emma and that world there. Between Emma and that Creole there.

Between their world and hers, between their speech and hers. Between their skin and hers. Between their gender and hers.

"Are you still hungry, Godmother? Have a little more breadfruit!"

From the beginning of the meal, Godmother fell into her plate like a gourmand dying of hunger.

"I'm not hungry for breadfruit purée, I'm hungry for mangoes!" gurgles Herminie the glutton, her lower lip glistening and greedy, still dripping sauce, while lapping up a gulp of that crisp Graves wine.

Saying this, Aunt Herminie squints at the full basket of fruits that Mammy Sonson just put down.

"Alas! Mango season is over . . . Do you not have one or two left? Would a Julie mango not tempt you, my dear? They're packed with vitamins. You would surely need some, to put some weight back on your little body!" This said, Herminie sways and starts to fish for conchs.

Emma has other appetites; the young newlywed feels other desires.

"A little coconut cream? You don't want to taste it? . . . It's light! . . ." Herminie yawns.

She's not hungry anymore, wants for nothing. (Especially not that slimy, unknown, whitish thing that the old girl is licking, like a little girl, salivating at the bottom of her spoon.) All her appetite for life stretches all her being toward the unknown, carries her entirely in spirit toward the mystery, the forbidden, fond of the shadowy enigmas of that other life, over there, in the belly of the distillery. She feels that it has something to do with her culture, with her heritage, with her being, with her own identity, but that everything is walled off. That she will not be complete as long as she is not admitted there.

Taking advantage of Godmother's nap and her drowsy watchfulness after her copious lunch, Emma slipped away, almost

Climb to the Sky

like a mongoose, to the outskirts of the Other World. Clandestinely, enjoying her disobedience, she crept outside without Mammy Sonson finding out about it, and even behind Sirisia's back, a person who knew "everybody's business."

Furtively Emma tracks the black giants from the morning, letting herself be guided by the river that feeds the windmill of the old sugar refinery, dashes toward the greenness of the bamboos that set themselves up over there, putting her trust in their leafy fleece.

But how to find her way around, in this unknown luxuriance, amid all these towering trees, like sentinels around her? Promptly Emma is swimming in the stifling atmosphere of the undergrowth. She is suffocating, is afraid of snakes . . . She rushes forward, her heart beating; her feet get caught in the roots, the low branches slap her face. Very quickly she no longer sees the sun, swallowed up by the foliage. Lacking air, she can no longer see clearly. Sweat is running into her eyes. She has never gone so far. Never has she gone so deeply into the woods, up to the extreme limits of the property. Is she going to end up getting lost?

It's break time for them, too, you'd say. This is normal: with Godmother, you have to serve early, out of respect for her old age.

A man is standing on the threshold; he is naked down to his waistline. After working, he slips on his undershirt so as not to catch his death. The loosened stitches of knitted skin adhere to his sweaty, muscular chest, gleaming in the glade's sun. Emma recognized him immediately: the voice belongs to him, the first voice, the clearest one, the one that best cuts through the air at each day's dawn. She would stake her life on it. What he needed was a good shower! But a cold or even tepid shower on a sweating body is just what's recommended to make you suffer. At least that's what the Adults preach . . . So, the shower forgotten, "there's no wriggling out of it!" If Mammy Sonson were there, that's exactly what she would say to him, by God!

Sweat, Sugar, and Blood

Just so he knows it . . . so that no misfortune would befall him . . .

The man with the wet shirt stretched his long limbs, then went in slow steps to crouch in the shadows, further away. Emma no longer sees his face. Only his grainy hair and his big powerful torso leaning over his food, and, like two cacao sticks, the curve of his strong brown arms with well-defined biceps.

Others joined him outside, sat down with him under the most bountiful mango tree or under the thick kapok tree. They took fat cucumbers, big breadfruit squares, fried ballyhoos, cod beignets, a torn-off bit of codfish from their satchel: it's Friday, the day of Venus, but a day of abstinence. You eat light. They chew with concentration, without saying a word. Wet Shirt pours around big draughts of clear liquid, country rum, certainly, or maybe just water, "to make it weaker," "to sweeten" the taste of the alcohol, as Mammy Sonson would say? (At this distance, she knows nothing about it. There is no label, neither on the bottles nor elsewhere . . .) He drinks without letting his lips touch the bottle.

Emma doesn't dare go talk to them. She doesn't even dare approach them. Is it their muteness that impresses her? She only knows them speaking, when she spies on them in the morning. It is first through language that their complicity passes, through the shared secret of all those words that she steals from them, day after day—these Creole words . . . Is it their silence that stops her, inhibiting her dash toward them, or the Insurmountable Fence between her and that universe there?

Insurmountable perhaps, but certainly there's a way to get around it . . .

She skirts around the group of men, always at a respectful distance, so as not to be discovered. She feels as if she cannot resist.

Almost on all fours, she reaches the back of the building, succeeds in getting into it by passing through the edge of a low window.

Climb to the Sky

Her blood spurted onto the sugarcane, splashed onto the stalks. The escapade at the distillery cost Emma three fingers, in the spouting of her blood. Such was the price. And only then because she screamed. And especially because the men, who had already run up, dumbfounded, believing there were zombies, at the sound of the machine that had inexplicably restarted, quickly got their wits about them before it was too late, while one of them, the strongest, Wet Shirt, clung to Emma's body with all the might of his muscles, tensed to the point of bursting. The man managed to hold back the voracious rush of the machine.

"Or else that filthy thing was going to crush all her fingers, her whole hand, and even worse her arm, and worse than that her entire body, who knows? . . . Tchip! Jesus, Mary, Joseph and all the saints, why did little Madam need to go play in those machines there? Can you tell me? . . . Well, Madam kept her body . . . It's not from a lack of having warned her, however! . . ." lamented Mammy Sonson.

A good doctor from among the cousins—another B.—called for the emergency, administered the necessary care to Emma's mutilated hand, and her ectoplasmic husband, torn from his study, made no comment. She was already punished well enough for her disobedience!

He had never been so quiet. She had never been so pale, at the bottom of her eyes a light that would never go out. From jubilation, yes, the light in Emma's eyes . . .

Having lost the use of the fingers that served her best, Emma B. lived, awkwardly—I refuse to say clumsily—her life as a lady from Fort-de-France, one single hand gloved, her left one, first in white, in her youth, as a symbol of her gushing emotion, then navy, at the time of her maturity, the color of the strange seawater eyes of Wet Shirt—the disconcerting ocean nuance of Wet Shirt's gaze where she had dived, panting, when the brown giant hugged her with all his might—and, finally, pearl

Sweat, Sugar, and Blood

gray, like the beading of their sweat, before slipping on a black glove, in her old age, as a memory of Wet Shirt's skin. She would have liked to put on a red glove like the insolent spatter of her blood, but never pushed her impertinence that far. Fools said: "Luckily it wasn't her right hand!" not knowing that she was left-handed. She let them say it . . .

Never did anyone ever tear the least word of this affair out of her, not a single detail—and especially not Master Emile.

Her single glove intrigued people. Some saw a mystery there, others a sort of disturbing charm; still others read a sign of peculiarity or a kind of provocation there, they couldn't say which. Very few knew which to stick to; no one was in on the secret of Emma B.'s rebellion.

When Emma died, in her 102nd year, on her deathbed— or should I say wedding bed?—it was the same one—Orestes, her seventeenth child, slipped the beaded white cotton glove on her, the first one, the one she wore until the day of her silver wedding anniversary. Washed, rewashed, ironed through Sirisia's expert attention, it wasn't even yellowed.

Neither crick, nor crack.
All this is not a story.
It really happened to my great-aunt, Emma B.
Thanks to that frenzy of sweat, sugar, and blood mixed together, Emma had one strong feeling at least once in her life.

Didier, 1992

The Three Musketeers Were Four

To Théodore

In you is my hope to escape from my evils. You see our misery and you arrive happy; share your good fortune with your friends; do not keep prosperity for yourself alone, but also take your share of pains in turn, paying to whom you owe your debt to my father. For one only has a friend in name without friendship if one is only a friend at the moment of unhappiness.
—*Euripides,* Orestes

It's completely fair if they haven't put the handcuffs on you, like a bank robber, a dreadful serial killer, or a fanatical terrorist, guilty of a "blind" assassination attempt, as they say, but spectacular. For the little thing that you did! If things continue like this, they are going to put you into police custody, like a vulgar criminal. They don't know what to make of you; they bustle about to get a superior out of bed in the middle of the night. The entire police department is turned topsy-turvy because of you. They give up interrogating you; so much of what you say is beyond them. They have asked you forty-two times your name, your address, all that.

When you say "Yich Lumina," go on; they ask you only if "Yich" is your last name or your first name. You explain to them that you don't care, that your whole name is "Yich Lumina Sophie dite Surprise," but this gets them all agitated. Not only does this name not tell them anything, but it doesn't tell them anything worthwhile. There's one that exclaims, "Yeah, it's like Élie-says-Cossack"! You counter learnedly: "Nothing like that! It's patronymic. Or matronymic, rather, neither a nickname nor a pseudonym. I'm not in hiding. I'm taking my true name again." And spelling patiently. In turn, they lose their patience. They don't give a damn about onomastics! They keep on questioning feverishly: "With or without hyphen?"

The Three Musketeers Were Four

You talk to them about a perfect union, an ideal communion, about fusion, a story of laughter. That doesn't make them chuckle at all.

So they drop it, they type, they're burning with a desire to hit you, the officer starts typing "YICH" in capital letters, beside LAST NAME, and "Lumina Sophie dite Surprise" in lowercase letters, in the space for "First name." He is tapping the table furiously each time you articulate "Yich Limina, if you prefer it in Creole, brother."

For the address, each time you chant: "60 Alexandre Dumas Avenue, 97200 Fort-de-France," they answer you that it doesn't exist, they don't have that in Fort-de-France. (You know that only too well!) When are you going to finish taking the piss out of them? The police officer fiddles with the Martinique telephone book, a little too nervously for your taste. Is it to look again for Alexandre Dumas Avenue, which cannot be found, which is unheard of, which is improbable, according to what all his colleagues are saying, or to give you a beating with it? You have seen that in movies: blows with a telephone book hurt, without leaving a trace: ideal. Certainly, the phone book, just the little mundane phone book from minuscule Martinique, it isn't the end of the world, but nonetheless . . .

But the limit is when they ask you your profession. There, they fall with their asses on the ground and then tell you to stop lying. They believe you are telling tall tales, that you're in full mythomania aggravated by schizophrenia. One of the Babylonians, inspired, even ventures "kleptomania"; he saw that on TV. They wonder if they shouldn't send you *directissimo* to Colson, to the knockers. They have had it with your delirium and your rantings!

They need to see what you have in your head!

"This century was two years old," wrote Victor Hugo, more gifted, as it were, at juggling meter than in arithmetical calculations, in evoking the moment of his birth. (In a more rigorous spirit, you note that that century—the nineteenth—was only one year old, if you're counting correctly, but to the devil with avarice! When you love, you don't count!) A respite from these

Climb to the Sky

impertinences, impertinent though they be! From what right do you have the impudence—perhaps double impudence—to dare to touch the patriarch who had "the art of being a grandfather" and Peer of France and national funerals? A little respect, shitter! It is like *Ubu Roi!*

In this year of Our Lord 2002, "the Hugo year" is thus being celebrated all over France and even down at the bottom of Martinique. A lot of good may it do us.

But Alexandre Dumas was ALSO born in 1802!

At the time when they finally dared to transfer him to the Pantheon—the homeland grateful to the great man, late in life!—the French town Villers-Cotterêts, a small village from the Aisne region where he was born, but where he lived only a few weeks, is upset, ten times twenty years after, about being robbed of the skin of the author of *Twenty Years After*, here is everything in his honor! May this good very François town—where François the First enacted the famous ordinance of 1539 calling for the use of French instead of Latin for official texts, laws, and judgments—be the birth city of Dumas, what a coincidence! What a symbol! Oh, Baudelairian correspondence that had everything to be delighted in heart and soul, in all senses and vice versa, you who show your fondness for the French language by mixing the love of Latin with the passion of Creole . . .

But remembering that the most famous French author worldwide, he whose Three Musketeers are famous over the entire Earth (the most represented, filmed, and cartooned characters from fiction), was born exactly the same year as the daddy of *Les Misérables,* you wondered why that year of Our Lord 2002 would not also be consecrated "the Dumas year." Why Hugo rather than Dumas? You were beside yourself at the injustice of it. You didn't sleep at night because of it.

You plunged into the dictionary to find the answer there to your question and to know more about him. There you only got that said "French writer" was the son of the general Alexandre Davy Dumas. Consternation!

My respects, my General! Thanks for the military rank, but

The Three Musketeers Were Four

for your Negress mother, no thanks! Total blackout on the black woman from Saint-Domingue, the African who gave birth to you, under the sun of the Greater Antilles, making of you, General, a half-Negro, and of her grandson a quarter—according to the idiotic distinctions in the Moreau de Saint-Méry or other nasal-talking eugenicists, capable of false notes as cruelly moronic as the cacophonic categorizations by which they label the different degrees of mixed races, calculating the proportion of "white" blood and "black" blood, in baptizing the mixed-bloods with the harmonious names of "mamluk," "sacatra," "octoroon," or "griffe," and you do without them and better . . .

You block your ears so as not to hear ever again the concert of detractors who amuse themselves spreading that this mulatto took Negroes to help him compose his monumental work.

Should the reason for this monumental omission be seen there? A mixed-race person from slavish descent, from "impure blood," the illustrious French writer, the most universally known in the world? That is not exported! That doesn't sell. That would sow disorder . . . Between Disorder and Genius, the motive for this iniquitous choice?! Is it that this black blood would stain, obscuring his immense work?

The Three Musketeers were four, they're accustomed to clarifying, with an erudite pseudo-smile: to Athos, Porthos, Aramis—d'Artagnan must be attached, evidently! They take pleasure in a slip of the tongue, trying, in order to point out the three Dumases, a play on words even more seductive than the three whose first names are Alexandre: grandfather, father, and son.

But what is never exalted is the existence of Cessette. What is proclaimed less voluntarily, what skins the mouth, is this Cessette, this belly of a Negress slave who gave birth to the first of the three Dumases, future general of the French Republic.

Cessette was her first name, and Dumas was her last name. Her first name remains vague; her last name has become immortal. Yes, the resounding patronymic, now immortalized,

Climb to the Sky

magnified for centuries upon centuries by the father of *The Three Musketeers,* is in fact a matronymic, that of the black slave woman from what is now Haiti, and not the hyphenated name of the Norman marquis Davy de la Pailleterie, an ancestor noble a little too generous to pass his title on to her . . .

Nevertheless, whatever the case may be, they want to brag about the charms of "our" Antilles for vacations, tourism, the beautiful beaches drenched in sun all year long, but you shouldn't exaggerate . . . After all, those Haitians took their independence, you should not confuse them with "our" people from the Antilles and French Guyana: they are not French themselves! They chose not to be French anymore, so now, let them manage! If they want to exist, to be recognized, to claim Alexandre Dumas, etcetera, that's their problem, not ours!

No, that wasn't possible! Not in the France of the Rights of Man and the democratic impulses against xenophobia and racism! Impossible to imagine that they would steal the memory of the most prolific novelist from the recollection of an entire people—a more serious theft, all things considered, than that of the Queen's Necklace!

Who would have had the gall to think, like his hero the Count of Monte Cristo, that Dumas would be compelled to reappear masked, clandestinely, decked out in a white iron mask to dissimulate the infamy of his yellowish-brown tint?

But to consummate what vengeance? Not a single one à la Edmond Dantès?

Your own revenge has nothing sterile about it. When you think that, in your childhood, you felt guilty about this damn middle-class mimesis that pushed you to identify with a Gascogne cadet or to ride behind a Knight of the Red House, without consciousness of your black blood? At the age of reason, you understood that there was no bad in that, that you were not renouncing your negritude by thoroughly enjoying these stories hooked to the History of France as if on "a nail," in their author's own confession. You believed it guilty, impure, this adolescent catharsis that made you in turns a "Don Quixote at the age of eighteen, an unarmored Don Quixote," "Don

The Three Musketeers Were Four

Quixote covered in a wool doublet whose blue color had transformed into an imperceptible nuance of wine-color and celestial azure," "noble like a Dandolo or a Montmorency," to take in good passion "a young woman of sixteen years, beautiful like love," a gifted creature "of a spirit not like that of a woman, but like that of a poet" . . . For already in you "a burning spirit was breaking through."

Besides, you hardly recognized that the "long and brown face" "the prominent cheekbone, a sign of cleverness; the enormously developed muscles of the jawbone" . . . this was your own description! You entered clandestinely into that skin. But the affair spoiled as soon as the fatal recognition of your mixed-race hubris jumped in your face: this portrait was not yours. Alas! Hell and damnation! Two lines below, they threw it in your face: these jawbones corresponded to the "unerring sign by which a person from Gascony is recognized"!

However, you, you bore these, these famous jawbones! In rage, they contracted. However, the yellow hair of the "Béarn bidet" hardly produced more disfavor than your skin of a yellow Negress. To be mocked, the victim of bullying, even a judicial error for the crime of your dirty look? All things that you knew. All injustices that obliged you to break some teeth, not long ago, in the schoolyards. Some new Dantès grew in you, stimulating the appetite for revenge. In this new generation, the Eumenides of a new era were pursuing you, in a hurry to consummate the vengeance of your scorned High Priest of Literature, your dear booed father.

You needed your catharsis, and, to get it, who knows? let loose a catastrophe.

You know that you are going to find yourself in a peculiar solitude, between the severe walls of Victor Sévère Street. You know that after what you have done, they dream of shutting you away, judging you, going back on their decisions about you. Condemning you.

Are you not condemned in advance by this tormenter of himself who raises his eyebrows at the words "Negro" or "Negress" as if they were abuse or insults? Ashamed of his own negritude, tormenter of his race, this sort of Creole *Heautontimoroumenos* wants to hear absolutely nothing of this abracadabra fable about the Haitian Negress ancestor of a great French writer. The poor devil is losing his Latin there (that he has incidentally never had). Go sing to him that Terence is also an African, from a slave father! Send that straight to Colson! First off, it's not in the dictionary. (They verify on the Internet, they have all the time to surf, that or the Dominican whores! They are cooler, in the air-conditioning, without risking a blow from a cutlass on the battlefield, in Terres Sainville or in the mangrove . . . And so we must do honor to the new technologies placed at our disposal! How do you connect, now? You're the one who shows how to navigate on the Net, you who have little distinctive about you.) Second, the Haitians sell bits and pieces and all kinds of cheap rubbish on the sidewalks of Fort-de-France, but if they hatched geniuses of world renown, that would be known, this is certain! He is resigned to it, nevertheless, not just sometimes! Knowing everything is his job. He did his studies, it may not be obvious, comes out of the Technique School (the high school with the same name should be understood by this, the Pointe des Nègres High School, not the ex–high school for girls, no, the other one). He even almost passed the bac. He took French courses—you better make sure you don't razz him! *The Count of Monte Cristo* was never presented to him as if it were born from a Negro imagination. Enough stupidities! The Three Musketeers were four? And the three Dumases mulattos?

The Three Musketeers, let's keep going: they know how to count to four. Shouldn't take them for stupid jerks. With d'Artagnan, that makes four. Affirmative! No need to count on the fingers. (Even though . . . What were they called again? Athos, Porthos, Aramis . . . Useless to whisper, you know it, you saw the film!) On the other hand, this story about the Negress! Alexandre Dumas, mixed-blood? They don't know it? This is why you are there. So that it's said. So that it's finally said! So that it can be proclaimed, it can be proclaimed loud

The Three Musketeers Were Four

and on high that this mixed-blood campaigned fiercely beside Victor Schoelcher for the abolition of slavery.

He, the descendant of an aristocrat, with his clear skin ("saved skin") could have lost interest in the question of the enslavement of Negroes! It wasn't his problem. He was well-integrated; his success was perfect. What need to compromise himself for such solidarity? Why did he need to worry about this black blood that boiled in him, by Jove? Why, free, rich, worshipped, would he run the insane risk of exposing himself, of ruining his reputation in the revolutionary ranks? Because, all mulatto that he was, Dumas felt concerned. He felt like he owed something to the Negress from Saint-Domingue whose blood he glorified.

Who treated the mulattos like traitors? Tired of the trouble of being mixed-blood, neither black enough nor white enough to be clear!

To turn the proverb into a lie, he found out how to remember that his grandma was a Negress...

Why so many homages to Schoelcher (a delightful library, the Schoelcher Bibliothèque, innumerable Schoelcher Streets or Victor Schoelcher Plazas in the tiniest communes of the island, the first high school of Fort-de-France, the proud Lycée Schoelcher, a host of statues depicting his haughty stature dominating the bunches of little excited Negro kids, drunk from a freedom given and not conquered, drooling with blissful gratitude, and even an entire commune, 97233 SCHOELCHER, a concert of "Viva Schoelcher!" in the four corners of the département), a consensual cacophony of "Hallelujah Papa Schoelcher," but nothing in homage to Dumas? Where is the statue of Dumas?

That the knight of Saint-Georges—a friend of General Dumas—be dropped quickly into forgetfulness although he was a great musician, that the passion he enjoyed within high society should dry up, at the moment of the restoration of slavery in the monarchy, because he, too, was half-Negro, was appalling enough. But for the whole world to hide, to neglect, not to know or pretend not to know that the Dumases were of

Climb to the Sky

mixed-blood is completely intolerable. Even more seriously, that at the very moment they decide to sing the praise of—in a relatively mediocre way—the inventor of the historical novel, they conceal from the public its Negro part, you couldn't tolerate it.

He was already chucked out like a bum on the day he presented himself to the Académie Française! He took enough rejection like that! Enough pokes and affronts for the most popular of French novelists! (Too "popular," perhaps, in the eyes of the jealous? Even though you wonder if it wasn't a godsend to be openly refused entry by this archaism-making inner circle of white men dressed in green, instituted by a cardinal in order to rule over the world of literature as it pleases, still indentured, thus, to a classicism corseted by very "splendid century" morals. A connoisseur of baroque plots, imbroglios, and fantastic quid pro quos, what would he have been doing bumming around in that old-fashioned gallery?)

The night before being admitted finally to the Pantheon, his spirits of the dead should be appeased. Act of vandalism, you say? Type all you want in your damn minutes. You have done propitiatory work.

"Act of vandalism with premeditation"? Type on, brother! All you want, type as much as you want. "Premeditation?" Says you! Because you had the plaques made in advance where you had the name of Alexandre Dumas inscribed, with the hope of engraving it in the memory of your people? With whom? In what workshop? They can frisk themselves . . . You're not close to selling a brother! He dreams standing straight up, the Babylonian! Sometimes, you feel like breaking everything, like taking a gun, shooting into the pile . . . You just changed the plaques there. What are they complaining about?

Why General de Gaulle Boulevard? Because it is—or should be—the Champs Élysées of Fort-de-France. You have nothing in particular against de Gaulle. But it doesn't make any difference when you cross Fort-De-France to and fro, you find Victor Hugo Street . . . (Okay, he was a Negrophile, the creator of *Bug-Jargal*, but only at the end of his pen, not to the

The Three Musketeers Were Four

point of receiving in his house the Negress who had made the trip to bring his daughter Adele back to him from the end of the world, from the faraway banks of Barbados and from the brink of madness) ... Nested deep within Terres Sainville, you find a Montesquieu Street, not far from the Petition of the Workers of Paris against Slavery Street ... (However, in matters of the abolition of slavery, the good aristocrat just tried to be witty, making laws, not at all, making do with creating comfortable irony and antiphrasis, sheltered from censure, dangerously scuttling his own argumentation when he deigned to blame the inhumane institution of "the slavery of the Negroes!") But you're seeking, seeking in vain: not an avenue, not a boulevard, not a street, not even the least little alley baptized "Alexandre Dumas," in your native Fort-de-France, the city where the mayor was a poet.

Oh iniquity! Ostracism! (Or maybe racism, without the "ost" ...) If it is noted that, among others, Hugo owes him for having been, he, Dumas, the precursor of the romantic drama, sounding the charge bravely with his Henry the Third and his Court ... Why does he have his Victor Hugo Street, comfortable, well-patronized, and Dumas nothing?

Or if it exists somewhere, Alexandre Dumas Street, it cannot be named, it's so ignominious, so seedy—because no one knows it, since nobody visits it—that it's better not to talk about it. This would constitute making the offense already done to the spirits of the dead of the Dumases worse. (Would they devote to august Alexandre the shameful ugly back of some courtyard?)

The Babylonian fiddles with the Martinique phone book convulsively. Ain't no Dumas Boulevard. Nor any Alexandre Dumas Avenue. He turns the pages feverishly, brooding: "No Dumas Boulevard." It's becoming deadly boring. Moreover, you would swear that the fellow is burning with a desire to knock you senseless; as if it were your fault, what's more! (You who wanted to remedy things! It's just for that reason that you are there!) He contemplates the phone book pensively, turns it, turns it over, twists it ... He has seen the same films as you!

Climb to the Sky

Are you shocked? You hardly have any choices at Madiana! ... And also, you have the same M.A.C. (Martinique Audiovisual Countryside!...) "Clean" work. They don't leave any marks, the blows from a phone book. That would put your ideas back in place. You would stop telling bullshit! After all, you're not a Rasta or a druggie or an alcoholic. You would even turn out to be a bit like someone well-to-do, rather ... The Babylonians only understand a squeak there!

"The Three Musketeers were four and the three Dumases were mulattos." You kill yourself reassuring them of this. The Three Musketeers were four and the three Dumases were mulattos ... The truth is elsewhere. Always elsewhere. But the Babylonians don't give a shit. What counts is that you admit to your crime. They want to gather your confessions? May it please the Lord! They would be well advised to hang on ...

You go to the Levee at night. You unscrewed, not without some effort, one by one, a half-dozen plaques—put up by the State Department of Technical Services or the State Facilities Department (yes, surely the State Facilities Department, you know nothing of it, there's no stain on you), where you saw spread out, white on blue:

CITY OF FORT-DE-FRANCE
GENERAL DE GAULLE BOULEVARD

Forgiveness to the Savior of the Appeal of June 18th! But he no longer needs that! He is covered in honors. What does he have to give a damn about, a boulevard in Fort-de-France, even if it's the capital of Martinique, he who shines in the firmament of the capital of France with the place de l'Étoile for him alone, and even an airport, so that everyone knows about it! And then, it's worse for him: every single person from Martinique knows that the president of the Republic on an official visit, the great man grumbled, the good man: "My God! How French you are!" in front of the black crowd that had run up to cheer him. Today they still laugh about it: reproduced by

The Three Musketeers Were Four

a Creole throat, the exclamation was transformed into "How dark you are!"

A shame they caught you too early. You only had time to hang two or three DUMAS plaques. And they were lopsided! The screw lines were all fucked up. The rusty screws snapped, no way to affix your beautiful new sparkling plaques, where you can now read:

ALEXANDRE DUMAS BOULEVARD

And you signed "YICH LUMINA" with a graphic that only those who kept in their memory the history of the people of Martinique could decipher. Those who still had in their mouths the bitterness of the blood spilled in September 1870.

You had thrown the old plaques in the trunk of your car, to keep from dirtying up your city:

Your city will be prettier
If you don't make a trash can out of it.

Stop taking the piss out of the world! You're making your case worse. "Property of the State": nothing to fight there. "Property of the State, therefore there is a theft!" screeches the raging Babylonian. "Theft" makes the list of your crimes longer. That's going to cost you an arm and a leg!

He had signed "Yich Telga," the unknown who formerly decapitated the statue of Josephine, this white man who was careful not to prevent his imperial spouse from reestablishing slavery. You, you signed "Yich Lumina." Is it political? You retort: "Everything is political!"

It was useless for you to do an exegesis of the Dumas genealogy; the Babylonians don't want to hear anything about it. They are all "colored," however. You're not at the local police headquarters—this is the National Police. Not a single person from Gaul among them. A lanky brunette with a horse's head, a light-skinned blond-headed mulatto wearing sunglasses even though it was night, a kaffir, a guy with mixed African and Indian blood, a light-skinned guy with gray eyes, and even a big beanpole who resembles someone from the Congo. But this business about Dumas with black blood is starting to come out of the brown, black, hazel, or iron-gray eyes.

Do you need to dot every *i* for them? Praising the excessive eloquence of he who led his life like a novel? Who wrote *Queen Margot*? Dumas. *The Viscount of Bragelonne*? Dumas. *The Forty-Five Guardsmen*? Still Dumas. *The Lady of Monsoreau*? Dumas. *The Lady of the Camellias*? "DUMAS, you know it!" shouts Iron-Gray Eyes, all proud. (Bravo, he takes himself as a champion on a televised game show; useless to wonder who wants to win millions . . .) "Okay, we understood! Do you take us for morons?"

You're amused: "Dumas, but Dumas the son." "But that's not the problem . . ." Iron-Gray Eyes gets tangled up, desperate.

Precisely! That a queen of France be compromised, that counts, viscounts, and beautiful women with or without all sorts of flowers from Mount-What-The-Hell-Do-I-Know or My-Asshole have anything to do with Haiti, from near or from afar, this is what goes beyond the representative of the police. It's beyond his capabilities. "The papa of the Three Musketeers came out of Haiti? Tchip! To others!"

To his gray eyes, Haitians are all thieves, swindlers, troublemakers of all sorts, miserable people who come to take work from the people of Martinique with good complexions, cause the unemployment rate to rise, as high as it already is, and dig holes into Social Security, enormous though they already are! And still, that's nothing: where he lives, in Guadeloupe, they come to blows, they lynch, they do pogroms of "immigrant" Haitians or Dominicans, blacks against blacks, but pay attention! Good French blacks against "dirty foreign blacks," undocumented down-and-out filth "who come to eat our bread" and make a string of kids to get benefits.

As for the example of the first black republic, it's better not to brandish it: it proves to be more repulsive than attractive to people who come from the French départements overseas in

The Three Musketeers Were Four

their Mercedes, their 4×4s, or BMWs. No help, no understanding, to expect from them, therefore. Who will come to plead your cause? The Haitian community of Martinique?

But what of Haiti itself? Has the Champs-Élysées of Port-au-Prince been baptized Alexandre Dumas Avenue? Is there even a Dumas Street in the capital of Haiti? In any case, if there is one, one thing is certain, which is that it's not the "principal artery," otherwise that would be known!

As soon as you are free, you are going to make a jump up to Haiti . . . just to see . . . Because they are going to end up releasing you! You haven't done anything bad . . . No, this isn't madness. You're neither marginal nor antisocial. You are even part of the notable people. You are a product of successful acculturation and strata of assimilation (not like the chlorophyll that flows through the Creoles but like someone from an overseas French territory) that have put down, compartmentalized, here and there, the vague attempts and starts for dignity.

They will say that you have lost it. The pain will not be heavy, unless . . .

You can already get your ticket for the former Saint-Domingue. But the crucial question suddenly appears: if, through the chance events of the Trade and the triangular traffic, the slave ship vessel had delivered its cargo of ebony wood to Martinique instead of to Saint-Domingue, the day when the slave ancestor who came from Africa disembarked, would today's people from Martinique have more enthusiasm for promoting and claiming the Caribbean origin of the Dumas? You will never know. And it's surely not Iron-Gray Eyes who is going to answer you!

The big beanpole slaves away at his computer's keyboard. In this night before the legislative elections, after the National Front jolt in the first round of the presidential elections and the republican frustration in the second, the Babylonians do not stop bellowing: "Is it political?" They believed that you were part of a band of poster hangers. They talk drivel, in a chorus, at the top of their voices: "Is it political?" So you pontificate, you repeat: "Everything is political."

Climb to the Sky

"Yep! 'All for one, one for all' is well known! You think we were born yesterday?"

And guffawing at their parodies, strongly, with ignoble expressions and gestures, the noble catchphrase of the Musketeers, which, in these libidinous mouths, becomes "All for one girl, one girl for all!"

With cynical macho, Iron-Gray Eyes barks the sentence right in your face, with a voracious lower lip, ready to give you one of those solid-iron blows that they would hand out so willingly. If you hadn't been picked up, the kaffir would have given you a simulacrum of sodomy more real than nature itself, whereas the light-skinned one would have shown his excessively large tongue, simulating without any ambiguity some rather unappetizing fellatio, with no possible doubt! The salacious jokes ring out everywhere, punctuated by "Girls for all, all for girls" and other sordid metamorphoses, each one more obscene than the next.

You feel vaguely that this has to do with you; you have a premonition that this is going to be your party, that you're going to ruin yourself. Everything is a hodgepodge with you, you bizarre, formless androgyne, bizarre, in fat shapeless jeans. Nothing can be identified anymore, your race, your sex, or your age, in the confusion of your bloods. Stop trying to talk to them! Impossible to communicate; all transmissions are blurry. Everything is interpreted the wrong way. Now, there will be blood, this is clear. Your face is unrecognizable. Sweat obscures your view. Your spirit is also confused. In the confusion of your senses, sounds also get mixed up: are they yelling that they don't want to waste their time with a "dirty assfucked androgyne" or someone that "dirty, in threadbare fat jeans?" What does it matter? You are not listening to them that much. You were dreaming in the Dalmatian language of the Musketeers until your dream broke, at the crack of dawn, on General de Gaulle Boulevard.

"Fuck your race up the ass!" hollers Light-Skin, who "did" ten years in France (Ninety-Third District) before finally getting his transfer to return to "the country." Is he going to join the gesture to his words?

The Three Musketeers Were Four

"Fuck your race up the ass!" Hold on . . . hold on . . . from then on everything is clear. Even though . . . fuck what race up the ass? All races, or none. It's not easy to find yourself in that muddle of mixed races! The guy had some difficulties doing two things at the same time anyway (talking, acting, thinking; hold on, that's three! But the third is optional). The insult is reduced to "your race." Fodder for groveling forever (in addition to the concave curves that you are getting on your face), or for erecting the superb on elementary principle, my dear Malcolm X or Y! You stand up, you swell with pride . . .

The light-skinned guy is having trouble with happiness. XX or XY, that isn't his problem! Go talk to him then about chromosomes! He doesn't give a damn. "Where there are genes, there ain't no pleasure!" he bleated. Dripping with lust, flowing from shameful phantasms, the gooey fat man is spreading. He fidgets, ensconcing his powerful clumsy shoulders in his seat. This sort of satyr salivates just looking at you, think of that! This smells bad . . . Satisfied with his spiritual features, the faun braces himself aggressively against the back legs of his chair. Thanks to this sudden curve, the animal spreads, sure of himself, two strong cloven paws, held out on massive hairy ankles. Puffy with self-importance, the lustful hirsute man is delighting in the spectacle of your distress. He's licking his lips with it, the old letch! Is an end of his shirt sticking out from him, under his belt, in relief, a monstrous hard cock? Upon seeing this, you open your eyes wide. Then you turn your look away, the hairs ruffled on your head, from shock and horror that he could act, not from a fortuitous outgrowth of tissue, inoffensive, made of tissue, but from a terrifying, sepulchral, unstoppable erection of cavernous bodies very much alive. In the face of danger, you just remain open-mouthed, a prey involuntarily offered to so much potential turgescence. Suddenly you catch your whole body crossed straight through by a dreadful spasm, as brutal as it is irrepressible.

From behind his Chanel glasses ("brand-name" glasses, if you please, with the two essential letters C entwined, "Have you seen how much these sell for, on Lamartine Street? Three hundred twenty euros, guys!" but the showoff got them for

Climb to the Sky

nothing—or almost nothing: "Just right: a little deal with a little crack dealer," he bragged a little while ago . . .); the other bearded owl becomes bolder in hooting sweetly, "Hoo! Hoo! One girl for all, all girls for us! Yahoooooooo!" soon relayed by the lanky horse, who is also entering the bacchanal: "One girl for all of us!" This gives him joy. What a menagerie! Is this a den of perverts or what? It's getting fiendishly hot, boiling . . . Your ass cheeks are beginning to get hot! And that stinks to high heaven.

With his thick hand, Light-Skin shuts up the hippomorph catchfly who's in rut: "No need to frighten this little treasure . . ." He imposes silence on everyone; you dread what he's up to . . .

There they are in great turmoil, these handsome well-hung officers standing at attention, aroused. (Not two pennies' worth of ceremony, their standing at attention, nor is it quite regulation! . . .) This good-looking crowd is slumming it in chorus, each one trying to outdo the other: "One girl for all, all for one girl!" Finally, this is their favorite variant. Facing this shapeless androgyne in fat, shapeless jeans, all of them have opted for this expression, without worrying that this is a case of mistaken identity; that squares things with them. Are they not going to gang rape you? They watch too much TV. Are you not going to get yourself violated right there? That would be the limit! To whom would you go complain afterwards? You see the title of *France-Antilles* from here: GROUP RAPE RIGHT IN THE MIDDLE OF THE POLICE STATION! This is starting to turn into a nightmare. You are really in full delirium there! They are driving you up the wall. They want to abuse you. To lose you in this solitude haunted by police presence. They are two fingers away from making you serve as a woman for them all. "One against all, all against one": that's what they made of your dear expression! Between two knocks, what strikes you is the insult: "AIDS nest!" It will save you. (The fear of contagion . . .)

Blessings! The Congo Negro calms them. He just reappeared, delivers you from the paws of these dogs, takes you

The Three Musketeers Were Four

under his probing yet beneficial protection. Some buffoons are still going to skulk around here and there on the ground, but out of bitter disappointment, from now on, more so than from natural desire.

"Fox, hoo! . . . Would you want to keep the young hen all for yourself? O-out! . . ." Chanel Glasses can still hoot . . . Let him get just a little bit close to you!

The most sinister-looking of the bulldogs sets himself up as Zorro's cousin in a *deus ex machina*! From a fox, there is only the name; you'd say it was Dumas's twin: it's the exact portrait of him that must've been darkened in walnut stain. (You had found him nice, the epicurean man of letters, already with his hair styled in a Jimmy Hendrix afro before Hendrix ever existed, crowning with black frizz his good jowly gourmet face, debonairly negroid.)

"Watch out! Fox is going to bite into you!" yaps Iron-Gray Eyes, swallowing the *F* greedily. "Don't trust his high principles!"

"Why does he have high principles? The better to BITE INTO you with, my child!" this light-skinned iron dog insisted uselessly and heavily. Congo comes back to serious things, if it can be said, willy-nilly, to his giant body defending, notwithstanding, the saucy little idea that was scurrying through his head obstinately anyway (for, although he refrained from it, the brave bloke would have paid dearly to know your sex finally; he would have even kept it to himself, for him alone, as a gallant man, refined despite his bestial outside, unlike his fellow creatures, if you had consented to reveal it to him).

"Where are the others?" barked Mr. Fox. "Where is the rest of your band? You're going to answer me, hoodlum, or . . ." hooted Chanel Light-Skin, to show off his zeal in front of his superior.

No way to make this infernal bestiary swallow that you prefer to act alone, that if you had exposed the least of your projects to your friends (including the most virulent of the militants), they would have dissuaded you vehemently. That there is not, to your knowledge, a single soul in Martinique who can

Climb to the Sky

vibrate in unison with an identical fervor. But no, you have no accomplice! No, you don't want to sell the plaques, you wanted to REPLACE them!

"What's going on here?" burps Iron-Gray Eyes, lost.

He's retiring next year, fortunately! The poor fellow doesn't understand anything about these youngsters. They're not that young, however, contrary to appearances. When you finally deigned to communicate your date of birth, tired of the war, after a thousand fruitless questions, then the cops also said that you were rambling. That you shouldn't mess around. Normally, people make themselves out to be younger . . . why age yourself more than twenty years? "Twenty years after . . ." you murmured gloomily. Iron-Gray Eyes is licking his lips. You ran across some pedophiles?

The pit bull didn't take it. He almost locked you up there. How many of them are there? It's the next shift. Or did they all spread the word that there was one crazy phenomenon of uncommon crime on their premises? It's coming out everywhere! They all come to look at you right under their noses, stunned by your unusual form of delinquency. Do these boys not have anything better to do? You would prefer to see them fiercely going at a serious investigation to find out who shot Dillon with a gun, right in the middle of the street, right in the middle of the day, last week. You would prefer to see them rush to put behind bars the thug who is in the process of calmly cutting the trembling windpipe of an old woman to steal her poor jewels from her, or rush to the home of the little unfortunate woman who just called the police emergency number because her lord and master is going to make her bleed with blows from a cutlass if they don't hurry. When are they going to decide? But when are they going to let you go?

Twenty years after? . . . Prevent yourself from creating unhappiness. You risk taking it on for twenty years.

Avenue du Professeur Raymond Garcin (and not Avenue Dumas, alas!), in the year of Our Lord 2002

The Virago

To Alexandra

Homo sum. A me nil humanum alienum puto.
(I am a man. Nothing human is strange to me.)
—*Terence*, Heautontimoroumenos

There are motorists who routinely hate people on motorcycles. But there are also irascible motorcyclists who know how to butt heads with them pretty well. Letting them step on your feet when you're ready to break your nose going 200 kilometers per hour is out of the question! If you can master 50 horsepower and tame a modern-day monster between your thighs, pick up with the strength of your own hands a mass of 150 kilos lying on its side, in the event of an accidental fall going around the bend of a slippery road, you're today's centaur, not a wimp. On one side there are the seated drivers; on the other are the motorcyclists, who become one with their machines. At least, if you look at things from their point of view, perched on a Honda or a Harley-Davidson, exposed to bad weather, so vulnerable, without a metal shell or seatbelt or back or head support. You feel less like a "seated person." You're adorned with risk, you growl, you squeeze through; you're no longer a lamb, you're a wild animal.

That's at least what they say, when fresh air bites your face and you confront it laughing.

What I say about it is what I assume, because I don't ride a motorcycle. I have never tried. I've been on the back of a motorcycle, occasionally, tightly clenching the waist of the person who's holding the handlebars. Maybe it's the same everywhere, but in Martinique, anyway, you are without a doubt special when you are enjoying roaring up hill after hill, into the depths and ravines, helmeted like a warrior from yesteryear, from long, long ago! You are not an ordinary person, with all

Climb to the Sky

those kilos of steel between your legs, squeezed into a biker's suit rather than set up in some air-conditioned compartment. You're not a common person, whenever you let go of your high-powered car on the only highway on the island, so short that you can see the end of it as soon as you gain momentum, once you've passed the constant traffic jams around the airport area in the Lamentin plain, our only large plain!

Exhilaration, a feeling of power, even superiority? An impression of independence, far from constraints, outside all barriers? I could not be sure.

At any rate, as far as I'm concerned, I met, under rather strange circumstances, a spectacular specimen of a motorcyclist who was one with a Yamaha-brand Virago.

I couldn't help but know the brand, displayed in gigantic letters on the scarlet curves of the machine. The model as well: Virago, in more discreet, more stylized characters. But this name made me smile: does it not evoke the Latin word that means "man" in the male sense (*vir*, as opposed to *homo*) to refer to a specimen of male-woman pejoratively? I don't know if the unknown person sitting erect on this Virago was aware of all that. The creature, dressed in leather from the booted feet all the way to the end of the gloved fingers, jumped from the metal mount. No way to make out the least glimpse of skin, much less to know the face, completely masked under the full protection of a helmet shining in the sun. I couldn't even see any eyes. Impossible to make out anything behind the blackish visor, as opaque as a switched-off television screen.

I, a poor car driver, was in the process of parking not too far from my new high school. I had just come back to Martinique a short time ago. Without understanding well what was afoot, for I was arriving right in the middle of an affair that had already started, I saw, to my great astonishment, the biker jump in one leap onto the front of a car that had, probably, triggered anger. The enraged android-like thing began jumping, jumping! . . . while trampling the hood, under the dazed look of the dumbfounded driver. I did not move, not believing my eyes. With a few well-placed blows from the boot, blithely dealt, toe,

The Virago

heel and heel again, then toe again, the cowboy boots got the better, in a curious dance of massacre of the metal's thickness. The sheet metal was completely dented. I saw the barbaric humanoid get on the Virago and leave as if it were nothing, the car driver start his car and leave in reverse without further ado. His passivity made me imagine that he probably did not have a clear conscience. I followed the Virago with my eyes until it disappeared at the corner of the street.

What a brute! I thought, while taking sides, deep down, without really knowing why. But the way it was done, the barbaric form that this protest had taken! . . . That could only be appalling to me. However, an incident on the street is never only an incident on the street, no sooner seen than forgotten.

I was coming out of my courses late the next day. It was almost seven o'clock in the evening when I was getting back to the parking lot at dusk. Suddenly, coming from behind me, a roar alerted me. I jumped, turned around, barely saw, making holes in the darkness, a shadow with reddening sides. No way! It's my Virago?!

I stayed there, without moving, as if I were waiting for something, wondering what the brute on the Virago was going to cook up next. Smash another car? Take it out on me this time? Had this become a mania? My Virago didn't look comfortable that night. Even less so than yesterday, it seemed.

What show will you put on tonight? I was saying to myself at the time.

It was starting to intrigue me; this was putting hot pepper in the daily grind of my high school, the backfiring adventures of the red motorcycle. Nothing to do with my regular little rhythm at the steering wheel of my little gray car.

Then, without worrying about my presence there any longer, the Virago was stopping beside a Mercedes, dismounting, trying to open a car door, then a second one. It was the fourth one that gave. I saw the silhouette sheathed in leather disappear inside the vehicle, then get out again immediately, brandishing a plastic box, one like housewives use to store leftovers in the refrigerator. One of the big gloved hands raised the lid, conspicuously waved a thick wad of bank notes, stuck them angrily into the gap of the jacket. Then, nothing else. Everything happened very quickly. I still had the roar of motors in my head when the Virago had already melted away into the night.

Like I was sleepwalking, I went up to the Mercedes. A piece of notebook paper scribbled in haste was tacked to the windshield. You could read a message on it; for me it was hardly understandable, with inhuman spelling, but in any case full of arrogance and contempt, where it was a matter of "dirty old men stinking of dough" who think they can do anything and imagine that all bodies are for sale. It ended, in unrefined terms, with a threat of reprisals. I wasn't far from believing that the Virago had found, in the plastic recipient, something with which to find vengeance far beyond expectations! One thing could not have been more explicit: the owner of the Mercedes had committed some act of disrespect, one way or another . . . (I had some idea about the matter in question, but I won't dwell on it, no more than the lecherous individual on four wheels had been able to dwell as he pleased on the object of his shameful desires . . .) In any event, the Virago had found the car again—Martinique is so little!—and carried out revenge.

It was better not to linger around. The letch from the Mercedes was perhaps not far away. I went back home.

Should I have denounced my Virago, my wild-child smasher of automobile hoods and emptier of bank-note boxes? I felt neither the desire nor base enough to go play informant at the police station by giving descriptions and blah-blah-blah. After all, I didn't know any of the protagonists in this affair. It was coincidence that had put in my path, two times, this raging Virago defending honor fiercely in a rather knightly way, outside norms, quite unconventionally, with maybe even a tiny bit of contempt for the law . . . But if the fellow with the hood dented by boot kicks had not decided to press charges, it wasn't up to

The Virago

me to do it. I just found myself at the show two times, that's all. As for the "old pig" in the Mercedes, what was he doing with all that money in cash in his car? Probably nothing upstanding. So, in these circumstances ... there's always someone more dishonest than you!

All that didn't prevent me from sleeping, and I returned to the high school the next day after a good night's rest.

But could that not be my Yamaha Virago? At this distance, how to tell? I know nothing about motorcycles ... Tchip! What does that enormous scarlet engine have to do with me, a well-dressed, well-heeled young woman?

It's certainly the same color. And the black of the leather clothing, and the same helmet, it seems ...

I need to make sure. I will leave when I have verified that it's the same motorcycle. Why I need to do this I don't know, and above all, don't ask me!

This time, I'm going to say two words to this little punk biker, I was saying to myself over and over without doing anything. I will get in my car as soon as I have seen if it's really the Virago. In the meantime, I stay standing there, looking, fascinated, at the dangerous saber-rattlings of the reddish engine that leaps and bounces on the slope, stops, takes off again, shoots off once more, in a thousand and one sultry turns! The hill in front of the high school is used like a slide. There it goes, it's coming down. No, it's leaving. It's drawing a long loop to attack the side of the hill, acting crazy, throwing clumps of earth, almost lying with belly flat on the machine. Going to commit suicide, I swear!

Dirty little pretentious macho man! Are you showing off with your scarlet thingamajig? Talk about an act! Is this how you flirt? Do you think you're impressing me? Come down from there if you're a man! ...

You look so clever, risking breaking your neck to impress people! I will laugh hard if you fall. I will be there to call the ambulance.

Yes, that's it. I'm staying to get help to you, in case you fall. I try to convince myself of that, at least.

Climb to the Sky

The motorcycle stops for a brief moment at the summit, its silhouette standing out, fiery and proud, against the roundness of the clouds. The hand signals me, as if to seal some peculiar complicity with me.

The being enthroned on the Virago had chosen an audience, following the example of a knight from the Middle Ages offering his victory to his lady, at the time of a tournament. I had a curious sensation, as if I felt chosen to be present at the feats and applaud the grand exploits.

And I remain there, stupidly. What good can this do me, whether this showoff's face is broken or not?

Alternately irritated and worried, I shrug my shoulders, then I tremble. I make a tchip with the end of my lips, then I bite them, out of fear that death will be found at the end of the acrobatics.

That's enough, you can stop now! Okay, you're the best, it's true that I have never seen so much. OK, no hands, no feet, in a little while it will be no teeth, if you keep up like that. That's enough. Now I'm scared for you. I would not like to see you die, right under my eyes, you whom I do not even know.

Everything goes very quickly on a motorcycle.

Hardly had I thought all this than the Virago completed its amazing parade of love, like a strange red-and-black bird, hurtling down the slope at top speed, coming to a dead stop right at my feet, almost running me over.

I made a scandalized start, opened my mouth to protest, to swear at him, you damn bully, really, who do you think you are? You're not going to squash my hood and make my money disappear into thin air! You'll see if I'm a pushover! I've already seen you at work, but with me, things will not turn out like that. If you think you intimidate me . . . Stop that bike from backfiring so I can tell you what I think! . . .

The biker lets me close my mouth again without having made a sound. Braced against the machine, taunting me while revving up the engine as if savoring a victory.

The Virago

The Virago is there, reddish, jovial, impetuous, a few centimeters from me, close enough to touch me... Really ready to take the plunge.

I will not cross your Rubicon! I am not passing through your Caudine forks! You came, I saw, you did not conquer.

But the die has been cast. Alea jacta est.

Suddenly the motor became quiet. The being of leather, plastic, plexiglass, and metal stepped down. Took off the leather gloves first, revealing to my haggard eyes delicate hands with long, polished red fingernails. Then the helmet came off slowly and a full head of mulatress hair shook in the full sun. Opening a beautifully well-defined superb mouth, made up with the same scarlet as her engine, the Virago exclaimed: "Hello, my beautiful! Are you new around here? Champagne, then!" In a triumphant burst of laughter her vermillion lips parted.

Awakened from his secular sleep by the racket of the motorcycle, the old devil who has haunted Gros-Morne since the death of the last Carib Indian and the descent into town of the last Runaway Negro—the last symbols of freedom of our good island!—found this dark tale of motorized man-women, lecherous blokes, and nascent feminine friendships so scandalous that he gave me a big kick in the ass for having dared to tell it.

"Holy peanuts! Kimafoutiésa! Who's stuck me now with such sorts of little light-skinned mulatto women who are quite simply going bad?" he grumbled in dragon Creole before falling back asleep, sickened by the new times and the smart side of Martinique's women of today, not without having drunk a little fire of country rum, in order to forget.

"What's this champagne affair? What have they got with their champagne? Rum is what leads to good!" he declared, yawning.

This is how we came to you, my story and I, quicker than we ever could've done on a motorcycle.

Casablanca, July 1993

Sister Soul

To Daria

> Ariadne, my sister, wounded by what passion
> did you die on the shores where you were abandoned?
> —*Jean Racine,* Phaedra

Because It Was He

He was one of those boys who believe that girls in miniskirts don't give a damn about anything and love life. For a good bit of time already, Mathildana had been watching him furtively; he came and went slowly on the airport pavement, like the "Caution Wet Floor" sign advises, but certainly not because of it. With a vague eye, a book in his hand, he could have walked like that, with the sweet air of eternity, in the middle of the nineteenth century. It was for this reason that she loved him, for this reasonable reason, this romantically serious look that the literature student felt around her like a reassuring perfume or like a balm, perhaps because, just a few months ago, her sister died, the little goddess! from hunger and immortality.

It was because he believed so strongly in this miniskirt affair, like iron, having an eye on her legs, which he found beautiful, and because she had this story of eternity in her head that they met, both of them, five hours later, still being and talking in the same place, huddled up on the same seat, each one close to the other, indifferent to the noises and the sounds of the strike, or secretly happy about the announced delays, from one half hour to the next, made by an angry loudspeaker that they might have believed to be their accomplice if they had had the intimate conviction of their perfect innocence.

Each new announcement of a changed departure caused exasperated shrugs among the passengers, discontented sighs, recriminations ... Only Terence and Mathildana invented a

Sister Soul

new joy from it. Each one, deep down, greeted this delicious setback as an exquisite opportunity. Without confessing it, without confiding it to the other, each of them secretly savored the obligation to stay there, in the "Icarus" room in Orly, permission granted, in a few ten-minute intervals, then suddenly threatened again, when the voice rose again, but granted again, for a few instants more, to sit there, side by side, as if subjected to the goodwill of an invisible divinity whose only emission, audible and parsimonious, would have commanded their destiny.

Afterwards, would he be beside her? Would they not be separated? They had not found themselves together at check-in. Could it be that fate would again put them near each other, once they had gotten on the plane? If not, all those hours far from each other . . . Eight terrible hours without each other . . .

She was going back to Martinique; this young man was going there too, but on vacation, for a month, at his mother's place in Anses d'Arlets. The loudspeaker regularly calmed the furor of the others, trumped the growing impatience of the annoyed passengers, but did not lessen their troubles. Mathildana and Terence remained in the same place, obedient, serene, and blessing the orders, with, on their lips, the same smile, the same eyes, precisely, infinitely indulgent to the chagrin of the others. They stayed there, docile and voluntarily passive, immobile, like well-behaved children, both abruptly youngsters again, as if to celebrate childhood, whispering about memories, anecdotes from their lives, for her, two or three noises from Fort-de-France, for him, episodes from France. The suburbs, a few snobberies of a wild child softened, peculiarly tamed by the miniskirt of this girl.

Everyone seemed more or less sickened by the wait that got longer and longer. From one twenty minutes to the next, from one half hour to the next, the clear, sweet voice became hoarse, repeating that they were changing the departure for obscure technical reasons, provoking complete panic. Everyone was grumbling. A few even began cursing, talking about bombs, attacks, booby-trapped packages, even about baggage that they had to explode, boundless losses of time, therefore losses of money! This was going around everywhere, shouting about theft, worrying about insurance, claiming reimbursements, compensations, making complaints . . . But Mathildana and Terence did not complain. They didn't have to complain. For in the middle of the screeching protests, outside the choir of shouters, they were enjoying their time spent together.

The Breath of the Ancestors

"Mixed-blood type, sex female, born in Fort-de-France (Martinique), according to the identification documents discovered on the premises. Discovered at 93120 La Courneuve, apartment 3517B, at the domicile of one Thanassia LEDOUX, 23 years old, unemployed, born in Capesterre de Marie-Galante (Guadeloupe), currently on a trip abroad according to the security guard's report . . . entry made by breaking and entering at the request of the neighbors, who were bothered by the smell . . . Discovered in the company of a child, sex female, mixed-race, distinctive characteristics: left eye green, right eye blue and brown . . . of indeterminate age . . . too scrawny in appearance to be the child registered on the passport and the family record book found on the premises . . . Waiting on the definitive report from the pathologist . . . talk of malnutrition . . . an unknown in the neighborhood . . . trying to notify the family . . . put on file under missing persons . . . ," the police report sent to the press for the "News in Brief" column said vaguely and laconically.

Rehvana had been found, the beautiful prodigal child of the enchantress islands of the Caribbean about which the brochures bragged so much, dead from hunger in a block of buildings in the northern suburbs of Paris, alone in the middle of the "Quatre Mille." At her side, nestled up stiffly, the cadaver of her little girl, Aganila, the child taken away by this same inexplicable malnutrition, the same atrocious and hermetic dereliction, at the peak of the twentieth century, on the threshold of the twenty-first century.

Sister Soul

In a gothic paradox, most worthy of the Antilles baroque, the woman from Martinique who suffered from chronic identity crises died with her passport in her hand, immediately identifiable, with all her identification documents (National Identity Card, family record book, etc.) dispersed on the carpet, around her overturned bag, all her pockets turned out, torn, and with her wallet ripped open, as if she had desperately been looking for something—a bit of money, without a doubt, a last forgotten bill, hidden in a fold?—before losing consciousness. The majority of the pages from the passport had been torn to shreds. It seems that Rehvana, in searching for her roots, got her feet stuck and fell, a fall from which one never gets up.

Completely emptied of her being by the strange end of her sister, staggering on the edge of insanity, insidiously penetrated by the ghost of Rehvana, by the chimeras of remorse and guilt, but accustomed to fighting and soon determined to win, Mathildana tried to get her life back together, attempted to tame the demons of her existence, piously gathered the heritage of so much sisterly suffering.

Nothing was easy for Mathildana. For her, nothing was clear anymore. Everything in which she had believed had dissipated into limbo. Disappeared with Rehvana. She who was accustomed to looking danger in the face, she who had led her life with serene energy, now saw everything through the mourning veil that had extended over the world, like a cruel filter, Rehvana's destiny.

However, she soon had to overcome her own pain, mask her own stupor and disguise it in energy in order to support her parents, who were themselves completely stunned and half-dead after the news. May they not lose one daughter after the other . . .

Once again, Rehvana had left to her older sister the responsibility of "mending things," the concern of "arranging things" while hiding the status of her own soul, like big sisters are accustomed to doing, from the very time that they are little, going behind the younger sisters to clean up after them or hide the foolish things they do.

The strength that Mathildana then had to draw from herself to revive her haggard mother, her despondent father, helped her to sustain herself, forbidding her to sink. From this came a flux of life that ran into her again, went through her whole body and anointed her spirit, thinned down the shadows of her soul. However this torrent, no matter how vital and beneficial it was, never managed to haul off all the dross of suffering that the questions linked to Rehvana's destiny left in her.

She wanted to decipher the scream, so close and so dark at the same time—so full of her accents that were her own and yet were strange to her—so Creole, so lost, so pure, that Rehvana had thrown to the world before leaving it. Now Mathildana remembered, upon coming out of a bitter daydream, that the two of them had almost the same voice, as often happens with sisters. But their scream was not the same. There where she herself was only fervor, assurance, openness to the world, she, Mathildana, the "Big Sister," Rehvana was lost, more and more each day, in an abolished quest. The little sister was drowning in an ocean of myths, wandered, tossed around, chimerical, halfway between two worlds, looking for a third world, never completely in one or the other.

In fact, Mathildana never stopped asking herself questions. Refusing with vehemence all delirium that would make her feel guilty, she wanted bitterly to understand. Even if life gave vigor and joy back to her, even if, in their whirling, her days enveloped her in sweetness, the anesthetic for happy times big and small, from one sun to another sun, offering her peace, love, what do I know? Mathildana would not stop wanting to have understood. It was there, oh yes, that the opaque sisterly heritage resided: living, and living after having understood why Rehvana, finally, only could have died.

She would ask herself for a long time if her little sister had died for having been just a little too black, in the land of the White folk, or, on the other hand, too light-skinned among the Black people. Neither a tall, full, and strong Negress of an

Sister Soul

undeniable blackness, nor a White woman with a capital W having the leisure, on occasion, when she feels like it, of clinging to the panoplies or the heraldic delirium of the so-called "superior races." Neither one nor the other, but mixed-blood, mestizo, "brunette," or "colored girl," as they say, or *calazaza*? Without a title, without a name, in fact, having to answer to so many uncontrolled names, alas!

Subnigger, Mathildana said to herself with a sad smile, inventing—in order to flee the stupidly held reality of this theory of labels, each one more grotesque than the last—her own name for a saint. A posthumous neologism through which she bestowed on her sister, insolently, tenderly—a term for all eternity for the departed little one.

Anointed with secular dust, thickened with sweat and blood, one word: subnigger, to be yourself, even if you're not completely either black or white; in order not to be completely a nothing (nothing never being completely black or completely white).

A delicate cameo of mauve and gray skies greeted them in Martinique as their plane descended, with the mildness of Lent that they hardly felt on their skin, such a caress in harmony with the sweetness that had spread, in them and all around them, since they met.

Mathildana and Terence soon wanted to taste their own Martinique, another Martinique, that corresponded to them, new like their newborn love, strong like them from the feeling of its difference.

But Mathildana led him to the places of her early childhood, a place before the Antony snows, before being in France. Hand in hand, they haunted the little dozing maze of Terres Sainville, souls united in search of a lost soul and calmed bit by bit, long silhouettes inhabited by dreams and memories and gliding, seeking other ghosts.

Eight hours in the flight between Paris and Fort-de-France had been enough for Terence to penetrate the universe of

Climb to the Sky

Rehvana, to learn everything about Rehvana, at least everything that could be said and that Mathildana had confessed to him, in a very low voice, her head leaning on her seat, looking straight in front of her, in one breath, without stopping, without turning her eyes to him, her endless hands sometimes tensed on her knees. She kept talking, even when everyone on board had fallen asleep bit by bit. They remained the only ones awake, he listening, she recounting in a murmur, as if in a confessional.

And now he proved himself so taken with this young girl who had been offered to him, by the coincidence of an airport and thanks to a strike, that he made her memories his own. Quivering, he found himself dizzy.

But Terence was not a man to make a mistake in the vain pursuit of zombies. Sister or no sister, Rehvana was dead and buried. It was very sad, very dramatic, he felt empathy for the beautiful Mathildana: he did not like only her long legs revealed by her miniskirt, he could respect her mourning and even share her sadness, but life was there, vibrant.

With night falling, since he felt confusedly that another shadow needed to be chased away and that he was one of those strong souls who does not fear dead souls, Terence hurried to give their flight an air of joy and life, played like the avid Caribbean Sea tourists in 77- to 80-degree temperatures like the hot peppers that Ma Jacques packed in crunchy fritters. He snatched Mathildana from the floating souls of Terres Sainville, where Rehvana had lived with her daughter, led her in a tornado of tours across the island on 4×4s, sunbathing in Salines and on wild races through the Savannah of Petrifications looking for an improbable bird-cat that meowed mysteriously at the bushy ridge of a tree, finding its natal Creole upon the hot contact of its bare feet with the mangroves.

"Gray or red fruits from the mangroves?" he asked while laughing, his nose in the wind, his big muscled body swaying to a vague reggae air.

He made her walk barefoot along the craggy rocks of an unknown Bath of the Goddesses, standing toward Senegal, on

Sister Soul

the boundaries of the southern shores, almost making her forget the rocky sisterly cavalry. They felt good in their skin, in their blooming crossbreeding. Their gaze turned toward Gorée Island, they communed as juveniles.

How long did they linger, did they stop to whisper, sighing, in complete pleasure, shoulder against shoulder, enjoying a holy communion, alone in this desert of loose stones? No zombie came to bother them.

Then, hand in hand, they began their ascent again. But it was becoming too physical. Mathildana couldn't go on. She slipped, dripping with sweat. Drained, the young girl from Fort-de-France let herself fall down. She was hardly accustomed to abusing her body like this. In her city-dweller existence, she didn't practice such sports. With a protective impulse, moved like a big brother, Terence softly massaged the sore feet with the delicate Egyptian curves.

However, this could not prevent twilight from discovering them, like thieves, knocking with a furtive hand on Ma Cidalise's door, Mathildana, all atremble, whispering feverishly "To To To!" in the Antilles way, and he, Terence, suddenly gripped with fever himself, an accomplice to he did not know what, under the stutters of the old Lady.

"Well! Well! Come on in! . . ." exclaimed Cidalise while still bending her old body to scrutinize the shadows, behind them.

"Mathildana, I see you just fine . . . So, you haven't brought my pretty little capistrelle?" she worried plaintively, pretending to look at the shadow beyond Mathildana, through her as it were, in order to see if, by chance, Rehvana and Aganila had not hidden themselves there.

Terence and Mathildana remained standing, lost, in the door jamb.

"Well, come on in, come on in!" repeated the old crippled body while frenetically twisting her stiffened, trembling hand toward the interior of her hut.

"What am I going to give you? A little fire? I haven't made the juice . . . I already know that my little capistrelle loves Cythera plum, but, with my rheumatism, now, my hand doesn't know how to grind it anymore . . . A titac shrub? Oh, no! Holy peanuts! I forgot that I have a good little jujube liquor, there somewhere . . . I locked it up about a century ago; I no longer know where I put it! . . . It isn't funny: jujube gives you forgetfulness! . . ." added Cidalise, who laughed with her two or three yellow teeth.

Her hand perilously gripped a dodine pole; the clawed other hand felt for the television remote.

"I have already heard enough about politics this afternoon! I need to chat with you. So, what news do you bring?"

Cidalise babbled and fussed over the silent couple.

"Ooh, where did I put it? . . . My head is rolling from right to left . . . I don't know what to do with my body ever since the day my old lady's cane just up and left me, like that . . . Well, give me some news!"

They didn't talk about Rehvana, at least not about her end. They couldn't talk about it.

Ma Cidalise pretended to long for her visit, as if she were going to come back, one day or another, under another sun, to comb her squeaking hair, to enjoin her to tell a story, after having put her sore, beaten body in the thousand-year-old rocking chair from Balata.

"Beautiful Balata wood . . ." Ma Cidalise hummed to herself with insight.

Thus she made sacred, at the whim of her fantasy, her only piece of Creole furniture, the only survivor of the old times. She would never let go of it again, since it rocked the dreams of "Poor dear Rehvana!" At that honey-soaked time when the pretty mulatto woman used to visit her hut, her ancestor gave her, hurriedly, her precious "beautiful Balata wood," curling up her body instead in the faux-leather sofa that had already started to smell musty purchased by her son "in the area," "in installments" "with one hundred percent credit" Ma Cidalise pointed out proudly: "My boy don't need no endorsements; Mistah is a civil servant, oh yes!"

"But look at that! The thingamajig is already all scarlet! They don't make anything good anymore these days."

Sister Soul

Mathildana found this colorful chatter delicious, these touching Creolisms, this way of confusing musty (*moisi*) and scarlet (*cramoisi*) that rocked her in her earliest childhood in Martinique, before exile, before being in France, before her sister sunk away . . . before Rehvana found herself, ill in her swarthy skin, on the sidewalks of Paris.

Ma Cidalise conversed almost gaily, made allusions to Rehvana just as if the only chagrin that she had had to suffer by her own fault was a prolonged absence, a sort of grave sin of which Rehvana was guilty regarding Cidalise. The old woman put Rehvana on the same level as her grandsons who never came to see her, or at least not often enough, leaving her to come to the end of her life alone.

"Me who only ever gave birth to little boys black like last night! . . . I had my beautiful little mulatto woman with long hair in my twilight days, like now, like manna from Heaven, because I sure deserved it! As you see me now, well I was born unhappy . . . I would like to see my little old lady's cane, well, Good Lord! . . . Quite simply."

The old woman was talking about herself in the present, she was dreaming of Rehvana in the present, but Mathildana knew very well that Ma Cidalise assiduously read the daily newspaper *France-Antilles,* which they brought to her at the crack of dawn, scouring the obituaries, that she listened to the death announcements on Radio Martinique, "at six forty in the morning, every morning that the Good Lord brought her, even before drinking her coffee," that she spent her clearest hours in front of her television, and that she had to know everything about Rehvana's fate. But a tacit agreement obliged both of them to remain quiet.

Or maybe the ancestor had really lost her head, found forgetfulness in the jujube? Following the example of the Lotus Eaters, on the shores of which Homer's Ulysses failed on his odysseys, did she have the secret power of distilling the liquor that heals nostalgia? The mythical lotus of forgetfulness . . . (jujube and lotus are brothers; do not both of them, in Greek, bear the same name, *ziziphus?*)

Climb to the Sky

An invincible and dark force had pulled Mathildana toward the heights of Vert-Pré, in the course of a long walk, then upon the crossing of Chère-Épice, pulled her deeper yet, past Morne Galba and La Charles, to this eroded depth where her little sister had lived (if you can call that living), not far from the place where, solitary and valiant, right in the middle of the banana fields, the great lady of the Café quartier was living.

This same implacable power brought her back there time and time again, regularly, like a ritual. Terence never sought to dissuade her from it. He accompanied her, however. Vaguely he understood that something was being hatched there, in that sordid decrepit hut, that something essential was happening under the tender gaze of milky cataracts. Some ancestral mystery was playing out there.

He followed her every time, silently, patiently, respectfully, with a morning religious fervor of resignation and superstitious terror, an amorous acolyte serving a strange religion, a choirboy with a tortured heart, playing the martyr, until the day when Mathildana deemed it was no longer necessary to return there.

The exorcism had been consumed.

At the time when Ma Cidalise was called Mamzelle Cidalise, at the age when Rehvana died, she was living in this same hut, in this same room where her grandmother, who had come straight from Africa in the last Negro vessel, was a slave and was talking to her.

From the faraway shores of Guinea, the ancestor had come back to talk to them.

Because It Was I

> In a month, in a year, how much will we suffer?
> My Lord, how many seas will separate me from you?
> —*Jean Racine,* Bérénice

Foolish remarks were made sometimes that appalled Mathildana: "Oh! If it had been a man! It would not have happened

Sister Soul

like that! She could have defended herself better, poor little devil!" Ma Cidalise began to moan, regarding Rehvana's end.

"It doesn't matter! Nothing to do with it!" retorted Mathildana, extending her talons. "This type of old archaic woman is capable of making you disgusted about being a woman, by annoying you with her stupid comments! How can a person be so narrow-minded?"

"You weren't ever tempted to get a sex change?" asked Terence, relieved, delighted to find there the opportunity to change the subject of conversation. Finally, to get away from Rehvana and her unsolvable problems!

"A sex change? Me? You can't be serious?" exploded Mathildana, from her long-contained furors. (Contained for centuries, perhaps?) "It's as if you were asking me if I preferred having dinner at McDonald's or chez Lasserre! You see, because of being a woman, there is one thing stronger than all others, that can make you stand anything, and that is the quality of pleasure . . . (where you get excision, women cut open and sewn back together and other sexual mutilations, all these barbaric acts claiming to deprive women of pleasure! In vain! . . .) You see, Terence, male pleasure is like sending yourself to McDonalds, whereas the feminine orgasm is like dining in a gastronomical restaurant, of the Silver Tower variety, or at the home of an officer of the King's Table, like Beauvillier . . ."

"Or at the home of Jean-Charles Brédas," added Terence, patriotic. (He himself came originally from Marigot, and it did not displease him to remember that there also existed great chefs from Martinique).

But Mathildana was fired up. Ignoring all interruptions, she continued savoring the metaphor of pleasure: "Before having you introduced by some sort of butler . . ."

"A majordomo?" funny Terence cut in.

Mathildana shrugged her shoulders while smiling: "Your table has been reserved in advance, you are met by the porter who greets you, parks your car . . . Upon entering, you admire the décor and you admire yourself, until the maître d'hôtel shows you courteously to your table, pulls your chair back delicately, kindly helps you sit down . . . appetizers and bite-sized desserts each more delectable than the last are served to you as if by enchantment, without your needing to ask for anything whatsoever, even if you don't have an aperitif . . . They give you the choice of the menu on a list that has no prices, because, when you love, you don't count . . . Then the dishes are presented one by one, slowly, voluptuously, you have all your time to enjoy . . . Regularly they ask you if everything is going well, but never at the wrong moment, and never named medium-rare. They worry about knowing if everything is pleasing you, they fuss over the esthetics, hygiene, and your comfort, they spoil you, they bring you finger-wipes . . . they are attentive to you, to the least of your movements . . . They anticipate the least of your desires . . . And the juiciness is varied, almost to infinity . . . Smells and tastes mix, ad libitum, unite, melt . . . Total ecstasy! . . ."

"Synesthesia!" punctuates Terence, Baudelairian, in order to prove his empathy, although he had a rather smutty play on words about "libitum" on the tip of his tongue.

"You also have the pleasure of the eye: from the moment you walk in, it's all about the presentation! And even in the names, in the words . . . All these delicacies are not named just any old thing! You think about the names again, when you sample, you repeat them, you savor them . . . You ask yourself again what that was called . . . For no other reason just to give yourself the pleasure of saying the words again . . . The better it is, the more you feel like talking about it at the same moment you're tasting it. You have already seen yourself whisper: 'Cheeseburger! . . . Oh! Cheeseburger-r-r-r' your eyes in space, looking capsized, in a fast-food restaurant, even if they have added 'Deluxe' on it to give it more style? In the highbrow places, on the contrary, you are treating yourself with words, from the hors d'oeuvres until the dessert, apotheosis! But when you think that it's done, it starts again, a new exquisite thing arrives: hardly have you sampled the sublime black chocolate cake than they offer some new sweet thing, they propose something strong, or serve you something fine, a citronella concoction, you suck mint bonbons

Sister Soul

... They make pleasure endure, and it's never you who pays. You would have to be crazy to exchange that for a hamburger on your thumb!"

"I understand why you don't feel like ... eating 'gastronomically' every day!"

"It's not that the Big Mac is bad; it's different."

Terence was dying to dance a little *kaseko* with her. He wanted to dance with her so much! He would be capable of dancing anything with her, even to the music of obituary notices. He didn't care about the rhythm, the ambiance; what counted was having her in his arms. "Okay, but I detest the salsa! Anything you want except the salsa." He succeeded in cheering her up, the train of zouks on vacation at the kebab parties on the beaches.

The month of August had fast fled. Terence, the "Negzagonal" as Mathildana called him because he was born in France with African blood, on the Other Shore, soon had to take his plane back to Paris, where his work at RATP was waiting for him, "at sunless Créteil-Sun," he said with a great burst of laughter. Mathildana had promised to accompany him to Lamentin. He had so much luggage, with all those mackerel scads, those sauries, those lobsters, those avocados, those Julie mangoes, that schrub, and especially all that rum that he was bringing back to his mother. Not to mention the famous flagon of jujube that Ma Cidalise had ended up finding under her bed, squeezed up in her "old hut clothes" that she was bent on keeping, "just in case," "if the need arose," in spite of the "special mattress for elderly people" offered by her oldest son, the civil servant with twelve credits and dust.

"As if you couldn't find that whole bazaar down there in Belleville!" Mathildana teased. "Mangoes, there are plenty of them in the Thirteenth Arrondissement, in Chinatown ... And avocados too ..."

"Old microscopic avocados from Israel that taste like water?! They are not like the ones from the property, untreated, with a local warranty!" Terence responded proudly.

"Still happy that it's not crab season! You would be done for if you brought them back still alive and they escaped during the trip and ran everywhere in the plane."

"This isn't Easter," Terence answered simply, laconic.

The airport . . . An airport again, like the one where they had met, hardly a month ago, that airport in Orly where every hour was a sharing, but for them alone, and for all others a torture. Terence was touched by the memory of their voluptuous ordeal, squeezed together on the hard plastic bench.

But from that moment on, two more days still, two more nights still, still their two lives side by side . . . Yes, who knows, for life, maybe? He would invite her to Paris . . . "You could come at Christmas. It isn't very pretty: an old building from the Eighteenth . . . Arrondissement, not century! The landlord cuts off the water from time to time, enraged that people are not paying, and it's even worse that he wants to chase us out to do real estate speculations, but, you will see, I have made myself a nice studio apartment."

Terence laughed, a little annoyed, when he said that. She obviously had nothing to do with it. A beautiful villa on Didier Street, and all sorts of unpronounceable diplomas. Thingamajigs that could not be understood. A string of studies of the great Greeks. (Just on hearing the names, his head went upside down.) Terence was offering her his life, but how would she take it, his life, his own life, outside Martinique, away from the beaches, away from the Zouks, her little Domian existence led in exile? He was afraid suddenly that making the water run in the other direction would put an end to their story.

Mathildana appreciated that he was not lying, that he did not feel obligated to show off to her. This proved that he did not rank her in the group of so-called vain girls who choose

Sister Soul

boys because of the type of car they drive, above all, then on the basis of the color of their skin.

"To To To! I said hello! So, son, what are you doing? What's new? Give me some news, little boy!"

All morning, while he was finishing strapping down his cardboard boxes, wrapping up his rum carefully, his avocados and his mangoes, Terence had a surprise visit. His father had deigned to come see him.

"Well, you're about to leave? You didn't forget the jujube liquor that Ma Cidalise sent for you, did you?"

"You know Ma Cidalise?"

"Around here, everybody knows each other. As for me, I know all the women from the country of Martinique! You can believe me, son. Biblically!"

". . ."

"What's more you've been seen a lot around Vert-Pré, in the Café quartier. Was that you? They told me that."

Without answering, Terence rummaged through his luggage.

"So, my good man. What news, boy, how are things going? You look good, elegant like a stylish dog! Let me tell you . . . It seems like you have a good girlfriend . . ."

The father fiddled with his Mercedes key, embarrassed, passed his hand over his face.

"Just like that, you want to get engaged without getting your father's advice? They told me that you were going out with little Mathildana? (Well, when I say "little" it seems like the little miss is even a little bigger than you . . . by a few months . . . there are four or five months between you . . .) You should not be loving that girl."

"Well I do love her. It doesn't matter, it doesn't concern you."

The father mopped his face.

"That's not what I mean. You don't need to be loving that girl."

Climb to the Sky

"What's gotten into you, Papa? You never worried about me! You let Mama leave for France without a penny to her name, to give birth almost in the streets, to slave away as a poor unhappy woman working as the hospital janitor, emptying the bedpans and cleaning up the shit of other people to raise us. We never saw you at home, and now you come to get mixed up in the affairs of my heart? What's up with you? What good can that do you, if I love or not?"

"You should not be fucking mademoiselle."

"But I don't want to fuck her! I want to make love to her: a nuance!"

"Well, you should not be making love to that girl."

"This is incredible! Now I have seen everything! Papa, the respect that I owe you aside, I feel like sending you packing. Why should I obey you?"

"Because I am your father. It is no more complicated than that. First, my son, if my job is to reestablish truth, I never left your mother. It is your mama who cut ties. I didn't want to give you the details, son, but it was she who left one day with the syrup spray. So, with what did you think that I was going to sweeten my rum? A man needs women. There are four women per man in this country, so you have to try hard to devote yourself . . . If not, all that about love would get lost! Secondly, none of that is your business. A little respect for your father! If you knew what my Calvary was! You were too little to see that! In the evenings, when I came home exhausted, I was convinced that I was entering heaven in my bed with my girlfriend who loved me so much . . . Madame only threw mud into the air! Always complaining about everything: jealousy. JEALOUSY, my children! I had picked the wrong person. Really and truly. One night, my son, I was so drunk on punch, I got up with a start, I didn't know at all where I was; I thought I was at one of my mistress's houses. The only thing I saw was the fat luminous numbers that bellowed in the dark: 'Five till three.' I shouted, 'It is five minutes until I LEAVE!' much louder than them. I jumped into my pants, into my shoes, into my shirt, that was dragging on the foot of the bed, I felt around

Sister Soul

for my car keys, and I was ready to go back very gently to the house, as if they would say that I was leaving the hut of an occasional girlfriend . . . My brain felt so sick, it was impossible to recognize that I was at my own house . . . Your mother was watching me in the dark. She said to me: 'Where are you going like that?' while still rubbing her eyes. I said that I was going to pee. She asked me, "Since when do men go to piss into cars, huh?' And that was it. As soon as it dawned on her, she didn't hesitate, she packed up and left. There I was, like a schmuck, fastening my pants, getting tangled up in my buttons. My son, I was really rolling along: unable to make those little whores of scrap-iron buttons go into their buttonhole whorehouses! . . . I had no idea how to answer your mother. All that I could say was "How does their whorehouse close?" When she finished dressing, very calmly, she said to me: 'I'm taking the BMW!' And she took the key from my hand. As a result, my pants fell down. They got tangled in my feet: no way to run after her . . . I found myself on all fours. I was back to square one. I had really picked the wrong person. Really. But you, my son, this should not happen to you. And you risk something far worse. This affair can be serious."

Terence shrugged his shoulders: "I don't feel like hearing this." Still bent over his suitcase, he wished he could cork up his ears.

"But you are going to hear it anyway. I came to tell you that you should not continue to see that girl like you're seeing her now."

"Enough, already! That's really something! What right do you have to talk to me like that?"

"I have that right because I am her father. She doesn't know it, you don't know it, but I know it. Her mama, too . . ."

Terence stood up; he watched, petrified, his father who was standing up to leave, his potbelly sticking out, a satisfied look on his face.

"Good! It isn't all that! Mission accomplished! You see, little guy, that liquor, the jujube that makes you forget, it's for your personal use. It dissolves even the thickest hairs! Moreover, I am going to send one to little Mathildana too! Go on, son, nice arrival!" said the father, stretching out his long body and pulling down his bakoua hat very low on his slightly balding head.

"Now I need to tell you two proverbs. Afterwards, I will be done with that. Here's one of them: 'When you have put your foot into a nest of biting ants, you don't know which one bit you.' Now, here's the second: 'You shouldn't buy a cat in a bag.' This is so true, my little man, that when in doubt, abstain! I can't tell it to you any better. Well! These two kids narrowly missed incest! Fortunately your papa was there, to react in time, right? And to prevent you from doing stupid things," he sighed, happy with himself. And he tapped his shoulder, giving him a dirty wink.

"I told you that I had around fifty kids all over, boys and girls, of all ages and colors, all throughout Martinique, like a biblical patriarch, without counting all the cuckold children from married women, that other guys have recognized as mine!" he proclaimed from the doorstep, no less proud.

"Back then, that would have made you laugh . . ."

Balata, 1990

Chlorophyllian Creation

To Jean-Benoît, sanctimoniously

It isn't by chance that the good people of the public (I am not saying the ignorant masses) worship publishers. It's because the writer himself has a part linked to them. A patron donated a country house with a garden in Strindberg, a peaceful retreat if there is one, that I imagine resembles the house of my childhood like that one I had in France, both of them curled up near a convent, making the good calm sisters my closest and most peaceful neighbors, or like my house in my Fort-de-France, the home of my birth, my birth, really, where I was born into the hands of a battle-axe midwife to whom goes all my gratitude for the prettiness of my navel; I owe her for having escaped from the unsightly prominent corkscrew model that looks like the end of a blood sausage that's spoiling, alas! the trademark stomach of my fellow countrymen. Forgive this brief outburst of acute self-centeredness and belly-button gazing, but I have an obligation to take advantage of this solemn occurrence to give prayers to the male-female aesthetic, as well as to that good doctor P . . . -F . . . (not that good, however, for he was sexist and superstitious: he should've been my godfather, but he retracted when he saw that I was being born a girl: that brought misfortune, supposedly; in being a godparent for the first time, you needed to be a godfather to a little male, said the fellow in essence, one of Ma's cousins). The brave gossipy woman and the assumed accomplice had both rushed to have me be born at home, at the end of Terres Sainville, on the street that bears the name of the first black senator, with a first name meaning "Love God" or "Loved by God," if you please, and with a patronymic that means "knight" in English, this other language of the Caribbean.

Being brought to life on Amédée Knight Street, number 3, at noon, into the hands of a godfather faltering because of an unsuitable, if not damned, gender!

Climb to the Sky

Oh, triumphant Negritude, enthusiasm from a holy number, a free Creole ride under the sign of the sun at its zenith! Who could dream of anything better, like a symbolic triptych, for a released creature, being brown from birth, will and skin, a future unbridled creator, deliberately brown, in literature like everywhere else?

Hardly having arrived in this world, this New World, if it is one, I was placed de facto under the sign and under the wind of Caribbean mixed-bloodedness and fierce liberation.

I was exposed, like my island, to the wind, like they named it, and like in ancient Rome, unspeakably barbarous, the newborn girls were abandoned because they were not boys (it's true: may the suspicious souls look in any encyclopedia in the "Abandonment" entry; they will find exposed baby girls there, it was official, legal, and typically Roman that when the paterfamilias refused to recognize them, the girls found themselves abandoned on a pile of trash), at crossroads, to the deleterious wind of pornographic threats, to the legacies of some enslavement or swindled femininity, under the plural feminine aegis that made my weakness and my strength, whether I want it or not, being born a girl, and being born a girl on this island, therefore by nature delivered to the mercy of the trade and southeasterly winds, doomed to rebellion or resignation, without there being any other alternative.

I never resigned myself to it.

I wrote, a stay-at-home nomad, an encaged adventuress.

I was traveling around a lot within the little island of my birth, forced to move, at the time of one divorce and a half, in the space of a few months and almost simultaneously, not from one house to another, like people normally do, but between five domiciles that were more or less unlawful: from the abandoned conjugal roof (because it had become hellish, in the bourgeois disorder concealed by the self-righteous), to the noisy haven, Bolivar Street, with an impure, sputtering peace, all the way up there, on the immense balcony in a Creolized attic, on the

Chlorophyllian Creation

rooftop of the building erected like an ocean liner right in the middle of Terres Sainville (formerly called "the district of the miserable," before that swampy plot of land was bought from Sir Sainville and from this lemon was born one of the most fecund developments in Fort-de-France), believing myself freed, boarded on this vessel, the tallest building in the district, but finding myself plagued, shipwrecked on a savage island, polluted with dust, polluted with noise, polluted with disturbed presences, far from being a desert island, cacophonic, finally deserted for the hotel Batelière, in Schoelcher, oh liberation! Oh symbols! Incognito there, I was "the lady who wrote" in the precious stillness of local celebrity "seen on the television" cautiously protected by a personal friend (in the manner of the great Colette, which exalted my enthusiasm, turned my embarking into poetry and lessened my suffering), on horseback with the satanic city Saint-Georges, where the demon who intended to possess me was vanquished, up to the redeeming residence in Upper Didier, a flight? No, an escape, rather, an upward and sensational escape, a synesthetic elevation, oh Baudelaire's beloved spirits of the dead! An evolution, in a spiral. The buckle was securely buckled, but I, never would I be buckled again, I, never would I be enslaved again, I, forever free, forever uncaged.

No, moving is not forbidden. Of her African farm, northern Karen had saved the memory, in the middle of Danish forests, whereas this other Marguerite soothed herself with her young nomadic years on an American islet. There was always something green, and even ecological activism! Going green . . . Writing like you knead bread, following the example of the lady in green, within the peace of friend trees. Is it not said that woodsy Marguerite put her patronymic Crayencour under a bushel with the anagram Yourcenar, seeing the symbol of a tree in the letter Y? Nearly three and a half centuries after the founding of that noble institution by Richelieu, always until then reserved for men, she experienced the supreme honor of being the first woman elected to the Académie Française, which, before establishing its headquarters under the famous cupola, had also traveled around a lot itself, holding its first meetings at the home of one of its members, Conrart, then at the Ministry of Justice, and finally at the Louvre, until the Revolution, before Napoleon finally set it up at the College of Four Nations, today called the Institute of France. What tribulations for these Immortals in green!

Similar to a "Little Pleasure," a thatched cottage in Sligo, at the extreme west of Ireland, green Erin, was a base for Yeats's summer vacation. It was here that the peaceful sower of dreams wove his heavenly tapestries—on which one must walk very gently. Regarding that other great Irishman who was Beckett, it was in the greenness of the vines of Roussillon that he took refuge, harvesting grapes, writing *Waiting for Godot* . . . From this same ochre from Provence, the sulfurous eloquence of the divine Marquis de Sade was nourished, in his Lacoste castle . . .

The filao trees, thus—Lower Didier—the great takeoff of my life, yes, for the taken-off Creole woman, up to that calm Clerc residence at the top of the Didier road that people quite correctly spell the wrong way, Claire, for it was there that I finally saw clearly in the confusion of my life. Elevation. The apogee of a geosentimental itinerary. It was there that I exhaled, finding there other tall, more beautiful filao trees, tutelary, the alliance of unbowed coconut trees, discovering there the pink splendor of a copse of zinnias pecked at by hummingbirds at dawn, in the shelter of an apricot tree and my lucky dracaena plant, in the shadow of a "traveler's tree" savoring the end of my wandering, far from the barbaric bougainvilleas in Saint-Georges, from the den of Satan with wrinkled bushy eyebrows on his devilish black look that carried suspicious thoughts.

It was there that I holed up clandestinely, over the weeks, over the months, unbeknownst to the two demons I fled, escaping their possession, exorcising their influence, a serene exotic refuge with a pretty stinking-toe-tree staircase leading to a scroll-sawn mahogany mezzanine, a sweet tropical chalet filled with plants and flowers. It was there that I finally breathed.

It was there that I was finally able to write without being read behind my back or defending my body. And write in the

Chlorophyllian Creation

nude. It was here that I finally acquired my first house of my own. There that I enjoyed the pleasure of being able to write completely in the nude, without the risk of untimely assaults. My first house all my own, far from the legal conjugal rapes and other verbal violence that deserved to be reported or written in police reports, without a fair trial.

Even if love slipped in there, one year later, I took a sabbatical year far from matrimonial Sabbaths or pseudo-conjugal frolics or psychedelic debates there; I prized it, drawing something like a new virginity from it.

For all that, be she given, bought, rented, or lent, changing in multiple relocations, like for Colette, in brief dances of *Three . . . Six . . . Nine*, or for Baudelaire, who was born on Hauteville Street, in the middle of the Quartier Latin, but who moved with a frenetic (or pathological, or splenetic?) cadence, the home is a place of writing, therefore a sacred place, a place of enthusiasm, in the purest Platonic sense, in other words, a divine place.

The home of the writer is neither a legal domicile in the police sense of the term, where one can only come knocking after six o'clock in the morning to evict, to do the work of low or high justice, for the writer does a work that has no cure for jurisdictions, censures, or other fatwas. The home of the writer is neither an address on a calling, identity, travel, work, or credit card, nor is it a blue card or a Green card or a gray card or a card of any other color. The home of the writer has no household tax, nor is it a headquarters, for what is created there is not calculable by any tax inspector. The home of the writer is neither an official administrative residence nor a home sweet home, nor a cocoon for cocoune (pussy). (Since the official government register proposes this questionable "cocoune," by refusing "cocooning," which would be an Anglicism, let's go with "cocoune" when even that would resemble "coucoune," a sweet way of saying someone is an idiot!) It does not pretend to be an interior for photos in the upscale decorating magazines, for what is produced in them only makes pages of frozen

Climb to the Sky

paper. The worst quality of paper will do. It is obvious that the home of the writer has no closed doors where creation would asphyxiate, neither a jail nor a penal colony, nor even a conjugal domicile that a judge could take the liberty of attributing to one of the spouses in the event of divorce.

Be it a minuscule apartment overflowing with books or a grandiose manor, or madness in the style of Dumas, like his baroque Monte-Cristo from Port-Marly, it is the LOCUS SOLUS, the first polished den of greenness.

Author of a *Guide to the Homes of Writers*, Pierre Assouline notes this constant in writers' houses. Do they revel in chlorophyll? . . . Chlorophyllian creation: breath!

One thing is clear: writers need a shelter to write. Even if it's a park for pigs. Really, the question does not lie there. When Musset, sick and "worn down from excesses" (according to the holy expression, but made holy by whom, Good Lord?), had troubles that were not jests, he found himself a patron so that he would always have a home, since a door is needed as well, be it open or closed! . . . A door and a roof are needed.

For Sand there was up until the end a Nohant where she could retire to enjoy her pipes until almost the age of seventy-two. There are, in the United States, these writing vacations offered to groups of authors, so that they can create, in complete calmness, within the immense peace of a forest. And if he flees a cramped world, the writer goes to seek refuge at the back of a café or a square, even within the peacefulness of a cemetery, like Sartre and Simone de Beauvoir in Montparnasse. There is always a green plant, be it dusty or bony, in the least of the bistros!

If my favorite, Baudelaire, moved so much, it's because he was looking for HIS house, since he lived, tumultuously, his frantic quest for the Ideal. To Balzac, crippled by debt, having arrived far beyond the human threshold of poverty, this convict of writing, paid by the line, a hack who knew splendors and miseries, a new path of freedom opened up, the right to cross

Chlorophyllian Creation

his own threshold, one day, finally, with money that he did not have. So he bought himself a palace under the foliage of a park but never paid for it.

"To be born, to live and to die in the same house": such is the bizarre recipe for happiness that Sainte-Beuve gave. If the critic from not long ago can still make torrents of ink flow with his sibylline formula, the Arver home, a corner building on Île Saint-Louis, on a dock where "the Seine and our loves flow," a door engraved on its stone the mark of the sonnet that made of this discreet poet from times past an Immortal:

> My soul has its secret
> My life has its mystery . . .

Always protected by leaves, the home of the writer mocks the fleeing of time, under the des Arts Bridge or under the Mirabeau Bridge that Apollinaire crossed at the other end of Paris, a few flows of the river later.

A few ocean swells farther away, having to take up residence in the stifling atmosphere of her birthplace, Terres Sainville booming a little too much, desecrated by a bypass for the high-powered cars of people in a rush (replacing the path of flame trees of her childhood in Fort-de-France) and by the fleshy Dominican hetaerae for men with pressing needs, so much so that almost nothing remained that was land (terre) or holy (saint), in Terres Sainville, on Bolivar Street, a new family residence (in spite of the liberating connotations of this beautiful name, BOLIVAR, with Latin revolutionary echoes) neither in the Balata gardens, visited too much by the public during the day, and private property with night watchmen with pistols and night rounds, nor squatting, at the foot of this sacred Balata Sacré-Coeur, in the ancient vacation resort villa of her mother's already commandeered by one of her very well-off relatives who fought to buy it but no longer even lived there, nor acquiring, from the hands of another old third cousin, one of the estates of her father's side of the family in Upper Didier, too expensive per square foot and rented anyway, and having met no really selfless patron, our writer unmarried one and a half times began dreaming about starting up for real and divine revelation, found herself dreaming about the Zion of the Rasta brothers, far from Babylon, about her real estate agencies, of her little advertisements ("Studio, F2, F3, F4. a view of the sea if you lean over well, security deposit, pay three months' advance rent, supply three pay stubs," and who could be still worse off than that! Chicken and worse with rice?), far from her exemptions, from her covering everything in concrete and from her false faiths fearing neither God nor man.

Burning with a juvenile ardor, in full regeneration, revival, her little mystical crisis was made.

Fleeing the dragon of Saint-Georges and the demon of Saint-Michel, ogres and poisoners, Bluebeards of all kinds and great mean werewolves, the desire seized her to rediscover original purity, to take refuge in Mother Nature. Jah's love, why not? Why not try it? Yes I! . . . Oh yes! Why not Zion, free like a lioness? Why not Zion, brown-haired woman? Well sheltered, well isolated from Babylon? . . . Yes I! Jah Rastafari! Each time she was loved only by abominable men or some kind of lesbian ogresses. The fantasy of turning Rasta seized her, like getting into a religion. If she had had twenty years more of pseudo-sentimental pains she would have grabbed her rosary.

She knotted her hair, her head laughing, laughing in her loins as well, natural nature, hid her legs under a long skirt, worn in the style of Haitian women, a woman of yesteryear, an upright woman, an authentic Negress, putting sandals on her bare feet, pulled them away from the town, and took the Trace Road toward the tropical forest.

Arriving at kilometer ten, near the Barème house, she abandoned her car to the pleasure of thieves and rust.

At a brisk pace, she set about climbing unmotorized, free, released, oh exaltation! up to the heights of the Clouds, humming Jimmy Cliff: "I can see clearly now" . . . Light was dawning in her.

Chlorophyllian Creation

All of a sudden the magical verses from Gratiant came back to her memory, learned in recitation in the Perrinon Street nursery school, there, below, in the Lower Town, when she was only a little girl, these words that marked her childhood, this Creole phantasmagoria that remained etched in her, with her funny quaint spelling, pondering etymology:

> An souè assou la route Balata . . .
> An ti boutique en bas an pied mango
> Toutt bête-à-feu ka lumin dans grand-bois
> An touff bombou ka crié con an moune
> An nhom passé-ou pié-nu san ou ten-n li;
> An gran coutlas té ka cléré assou bra-ï . . .
> . . . .
> An-ni songé, chè, an-ni songé . . .
>
> One night on the Balata road
> A little shop under a mango tree
> All the fireflies twinkle in the woods
> A tuft of bamboo screams like a human
> A barefoot man overtook you without your hearing him
> A big cutlass shone at the end of his arm
> . . . .
> Remember, my dear, remember . . .

And she yielded to the invitation, she found herself dreaming, dreaming . . . That evening, in climbing up the same Balata road, a half century later, watching out for "the fireflies in the woods, the murmur of the bamboos moaning like a person, the rustling of the barefoot man, a big cutlass gleaming at the end of his arm, the barefoot man who just overtook you without your hearing him, and that smell of oil that will follow you like a dog" . . .

She dreamed about it, she dreamed about it . . . With the fear that dreaming about it might make her dream too much . . .

Climb to the Sky

A double set of conditions: the Jamaican singer friend, although far away beyond the seas, and the poet from Martinique, although deceased, warmed her up, filled her solitary march in the coolness of the evening falling on her shoulders. She felt good in her skin, her skin frozen by the calm of the twilight, finding serenity in shivering, proud and nervous.

The image of the man with the cutlass would be that of a brave yokel going to cut grass for rabbit feed . . . And the thousand animal or vegetable presences, crazy bamboos, fireflies, large woods, were familiar, welcoming, so many allied presences . . . A humble hut made by helping hands, deep in the tropical forest, in the shadow of a mango tree, to write there as she pleases, among the Brothers, YES I! . . .

Yes I, Yes I, Yes, I want it!

Ah! May she arrive in Zion quickly, there, where "I and I" is said and not a single "we," making expressions like *homo homini lupus* (man is a wolf to his fellow man) and men are piggier than real pigs amount to nothing but lies! . . . She runs toward the Lion of Ethiopia . . . Ah! To withdraw from morbid miasmas, to find a healthy refuge, to warm her body and her soul within a group of pure people! . . . Elevation.

But the road passed through Colson.

Hardly had she left the firing range of the soldiery's camp, after the place called "The Clouds," than she plunged into strange dense billows, penetrated into hallucinating teal blooms, sunk under an arch of spirals formed by the arborescence of creeper vines and intertwined ferns, then happened upon a madman in full abracadabration, brandishing an enormous cane and an authorization for discharge from the psychiatric hospital located at kilometer thirteen, who released, to all of them, clouds, billows, rejuvenations, lit sticks, phantom shots, and prophecies, all except the white page (but let us not forget that the Sister is a writer, and an inspired writer: the mystery of the white page does not frighten her!), all almost flanked her, flap! a ferocious whinny.

Chlorophyllian Creation

The madman traced extravagant spirals with his official paper with his left hand, while playing with his cane on a nonexistent conga, an imaginary *gros ka* drum or a wild goatskin with his right hand.

Terrified by all these clouds, all these chimeras and the darkened thoughts of the single human being around her except the even less reassuring invisible military shooters, shivering with cold and fear, our writer never found Zion or any trace of smoke or any odor of pretty short grasses that could have pointed out to her, oh solace! oh heartwarming fragrances! any Rastafarian presence.

She only found the courage to climb there to the height of the lanky *piopio* bird and turn tail, weary of forcing herself to forget mygale spiders and fer-de-lance snakes through self-persuasion, weakened more and more!

They inevitably threatened her, all those beasts, crouched in the suitable shadows of the arborescent ferns . . . She realized suddenly that night was going to fall on her swiftly! . . . Our writer lifted no less swiftly her overly long potential-apprentice Rasta-woman skirt that hindered her running, tearing down somehow or other, twisting her feet in her African sandals along the sides of Césaire hill, tumbled down, shook about, giving thanks to all the saints of Catholic heaven, the only ones she knew, at the time, not knowing the Rasta saints, thanking divine Providence that the return path and the path to salvation were by chance on a descending slope (contrary to what mister priest affirmed in catechisms), so well that she found herself short on benedictions when she caught sight of her car, her dear little car, quite recently doomed to contempt, appearing barely undisturbed in the evening humidity, faithful, still in the same place, and from which, Thank God, only a hubcap was missing, stolen by some unknown Brother.

And which even started up right there.

She blessed technology.

Port-Royal, July 1994, and Upper Didier,
Good Friday, April 13, 2001

Oedipus on the Train

To Michou, half-goat, half-cabbage
The man who loves danger and play is not displeased to see a woman change into an Amazon as long as he keeps the hope of subjugating her . . . The true victory for man is for a woman to recognize him freely as her destiny.
—*Simone de Beauvoir,* The Second Sex, *"Myths"*

"Excuse me, Miss, if I'm looking at you too intensely. But you resemble my mother: the same eyes, same hair, the same fine nose, the same long hands . . ."

The guy came into the empty compartment gently. A train between Liège and Paris, in first class; during that period of full winter, it's never very packed.

She is coming back from a literary conference on "women's writing" and is still wondering what such a thing is . . . "Antilles literature" is still okay . . . She very much wants writers to be classified culturally, and certainly accepts that they glue that ticket on her, even though there's still a lingering odor of racism about it, even some remainder of baby talk, in these categorizations, but the feminine ghetto where they stubbornly insist on shutting up women who write has always exasperated her. She loathes ghettoes.

She was there, very peaceful, all alone, warm, quite calm . . . She had started reading again, after coming out of her meditations, and here this unknown man interrupted her from her reading. She didn't even hear him come in. She just raised her eyes after she suddenly felt a presence, there, very near her, on

Oedipus on the Train

the opposite seat, when he sat down in front of her. Since then, he has hardly moved. She had started reading again, without worrying about him anymore, but his voice made her jump. What's he saying? Funny flirting. She has known flirts, liars, hucksters, and other people who give compliments, almost professional playboys or occasional seducers. All the ones who give the impression of doing their male jobs in attacking everything that moves. But never has any one of them compared her to his mother! Original, that one there. Just for that, she lifts her head, assesses the eyes of gallant Oedipus with a quick glance. Nothing heroic about him. Nothing sovereign or mythic: a brown-haired man with stocky shoulders. (But is it not his vest that is filling him out?)

She ventures a vague smile, then plunges herself back into her book. If he hadn't come up with this story about his mother, she surely would not have smiled. But that had made her tender, that thing, even if it's a flirt's thing. As a result, he's overdoing it, the cunning devil!

"My mother died when she was about your age now..."

What does he know about how old she is? There it is, the dead mother, now! Unbelievable, this guy's cheekiness. He's not going to start telling her about his life? Does he not see that she feels like reading?

"She was so beautiful, so sweet, so fine, so loving... I caused her a lot of pain: I only did stupid things when I was little. Around the age of fourteen, I was a real delinquent. I got into stealing cars, yep, you know that in Warsaw, you had to know how to get by..."

And a delinquent from the East, on top of it all! Since she just visited ex-East Germany, she could use her recent memories to tease him a little bit about Stalinism, in passing. She has to say something... and he doesn't look very mean. Anyway, he's the one who's doing most of the talking. She listens, ironic, letting two or three smiles emerge.

"I live in the United States and in Paris. Now, I'm in business ... I'm still doing a little work with Poland, but it's different today! It's a little more honest, the business that I'm doing now, and I'm earning a lot more money! I would've really liked for my mother to be there to benefit from it . . . She would have been proud of me, she would have loved America. And Paris! The poor thing used to dream about it . . . But she died too soon. I was too young, too crazy. I did so many bad things to her! Oh! It's crazy how much you look like her. You look exactly like the picture, the last picture I have of her . . . Just before the accident. I had just celebrated my fifteenth birthday; she was thirty-one years old. That damn factory! No safety there . . . They are criminals, those people!"

"She had you very young . . ."

"*Voï*, yep, very young; with a guy from the Party who didn't make her happy . . . I saw my father very little. He didn't help me at all, when I started having problems with the police. He rather pushed me into it . . . At any rate, to wrap it up, he ended up dumping me. A self-called moralist who lived off Russian vodka from the black market and preached obedience to holier-than-thou Moscow . . . Go figure! He loved everything Russian! I even wonder if it was he who denounced me to make himself look better and get an apartment in downtown Warsaw. Can you imagine, he got it two months later, as if by chance . . . A three-room apartment, do you realize that? The top of the world for my father. I suspect that he sold his only son for a three-room apartment right in the middle of Warsaw. He was certainly capable of it . . . I have one of those feelings like I'm going to throw up when I think about my father and that band of barbarians!"

And forward on to a resounding verse, a model of anti-Stalinism. The "communist" father is painted in the darkest colors; the mother, she is adorned in all possible virtues. That doesn't shock her too much, since she is a woman from Martinique. She is so accustomed to the idealization of the Creole ma. Even if it's a bogey-woman mother who hits with a leather belt or gives slaps on the head for a yes, for a no, for a bad grade at school, a cake that the child drops on the sidewalk,

Oedipus on the Train

shoes that the child doesn't want to put on, she is the best of mothers, the Creole ma!

"You see, I could not resist the desire to tell you how much you resemble her. And even when you spoke, you also had her voice. I was sure of it. I wasn't even shocked. But I have not introduced myself: here is my card."

"What? Starsky, like in the TV show?"

"No. STARKY, without the second *S*. And it isn't a TV show, they call that a 'series.' But that isn't important. Say Starsky if you want. I think that amuses you. *Voï*, yep! . . . It's good to see you smile. I would have really liked to make my mother smile like that. Instead of that, I made her cry. I made her die of worry, die of shame, when those Stalinist bastards put me in the reformatory. Oh! Seeing you happy, that gives me the impression of patching things up, of giving joy to my mother . . . If you knew, if you just knew how that does me good!"

She, today's mulatto woman, has some trouble seeing herself as yesterday's Yiddish mama. But go on . . . The traveler is touching, he talks with that suave accent that she has already noticed in Jews from Eastern Europe, the ones she met in Paris, at the Sorbonne, when she was doing her studies there. He brings happy memories back to her, true enough, this strange Oedipus from the East . . . The smoke-filled bistros, winter, and the acrid smell of coffee, the woodwork and the monumental paintings of Henri Martin, under which they used to sit to hash over literature, the world, life . . .

Coldly the small villages from the North flashed past at great speed: factories with broken windows, a humid grayness. Batches of children all bundled up . . . They sure make rabbles of kids in the North! Even more than in Martinique! Silver zippers, they must say that in Picard, in Wallon, just like in Creole!

He spoke so much about his mother, about America, about Stalinism—not to be confused with true socialism—that she hardly spoke about herself. He tries to find out her address and does not manage to do it. He contents himself with her first name, which he was able to pull out of her because of the initial R engraved on her cigarette case.

"Rachel! Oh! I was sure of it. That's my mother's first name. My uncle said *Rochele*. It's a good biblical first name that suits you so well, just like her ... But it's also the name of a great actress," he insinuated, dreamily.

Not a single direct compliment. Everything went through the mother, the resemblance to his mother.

She did not say much about herself. Imagining their arrival in Paris amuses her, and she smiles again, when the train enters the northern station.

He would like to have dinner with her. No. To see her again? That will certainly not be possible. There are no vacancies in her schedule? It's repugnant to talk about one's self like toilets, vacant or occupied! Is she married? Faithful? That's good. That's biblical, like her first name.

"I said 'married,' not put in a cage! I will call you maybe on one of these four mornings," she said, wagging the visitor's card with mischief that he had been extending toward her for a century, that she ended up grabbing.

But he is already a little sad, a little bit like an orphan, again. An orphan for the second time.

Just before the train stops at the station, she checks to see whether he is handsome or not, if he would have been worthy for her to have a son like that. She observes that he is not very big, when he gets up courteously and takes down her suitcase from the luggage rack. Not very big, but very gallant. Not big, but with beautiful, curly, well-arranged hair, bright-eyed. A nose with fine, living bones, good olive skin, twitching hands, supple body: no, she would not deny that. But she smiles again. (This time it is not for nothing, at least not directly.) She has a good time thinking about what is awaiting her on the platform.

He tried to prolong the last minutes of his torn dream of filial love. The last seconds, now ... He grabbed hold of his suitcase, her suitcase. He goes down, walks on the platform,

Oedipus on the Train

carrying her suitcase, insists a final, final time on taking his dear mother's twin to dinner.

"Mama!"

A big young man hugged her. Very big, very handsome, and very svelte, he has the same curly hair, the same dark eyes, the same fine hands.

"How are you? Did it go well? Was the conference interesting?"

She embraces him, drinks him in with her eyes, with these same black eyes that gallant Oedipus loves so much. She covers the boy in kisses. Schmo-Oedipus stays there, petrified, all stupid with his suitcase at the end of his arm. So much suffering in so little time! So much pain on the train station's platform, not on the occasion of a departure, as is normally the custom . . . No, this pain is a pain of mourning. Of an unbearable reception. A second mourning, intolerable, in the irritating effervescence of the hugging and kissing, of handshakes, of the "Did you have a good trip" that ring out all around him.

Their breaths are so visible, so raw in the frozen winter air. He shivers, he is an orphan. More orphan than ever.

"Jeremy, let me introduce you to Mr. Starky, without the second *s*, not to be confused with Starsky from the series, that you must not confuse with 'TV show,' no more than you should confuse Stalinism and socialism!" she reels off in one go while laughing. On the train, she just smiled. Now, she is bursting out laughing.

She added, a hand tenderly posed on the beautiful shoulder of the young man (*voï*, yep, so tenderly and proudly): "This is Jeremy, my son."

She was already dead to him. And he was half-dead.

The adolescent with the same olive tint and the same sumptuous look hardly grazed him with his own sumptuous look. The young man ignored him. (In his eyes, the Oedipus from the train never even existed.)

Everything happened quickly. The man felt that someone was pulling away the suitcase that he was still holding, to which he was clinging tightly, as if to a last relic of her, fist

Climb to the Sky

tensed. Provided with his mother's suitcase, the young man went away quickly, an arm affectionately slid under her arm.

The mature man watched them walk gaily side by side for a long time, until he lost them in the crowd.

Nothing else happened: there was only, between the two sons, a furious exchange of luggage.

Between the son of the Jewess from the East and the son of the light-skinned redheaded woman, the *ouaïe-aïe-aïe* from Martinique, nothing more was exchanged.

Fort-de-France, 1993

A Little Child Is Not a Speck of Rock

To Samantha

Oh! Never insult a woman who falls.
Who knows what a chain the poor soul enthralls.
—*Victor Hugo*

She hauled her own galleys, in full sun, alone and proud. Something had made her into a girl cat, she didn't know what. Something or someone, perhaps? She had had her victories and her defeats, her hopes . . . And she had decided that never, no, never again, would she allow anyone to try to enslave her head. Neither her head nor her body nor anything.

A rustling made her jump.

Her head, she held it high, her mane flaming in the wind. A sort of animalism had developed in her, by carrying her humanity to the highest. She had struggled so much, oh! Struggled time and time again! Causing Femininity to be respected in her, the non-male, the absence of a set of balls and cock . . . they call a cock a coconut in Martinique . . . and its little testicles, seeds . . . Grumbled so much that she ended up admitting that she had incorporated the coconut seeds. And that this wasn't weakness, but a living force, the integrated coconut seeds. She breathed.

The chains, she wore them on her neck, on her wrists, in cascades. They were jewels, transgression. They were not chains of slavery. They were emancipated gold, gold of a mulatto woman braving the forbiddenness of the *Black Code* and the old Law of Twelve Tables and all the pseudo-laws, Napoleonic codes or others, that had claimed to make of her, a free woman, practically a Negress, the object of a master through slavery, made a man's half through marriage.

Since she had understood well that having gold, for a woman from the Antilles, was answering with "tchip" to prohibitions;

since she had learned also that prostitutes and courtesans from ancient Rome didn't have the right to wear jewels in public either, she sent out a formidable TCHIP! to the two worlds, the ancient and the new, the antique and the modern while shrugging her shoulders, which were beautiful and brown.

And this tchip from a coal-woman from before the eruption of Mount Pelée, this disdainful interjection from a fishmonger-woman seated at the end of the Levee, her thigh quarters spread, her skirt folded in the crease, this ancestral Creole grimace bunched up her lips, which were full and swollen with blood—with a blood the same color as that of all human beings, for all that.

With a tchip, she rebelled. With a tchip, she started off. With a tchip, she had gotten unmarried, as soon as she had understood that in certain languages, around here or on the Other Shore, in beautiful French from the classrooms just like in Creole from the pits where police informants cackle to make cocks fight, in these two languages, thank you, my Lord, a godsend from the diglossia that gives two languages to an island only fourteen kilometers long when immense countries only have one, in these two languages there, most assuredly, slavery and marriage rhymed and agreed like two gossipy women.

She had all that in her head and in her body when the rustling just made her body jolt. A voice made her head move. But you see that it was very necessary to tell you what head, what body, and what she had in her body so that you would know, like me. (So-called omniscience, I share it voluntarily with others.) The arrogant carriage of the head of the surrogate mothers of long-ago yesteryear, she was absolutely not obligated to show it, that woman. All the women from Martinique have not come straight out of a page from Lafcadio Hearn and do not step over Martinique from Grand-Rivière to Salines with a load of fifty kilos on their heads. She bore that load truly, without fatigue, without a tremor, this imaginary load that weighed three times her weight, her own weight. And it is this chimerical burden that makes her carry her head that way, this absence

A Little Child Is Not a Speck of Rock

of failure that makes it seem astonishing that she jumped, suddenly. Jumped, jolted.

"Jump," said the voice that reached her:
"Excuse me, did I make you jump?"

A shudder from the feline hair that she let wander in the wind to affirm her brown soul, a rebel to all straightening, to cold, to heat, or to steam, one of those fierce shudders prevented her from seeing the fellow. Only the voice, unquestionably deep, warned her that it was a male. A male, and nothing less.

You know what they needed, all these stalling tactics and these apparent digressions about slave jewels and codes of all colors and servitudes, studies and all these holy words in -tude, to make you an accomplice, reader! And now I'm addressing you informally. And don't be surprised seeing her jump like that and seeing her, yes, with your own eyes, without my needing to say any more. You know her head so well, from now on, that you guess what is inside it. You know, henceforth, my male mate—or female mate, if you prefer, that she is inevitably alert. She is not an American woman doing study abroad on the U.A.G. campus (Université Antilles Guyane, remember?) who is shocked by the prevailing machoism. She is not a Canadian woman on a pseudo-sexual vacation or a white person from France who wonders what truth there is in the fable of the famous Negro calluses: "Do they have colossal cocks, yes or no, holy pistachio?"

I won't slice off, no matter how much I feel like it, oh! Not in the manner of the conjugally raped—originally latino (or should I say latina?)—an immigrant therefore—who sliced off her military husband's coconut, a good U.S. citizen of the proper tint, white, that is, Anglo-Saxon, etcetera etcetera, irreproachable in appearance, in other words, but in appearance only. (For who knows what was happening in the closed universe of this couple? It was, however, necessary that shocking things happen, in the intimacy of these people, for them to arrive at such a point!)

Climb to the Sky

In my capacity as a mixed-blood in confluence with all races, I could enjoy taking part in my own experience, singular and plural, and interracial, if you please, in order to issue an opinion, an "informed opinion," isn't that what they call it? ... No, that will be for another time. Writers from the Antilles can do without, from time to time, giving themselves over to filthy things or neo-doudouist folklore. We don't have anything other than fantastical stories about pussies and cocks to tell!

Pussy, coconut, callus, potato, seeds, asses, tongues! ...

"FOUT FOUFOUN FANM FODFWANS FANN FON FOUT!" There. Good job gargling, yes? What? Some people want that translated? If I do it, it's at our own risk and peril, and without alliteration, on top of it all, or in sweetening it: "The cracks of the women from Fort-de-France are split deeply!" The answer to the enigma is there, I will say no more about it. Let us kill this discussion!

You know therefore that she is not the sort of woman to let her body go; she's a single woman and a fighter, as I have said. You know that, without being stiff, and although having this sway deep down in her loins, this Baudelairian nonchalance, this grace of a dancing serpent, following the example of a present-day Jeanne Duval, but not with a grade of minus seven on her bac but with a grade of plus nine for good measure, you know that she is obliged to put up all around her and around the roundness of her ass a complete network of defenses, if she does not want to spend her time with the weight of a man on her body.

You already know her eye. Her black look like yesterday evening that takes in the height of the man, measures him without recognizing him. You know also that in Martinique, you know to be well trained in this sport of greetings: this isn't Paris or New York. You run across someone that you know at the end of any sugarcane field (let us creolize the expression, to regain possession of our sayings, our thoughts, our being ... our soul, and who knows where we'll end up? Let us suppose

A Little Child Is Not a Speck of Rock

that that can work). So, may the Madam watch out, she who would decide not to greet anyone from the masculine tribe! She would put herself in great danger of a poor social state in the microsociety of Martinique. Well informed of all these things, our brown-haired woman evaluated her sudden interlocutor.

"Do you not remember me? You taught a class for me . . ."

The voice was virile but imploring. The introduction is good enough, though clumsy. Such an introduction makes her lower her guard, soften, almost smile. (Yes, makes her lower her guard: where I live, they say it like that. Between a certain French grammar worthy of Claude Favre de Vaugelas himself and a hardened subordinated infinitive in Latin that is found also in Creole—thank you, Papa Cicero!—I can offer myself the distinguished luxury of opting for Latin-Creole willingly.)

Forward to the reproduced accusative on the subject of our infinitive, and a bravo to Caesar also, and kudos to Mister Schoelcher, and viva Master Jules Ferry who made all children go to school, and hooray for regionalisms, even if all these insolences are pulled out of the wrinkled hair of my mop! . . . (Did you not pull my tresses, mistress, at the Ile-de-France elementary school, to "see what touching" the semi-frizzy hair of a mulatto woman was like!)

Dear Mister Vaugelas, you were anti-Latin at a time when my Negro ancestors were being dispossessed of themselves and their African languages. You preferred the habits of language imposed by the "good taste" of the Court and the City, *vous prônâtes,* you advocated—with two circumflex accents, my God, how snobby that is!—resorting to the usage, and you proved anxious, not to establish, but to regulate—the French language. Allow me to grant myself that same tiny liberty today. You have understood without a doubt that what I value above all, in writing and elsewhere—is truly freedom.

She examines the open face, him smiling too. She asks him what year he was her student. She questions his look and his memory as much as his lips . . . But how to find a forgotten

Climb to the Sky

adolescent among this great adult bundle of muscles gleaming in the sun? Where to track down the little clumsy being that he was, ten years earlier? Certainly not in these wide, broad shoulders made stronger by sports, certainly not in this big body of a man standing there in front of her and taller than she by a good head, although she carries her head high, we are not going to repeat ourselves . . .

You feel that he's warding off a snub. That it is he who is on his guard henceforth. It is he who fears she knows not what from her. A slap, perhaps? A slap from a woman bothered by the sweet talk of this fellow? . . .

And it was there that she recognizes, yes, in those eyes there, in this fear, in this imperceptible moment to ward off the blow, instinctively, to confront the scathing words that she could shoot at him, if by chance she took him for something he was not. This fear mixed with love drowned at the bottom of his look is what she recognizes in him. The same fear and the same love that he must have had in his eyes ten years earlier to protect himself from other blows, from another woman . . . He shifts from one foot to the other on his long legs, carries his long, strong arms forward where she sees a knot of vigorous muscles taking shape.

But in this movement in which he gives a hint of extending his arms to her, in a burst of sympathy, she reads an old fear, an unconscious, involuntary, touching palpitation. And his smile broadens, and it is with no surprise, other than being a discovery to her, that she follows, with a shudder, the line of the scars, violet, faraway, puffy on the forearms of the colossus. She smiles, thinking that he might be a Hercules. She knows what he is going to say to her. What sort of vibrant complicity the deep male voice, so virile and strong, is going to reestablish between the two of them. Yes, she has goose bumps, she shivers, but she is fulfilled. For she will hardly hear when, with his male voice, he will say, making his beautiful muscles roll:

"They can no longer do anything to me now."

No more than he was ten years ago, he will not be very

A Little Child Is Not a Speck of Rock

chatty. He will not give any details. Prudish like her, and restrained, he simply opens his arms to her.

She knows these arms well. These are the ones he tried to hide, ten years earlier, at the time when he was puny, affection-starved, and mistreated. What no one wanted to see and he was afraid to show. Fear, shame, and something else . . . Something akin to love for those same arms that once beat him? . . .

To her, to her alone, eventually, he ended up saying where his scars had come from and that he didn't get them climbing coconut trees.

They had broken the silence, in two or three words, uncertainly, they had vanquished fear, filthy fear, but it was understood that it was not the fear itself that was filthy. They had done that, ten years ago. Lived through that intensity, shared that emotion. And now they savored it, these two former weaklings, silence. Sampled it, partook of it like a liqueur is sipped, their tacit satisfaction.

She had done everything possible to alert her superiors. She had done her best, ten years earlier, to shatter the famous wall of silence. It had not been easy, because at the time there was neither a "Child Abuse Prevention Society" nor a "Declaration of the Rights of Children" nor anything whatsoever, in Fort-de-France, for mistreated children. You couldn't even talk about it. It didn't exist where we lived. It was at the very least whatever people believed or wanted to delude others to believe. And she herself started, freshly out of her competitive exams, having just gotten back to Martinique, after her studies in Paris. It was her student teaching class, her pet class, so moving, with good, adorable adolescent juvenile faces that she would never forget.

But he, the ebony Apollo, it wasn't only his face, it was his bruised martyr child's arms and his look that she would never forget. And they left in a burst of laughter, showing all their teeth, only to discover each other, so strong, so well-adjusted, ten years later—she, from a fellow who almost massacred her psychologically, and he, the former beaten child—both vanquishers of liars, hucksters, and tormenters, those who claim to love you and make you suffer "for your own good," those societies and codes and laws and fanatical religions and villainous dogmas and sacrosanct families and the secret of private life and the closed doors of houses and the weight of education and the burden of ideas received and well-maintained opposition to the spread of knowledge, the tyranny of prejudice and prevailing hypocrisy and cowardice: courage, let us flee! And human brutality and individualism as king, and subjection to the powerful, selfishness imagined as an ethic and the rampart of blinds closed tightly on the crimes of intimate enemies give the right to do harm to you with impunity, until . . .

It is true that there are closed houses that must be opened. It is true that there are homes where only one sweet fire burns and that resemble hell.

Yes, Mr. de la Fontaine, the reasoning of the strongest is always the best. For there is strength in the weak that is Reason.

A little boy is not a speck of rock, and a woman fallen is never hopeless.

Fort-de-France, September 1994

Written in Lime Juice

To Dany and Fernando

First Month

Is confining yourself to madness the same as consenting abruptly, after coming out of a hegira of obstinate silence, in a rush all the more impetuous since it was contained for so long, to engaging, because it certainly deals with that, in this shameless, even obscene act, brain-destroying and immoral, the act of writing on her part?

Is it feeling deep within you a great emptiness that constrained her to have an everyday cohort proliferate inside her, ephemeral troublemakers, sniggering parasites, morally sick characters (but there is an Army for that!) and who, hardly named, behave like masters?

No, this would be an overflow, rather. You would think that she is going to explode, that a dismal explosion rumbles in her. (Or an implosion, who knows?) That she contains a burning cloud impatient to gush out of her. "Volcanic," her mother said, when she was just in her childhood, a mulatto woman, light-skinned freckled woman defying the snows and the foggy winter weather over there in France. She transported Mount Pelée within her from her island, a Pelean woman deep inside Ile-de-France. Proud of her natal vulcanism, full of incandescent lapilli, she took delight in magma without worrying about the cinders. "Iron breaker," her ma said. She found herself writing.

As far back as I can remember, she was in front of me, writing. I keep the traces of the first stutters in my memory.

She beats my existence with her writing. Without a doubt, she would be better off going to take care, on some divan, on some island, of her destructive schizophrenia before imposing on me and delivering her blasphemous logorrhea to the world, this story line torn from inconceivable self-sacrifice and cruel cravings—alliances with multiple meanings, bridges thrown up to improbable possibilities.

But may she take for herself all the sarcasm of Alceste, and may she take care to show this to people! Everything that is not writing, everything that is another task, be she a housewife, a professional, a cook, or something else is all the same to her, discourages her, or is accomplished in the most casual incoherence. She lives, acts, manipulates objects, talks to people, and yet within her writing this inert and tyrannical thing exists that she created and that obsesses her, imperious, fearsome invasion, little grotesque despots, always shut inside the closed doors of her head, puppets more or less connected, automatons, sordid gnomes to whom she gave life and who from that moment on haunted her, laid siege to her, surrounded her to the depths of her being, even into the most ridiculous moments of her life, so much that she can no longer beat an omelet without leaving the fork in suspense to run off to scribble notes on the grocery list reminder, between scouring powder and powdered sugar, to such an extent that she can no longer shampoo her hair without surging out of the bathroom, dripping, to dissolve on her desk and splash, bare-chested, breasts in battle, tawny mane soaking wet, the virgin paper where her writing and the avid beings who speak to her, call her, convoke her, demand being told, insist on being, wince.

What does she hope to exorcise? To whom is this discourse addressed? From what tears, from what pouts, from what gnashings of cynical teeth does she intend to nourish herself?

What shovelfuls of dead rats does she want them to throw in her face, she who, of her own will, violated her secret Sahara, where every sermon was good to tell, propitiatory, to serve herself up to foreign, certainly hostile souls?

What did she knead that was stolen in the full light of day? She exults, vain writer, she shows her feelings and gets drunk. Such a bacchanal, she gets intoxicated, uninhibited, dragging me in her drinking-song crisis. She makes herself a servant of Liber, the god who delivers; she expresses herself.

I would like her to be more discreet. I want to keep her

Written in Lime Juice

virginal, to hold her unviolated. I don't want her to give it up. Why would she turn herself in to people other than me? But I can only practice, in what she decides to write, the censure to which she consents. All the corrections that she imposes on herself, issued from her self-criticism. She hates any external constraint, rejects all form of intolerance born from the forbidden or taboos. She wants to be free.

Second Month

I had granted her a reprieve.

She had begged, confessing to me that she loved words so much, to make them sometimes sing, to make them sometimes caper about, to make them sometimes rustle, to weld them to the enthusiastic chorus of a solitary hymn, to magnify them among the trochees or the rattles, to glorify them in unique chants alternated with cleft confusion.

But she began to lick her lips in an unbearable way, to take unrestrained delight in her infectious mishmash.

Where are they now, the liquor on which she got impaired, the ambrosia on which I want to feed? And the Lotus Eaters' jujube, that procures the magic of Forgetfulness? What has she done with them, in order to feast on malignant evacuations in the slow stenches of the poorhouse?

Is this what merits intercepting everything in her life, and daily like a trance or a monastic rule, bringing her back, perched there, so close to me, to touch me, be it in full light of day or at night, even in candlelight when the electric current goes out?

What pleasure does she take in delivering these cruel emanations, as if they had come out of an ectoplasmic substitution, that, coming out of nothingness, cross her entire being, kill her, in order to gain access, triumphant, to the visible part of the blank page? A sadomasochist, that's what she is.

She approaches me only from time to time and then turns away from me. She uses me when the notion seizes her, then abandons me to return to her papers, to her pencils, her pens, these objects of which I am jealous. (I can't stop it. Although I

Climb to the Sky

defend myself from it with all my strength, I loathe confessing it, these are rivals that I abhor, primitive brutes that steal her from me.)

Third Month

And she perseveres, oh blasphemy! She seems to tolerate this self-consuming base act without any problem. Because I did not note any sign in her, no manifestation of rejection. All these people occupy her from now on like a free room.

Mown down even in the most intimate movements of her life by all these unknown people with unbearable existences, with exaggerated names, with ridiculous obsessions (or with grotesque first names, with reckless obstinacies, unless it has to do with strange fates), she sprawls out, opens up her heart, tarnishes me and scares me in the end.

I cannot let her go on, mistreat me with impunity, manipulate me without remorse, when I have, after all, the power to put an end to this macabre game.

I had taken a malicious pleasure in seeing just how far she would be capable of going, believing that she would stop herself. But since nothing comes of it, since it also seems that she is determined to continue, I will set everything in motion to dissuade her from it, since I have to prevent it ultimately by force.

There she is torturing, omniscient and perverse, her poor haggard creatures. (Should I say: *supposedly* omniscient?) There she is closing the demonic jaws of the trap on them again; there she is, the writer, monstrous, voracious, finally free.

For it is permissible for her to deliver, transparent, her creatures to her phantasms, to bend them to her designs, in order to spur one on better and to straddle it, death-bringing, in her gallop of sadistic ubiquity, until the little girl gets lost, until she begs for mercy, until she can do it no longer.

I deny her this morbid license, this power of holding the reins, like the power of ruling, sovereign, over a destiny that is not her own. But with what right does she influence the life of the Other?

Written in Lime Juice

There she is assailed by the sin of pride, there she is stretched out, greatly shameless in the exhibition of her ego.

And I become enraged seeing her still writing, defaming my memory, unbridling her thoughts, flaunting her retreats, accepting being read by imbeciles or cheats, even by others.

Like King Midas's barber, I would like to be able to dig a hole to scream her secrets into it. In what polluted postmodern gold mine does she think she can immerse herself without getting stained?

I would have wanted to be her accomplice, her sorceress trickster, when she plots her sentences, in the alchemy of her language. Yes, I angle for the role of acolyte, choirboy, within the mystery, in the high mass of her words. To be in empathy with her, for her to associate me with the genesis of her stories! Instead of that, she always puts me before the fait accompli. She is the sole master of the mystery. She asks only little from me, using only an infinitesimal part of my possibilities. However, if only she wanted it! . . . If only she requested it from me! . . . Of what am I not capable? But she never wants us to go to the limit of my performances. Everything she has in mind is writing, to set the vertigos that come up within her from I don't know where, resuscitated through I don't know what. Acknowledging the emergence of all the fables that she invents and that I myself have to accept! I have to gather everything without the smallest reaction, without emitting the least comment. I have no voice in the chapter. I only have to record, and woe to me if I get stuck! I have no right to speech. I have no right to look.

She scoffs at my poor glassy eye, pretends that it is inexpressive. She would like for me to be insensitive; she appeals to me only to submit me to her caprices. She damns the greenish light that ignites in the bottom of my eyes when she presents herself in front of me, full of all her creations like a pregnant female. Adulterous and clear-eyed, unfaithful, moist from her indiscretions, proud of having rubbed with men, by everything that she brings in from outside and from her frequenting of the world, daring to look at me solidly, right in the eyes, without blinking.

Climb to the Sky

When I contemplate all this swarm, I become terrified. I detest this frenzy that scratches and tears her entrails. I would like to set myself up as Haruspex; I would dream of having this function, in order to detect omens, to know if they are good or bad. I hate this Socratic or Platonic demon that camps in her, a parasite, an epiphyte, a buffoon that she tolerates in her lap! From it comes her enthusiasm, in the etymological sense, she insisted on specifying, making herself proud of an orphism that surpasses my understanding and my threshold of tolerance. But I despise this suffering that she has made her own, this torture more abominable than any birth, patient, impassioned, not passive, this terrible work, timorous, such a voluptuous torture, violent and voluntary torment. (I myself am also going to give her some, in the proper sense, denotations and all the connotations of the infamous pillory that breaks her, to work these lexical fields from this almost animal fear of finding herself barren!) May she let it suffer, this work!

For I know that the child to be born is as uncertain as it is hazardous. Its pain is unbearable to me. All my senses awakened, I am present, terrified, at this monstrous birth that I myself had not wanted, and that I would not know how to want.

And she dares to find me dreary? She dares to complain that I tire her, that she is sick and tired of me! She dares to make me responsible for her red eyes, her doubts, her lacks of progress, her deletions, her frenzied trials and errors, her pompousness! Her pride is teratological. Her ego is oversized.

Now she makes fun of my sophisticated side! She detests everything in me that she considers complicated. It even occurs to her to suppose that I am on the fritz, that I am not up to it. She imputes her own errors to me, accuses me of her own mistakes! She claims that I am keeping in my memory what she urges me to forget! That it is my responsibility, my role, practically my only usefulness. "Utilitarian," that's what she makes of my function: this is what she has reduced me to. Madam would dream that I inform her desires, but she reproaches me for any initiative! She refuses to consult me.

I would have liked so much for her to listen to my warnings:

Written in Lime Juice

she does not know how far writing can go, the Thing Stated, or what throes lie in wait for her, if she persists. This living together with abject beings is worth nothing to her.

However, I hesitate to act: I see her so sensitive, so vulnerable! I would like so much to take her away from those people! She only pulls a long face about it, and revels in this pernicious cohabitation. She is henceforth, heart and soul, plunged into her world of chimeras. She got bogged down in it little by little, to such an extent that I dread, if I devote myself to demolishing this world, hurting her with a blind remark. If I come to breaking down the universe that she entered, I run a great risk of destroying her too.

My indictment has, contrary to all expectations, become a speech for the defense. I plead for her now. I am apprehensive about all the evil that she tries to inflict upon herself.

It is said that first novels are always autobiographical. This is why she retorts rather quickly, by affirming, with bravado, that she has started directly with the second.

In truth, it is I who had been the first to destroy: I had only, alas, pushed back the due date and obeyed her orders.

She says that she must go on, that she likes what she does and ignores the dangers . . .

And yet I feel that she is crumbling away, that her entire person is dissolving; that these beings are gnawing at her and nourish themselves from her relentlessly.

At any rate, it is too late: now, she is much too involved.

Fourth Month

But it's that she takes herself seriously and even considers that a real job, that calls her, absorbs her, and keeps her busy, that goes before everything and even gives her, when she does not deliver, the bitter feeling of work not done, a true guilt complex when she is not there, writing.

She dares to tell me, in her defense, about the agony of the great Balzac calling for the Horace Bianchon of the *Human Comedy* at his bedside, the doctor born of her own imagination: this is all that this presumptuous woman was able to find

Climb to the Sky

to convince me, to justify the presence in her of this crowd of individuals, of things, of noises, of dances, of words that bang together. This swollen and sterile gestation, for whom, for what?

And she tosses and turns. And she expels, parturient, gives life to existences, boasting about them, as I reason it: for what life, toward what end, all these shadowy nativities and these deciduous shoots that become bare in full sun but will detach from her sooner or later, I know it?

For me, I deny all these things, or at least I felt the desire to do it!

I have the power to shut her up and I will use it.

I cannot tolerate this massacre any longer.

As I have said it, I have already disintegrated her first novel, autobiographical if there ever was one, since they maintain that all first novels are. And in spite of that, she took off again from zero, decreeing that this one is the first. That any novel to come is an emotion first, just like the "first time" in ideal love affairs: when you fall in love, each time it is the "first time."

She runs over me, hides her papers, draws up uncontrollable things, that I discover only when it is too late. She follows a preposterous story line.

Even if I destroy the words, the Thing lies in her, now.

Fifth Month

I no longer know where she is. She switches round, inverts . . . I get lost. (However, I have a memory that is more than human.) She fights me with lies and duplicity.

She lies, but something tells me that she has fallen back into her trances. She had feigned being busy, having pretended to accept, with the greatest grace in the world, the distractions I had created for her, and that I anticipated would turn her away from her useless work.

God, how she annoys me! She worked, chatted, she even went dancing, as far as I could understand; she tricked my vigilance by pretending to hear reason, to bend to my reasons . . . Even devoted herself to my games . . . Stopped underusing me

Written in Lime Juice

... Deigned to abandon herself to me, to get pleasure out of my possibilities ... Was this to dupe me better?
She will burst from it, from her need to communicate! With what does that rhyme? Do I myself communicate?
If at least I knew to whom she talks, to whom she screams, what she means, and, especially, to whom she is writing ... I am weary of going astray.
But in her rage to tell others, she quite simply renounced justifying herself in my eyes. I am not sufficient for her. (Is this surprising? I am not sufficient for myself. Without her, I would have no grounds for being ...)
This is silence between us.
Worse than her revolts or her tears, it is mute determination, toward whom, toward what?
I am in the margin. It is to the margin that she wants to relegate me.
She exhales a deaf complaint, unto me, opens herself to a solitary, universal communion blindly, without knowing who is receiving it. She establishes, in the vagueness of possible things, an enormous multiple, and resolutely refuses all dialogue with me.
She hurls insults, gives orders, even poses ultimatums, exhorts me to take the time to judge before condemning, to reflect before judging. Because condemning without judging is no longer criticism, she replies to the least of my objections; it is villainous crime, murder, summary execution, even premeditated assassination, making you a common-law murderer.

Sixth Month

The leaves blacken, and I hold vigil. I curse silently. The days pass, the unclean work swells and rises, but my vigilance is total.
All virginal whiteness is tarnished bit by bit; however, I observe and appease. My role is not so secondary. I am not just a receptacle!
On the other hand, what is this still? What has she invented, in order to lose us? When French no longer suffices for her, she pleases herself: here she resurrects Latin, even Greek! Here she

packs together I don't know what else again, ancient or newborn languages, and even, my word, Creole! For this demented *why have you forsaken me* that no god will want to hear.

Ah! I have my hands full with her! My torment leads me to undermine, to deny everything that comes from her. I require her to inform me on the hour, if not, I will sabotage everything! Or I will give all this a completely different turn of phrase . . .

Yes, I will show myself to be incorruptible, lucid, severe, and helpful notwithstanding.

Seventh Month

She is haunted.

She causes traffic jams in order to scribble in her car because a fickle idea crossed her mind, because one of her characters hailed her all of a sudden right in the middle of the Rise. She calls that inspiration, the desire to write, she says it does her good.

She promulgates that it is necessary, throws herself into it and no longer listens to me. She only turns to me afterward, brandishing her bundles of drafts, her sheets of papers, and her sparse notes. I believe they could put her in prison if they didn't beat her too much. I believe that she would accept the dungeon without even seeing the bars, provided that they left her a pencil. Then she would see only the virginity of the walls and would cover them with inscriptions. She would not even need me!

She no longer puts up with me telling it to her, she yells, "But no, I continue to live," but I hardly see how she hid from the world and how the updating of the ones she created was done at the cost of her seclusion.

Would I dare to speak of alienation?

What does it matter to me? I dare. Such is the extent to which, possessed by others, she no longer belongs to me.

What scares me the most is not knowing, outside those from her story (the ones who knot and unknot their alliances, seek and wander), who these others are to whom she has given and given herself. I can neither measure the part of me that she sells

Written in Lime Juice

off cheaply, nor evaluate how much that amputates me. I do not know, truly, what my participation is in the chaos that she organizes with my brain, my ink, and my tamed intelligence. My revolt aside, I have only a vague idea of the damages that she concocts in me, since all my various characters as well have been, like the rest, annexed, all my moving parts controlled by her, and my thought vanquished. All my rigor thwarted. All my logic perturbed.

Eighth Month

You have the power to destroy. If not, I will do it.

I can do damage and I will do it. I therefore said I would.

I have to uproot this lost hallucinating woman from my life, helpless and hyper.

For what need did she have to tell these things? She penetrated, with her head high, into this stagnation that she believes to be outside herself, and she has fun and gets drunk, hysterical. She takes pleasure in writing this thing that she believes to be a novel.

How can she feel like telling these intimate things (for they certainly cannot be that) to people she does not know?

She was not able to resist desire for long. And yet, from as far back as I remember, she has always, lily-livered, dreaded this assault, taken my warnings into account as well as my deprecations.

With what insane silt had she suddenly found herself fertilized?

What impudence did she have, this sow, to birth nine little ones with almost identical appearance, who weave their way, disobedient, curl up voluptuously and cross in her mangrove? What audacity, what impertinence? . . .

But now crawls within me, but now worms inside me, in my entire being, intolerable desire, rage never edited.

The tolerance of desire, the ardor that this enraged woman made herself responsible for telling.

Climb to the Sky

Ninth Month

When I intervened to put an end to all that, when I asked her the reason for all that, she had a doleful smile, as if I were arriving too late—a provocative smile also, curving an eyebrow fleetingly—and it took her a long time to be persuaded to answer me. I even believed (do you remember?) that she would never again consent to open herself up to me.

When she finally decided on it—or perhaps she forgot herself, denying my presence because it was just called a breath of air, and held well—she was only able to put forward this incomparable and questionable formula:

"I write for myself, for my friends, and in order to sweeten the passage of time." Yes, she only gave me as an answer the magical sentence of Borges.

So it was now clear that she was borrowing from others, she was now refusing to offer me anything that came from her whatsoever. It was also clear that she didn't count me among the number of her "friends," that I had not, well, done anything to earn that, and I agree with this; my only outlet would have been to melt myself as quickly as possible in her ego if I had wanted her not to write anything outside of me, not to put me outside myself!

I understood that there were at present no longer any words, except those that were addressed to me by her; that she would never say another one to me, no, not a single one, no! Not the least word, except those same ones that I vowed to destroy!

Now, I tell myself, it must be done like this. There is no alternative: the ego must be reintegrated. It is necessary to go along repeating the Formula many times over, until I understand, as I do presently: everything that she wrote, she wrote for me.

A voice softly singing with the syncopated accents of a child from Terres Sainville with runaway syntax, outside standardized norms, suggested to me from inside: "Let us keep it for ourselves!"

I no longer feel like destroying, I feel like piecing back

Written in Lime Juice

together, tying back together the broken unity, to recover it, to find myself again, I no longer know.

I am no longer afraid for her. It is no longer she who drives me crazy: now I tremble for us, I am irreversibly afraid of everything that is outside us.

This morning she tore the disk away from me, and then she sent the manuscript to the editor.

I no longer need to read it: it is I myself who wrote it. Me, her writing machine, her record-life laptop computer, the computer of her great works as well as the lesser ones, with an integrated dictionary, that knows thousands of words, in French and even in Creole, in addition to her personal lexicon! She has not given a name to me. She hasn't even given me a name. I am entitled only to a number, that she doesn't know furthermore and that doesn't come to me from her, a vague and vulgar reference on a bill, a series of numbers and letters without any meaning. I don't want it.

To the Other, she gave a title: "WRITTEN IN LIME JUICE." To this work that is not mine, that swelled at the bottoms of my entrails, that is going to blow out my circuits, this creation of which I am only the instrument as well as a great altar at the same time, the translator and the monstrance, even the Cerberus!

I am the Negro of the mulatto woman. I am her property, one of the assets from her inheritance, like the Other can boast of being part of her "literary property." (What a pompous name, the name of a byte!) But I am the holder of it. The Other would not exist without me.

May she be wary of my servitude: the old Greek Aristotle said that there are two sorts of tools: the non-speakers, such as ploughs, hammers, anvils, etc., and the speakers, slaves. I am of the second category: I have intelligence bestowed upon me. One that has nothing artificial about it. May she keep on her guard, the author!

Following the example of the slaves from the Antilles and America, formerly subject to the somber law of a *"Black Code"* (who did not belong to themselves, could possess nothing but could be guilty of theft), a similar paradox, with equally perverse logic, has simultaneously made of me an irresponsible object, subject to tallage, and an indispensible collaborator in whom confidence is placed.

Written in lime juice, in the guise of pleasant ink, that remains invisible, illegible, as long as it is not submitted to the actions of a body with which she is on friendly terms.
  But it is she who has signed.
  DELETE!

Balata, Carême, 1988

Afterword

EDWIN C. HILL JR.

Suzanne Dracius's *Climb to the Sky* actually weaves together a series of descents and escapes. The *métisse* protagonists in these stories all represent, each in their own ways, historic and modern-day *marronnes:* women who risk life, limb, mind, heart, and soul to make a break for it. The stories are set in Martinique—which like Guadeloupe and French Guyana served as one of France's slave colonies from 1635, before becoming overseas departments in the mid-twentieth century, and now part of the European Union's twenty-first-century "ultra-periphery." If the island's political and cultural situation exposes the false pastness of the colonial in "postcolonial" modernity, Dracius and her characters negotiate the seemingly never-ending temporal and spatial confines of colonial patriarchy (and the equally never-ending debates of postcolonialism) through literal and figurative dynamics of mobility. Whether in the form of sneaking out and running away or in the form of dancing, sea diving, or motorbiking, Dracius and her cast of characters work through the historical binds of gender and race by relocating their bodies in space and time.

Not all of these women achieve or even seek out a complete rupture from colonial society; rather they find and make room to maneuver within it. Through their own mixed and transnational histories and genealogies, their limited but inventive modes of literacy, their creative ways of reading and writing their place in the world, they boldly remap themselves through historic matrices of exclusion. Many types of body movement constitute this type of *marronnage,* a critical gesture that refigures the masculinist mythology of the *marron* to include a range of action, punctual and habitual, in the everyday lives of everyday *métisse* women. Fleeing the paralysis of island-paradise mythology and breaking from their position as a figure

Afterword

stuck in someone else's dream, these women engage with a long history and *lieu commun* of Francophone Antillean letters: the project of creating totality and continuity through the aftermath of historic violence (see Nick Nesbitt). Piecing together a sense of cultural and psychological "wholeness" from the torn and heteroclite fragments of the past, Dracius's protagonists strive to find their own place in the present while forging paths toward a more liberating future. Dracius creates a model of Creole identity that explores the possibilities of productive relations between *marronnage* and *métissage*, a dynamic that is both a breaking free from *and* a weaving together.

Dracius's contribution to discourse on Caribbean identity and Creole hybridity is most substantial in that it consistently imagines *métisse* women agents at its core. In the French West Indies, as the Guadeloupean novelist Maryse Condé and others have shown, "the founding fathers" of Negritude in the region (Aimé Césaire and Léon Gontran Damas), of Antillanité (Édouard Glissant), and of Créolité (Raphaël Confiant, Patrick Chamoiseau) issue ideological demands and writing orders that leave little room for the representation of women, women's sexuality, or stories of romance. Dracius takes these charged themes and representations head-on. Why are these themes controversial? The stakes of representing women, and of representing the island as a woman, have their profound ideological roots in the deep colonial mythologies of the French West Indian tragic mulatta: the *doudou*. The latter represents the exotic object of love and possession for the white colonial explorer, and constitutes a favorite subject of colonialist fascination spanning from the early history of Antillean sound texts in the eighteenth century (for example, the—infamous for some—folkloric song "Adieu Madras, Adieu Foulards"), to historic travel narratives (Lafcadio Hearn), to popular novels (Albert Bérard), to highbrow poetry (Saint John Perse).

At the same time as the representation of women protagonists and experiences was exoticized on one hand, and sidelined and shunned on the other, the literary expression of women of color themselves has long been effaced, suppressed, and

Afterword

overwritten in Antillean literary history. The early-twentieth-century writers Mayotte Capécia (vilified by Frantz Fanon in *Black Skin, White Masks*), Suzanne Lacascade (semi-forgotten until recently), Suzanne Césaire, and Jane, Paulette, and Andrée Nardal (marginalized in Negritude discourse and without white male patrons to champion them in the publishing world) are just now beginning to receive their due in critical thought and literary history.[1] Why have women's voices been thus marginalized? Why is there only a handful of active women writers in Martinique being published today? If, for many, "it is obvious that neither Suzanne Lacascade nor Mayotte Capécia had a particular gift for writing," as Condé writes, it is still true that "the oblivion in which they have unfortunately been relegated is not due to their lack of literary skills. Whenever women speak out, they displease, shock or disturb. Their writings imply that before thinking of political revolution, West Indian society needs a psychological one" (131). Since the time of these early-twentieth-century Antillean women writers, Guadeloupean writers like Maryse Condé, Michèle Lacrosil, Simone Schwartz-Bart, and Myriam Warner-Vieyra have masterfully rewritten women into French West Indian letters, but publication of novels by women writers in or from Martinique has been more limited.

Considering this patriarchal history and contemporary disparity, Dracius offers a crucial perspective in a corpus of work on Creole identity and subjectivity. As she notes in interviews, "the issue of métissage is linked to the feminine condition" (Rinne, quoted in Vété-Congolo 16). Dracius herself, like her characters, reflects "this multiple identity, firstly feminine. . . . It's true that I define myself as feminine, I live my life as a one, but in the plural" ("Entrevue avec Suzanne Dracius" 1216, 1217).[2] Born in Fort-de-France, Martinique, Suzanne Dracius has spent her life between the Antilles and the *métropole*. Dracius's work speaks to the way *métisse* women come to terms with the double bind of colonial exoticization and negritudinal marginalization through dynamic gestures of relation to the plural.

Afterword

The body lies at the center of Dracius's set of relations. The very formulations she employs in her interviews, "I define myself" (*Je me définis*) and "I live my life" (*Je me vis*) indicate a taking hold of one's self and one's body that cannot be taken for granted. Later in this same interview, Dracius comments on the way Creole avoids this grammatical structure of "myself" (*je me*), instead preferring the "my body" (*mon corps*): "For example, we don't say 'I'm going to wash myself,' but 'I'm going to wash my body.' Similarly, instead of saying 'I'm letting myself go,' we prefer 'I'm letting my body go'" (1218). To continue in this vein, for the women of Dracius's creation, "to free themselves" is primordially "to free their bodies." In this way, the body, and especially the woman's body, in its socioculturally determined histories but also its self-determined movements, serves as the locus point for strategies of self-realization and self-inscription.

The opening short story, "Her Destiny on Climb to the Sky Street," sets up the collection's broad discussion revolving around the renegotiation of violent economies and genealogies of bodies and historic texts. Leona's grandfather, a runaway slave, must endure the biting recitation of the Code noir while enduring the lash of the whip for attempting to break free from the dominant flow of these economies. Leona, like her grandfather, must endure the recitation of official genealogies of authority and respectability while Madam delivers corporeal punishment and verbal humiliation. Her boss calls her a "vagabond" in fits of rage to insult her; yet Leona's boundary crossing and *marronnage* suggest Madam alone felt the horror of the designation. Leona is proudly the *major de la pêche aux Totors* in Saint Pierre, better than any of the boys or girls chasing and retrieving coins tossed into the sea by tourists on transatlantic liners.

And like her deep relationship to diving, Leona's deep engagements with texts transgress the gender, racial, and class codes of Antillean colonial social order. She reads the papers Monsieur purchases and leaves scattered around the home, and that Madam holds in disdain. She steals away books to

Afterword

painstakingly decipher what she can by candlelight in the wee hours of the night. Building up her own worth through them, Leona, like her grandfather before her, prepares to take flight.

> The wax, in melting, formed a Virgin. That was a sign. Leona gathered her things, and then she closed up her old clothes in her Caribbean basket. The puny basket concealed all her treasures: her wax Virgin, a novel by Alexandre Dumas with the premonitory title *Twenty Years After*—her most recent petty theft—the pencil portrait of her mother, languid in a rocking chair, nicely "sketched" in a rush by Paul Gauguin, and the solitary Totor earned at such a great cost. (12–13)

Plotting her life and trajectory through the signs and symbols of European value—the coins, texts, and sketches retrieved from the beyond, fragments not fully understood but cherished as one's own—Leona reads her own signs in her own ways, and uses them to gather herself up and find a way out just in time.

Dracius's reference to Paul Gauguin recalls the artist's time spent in Martinique, and the letters he wrote to his wife where he speaks about the oft mythologized beauty and charm of Creole women. In one such letter, for example, Gauguin writes to his wife: "I swear to you that a white man has a hard time keeping his clothes intact because the ladies of Potiphar are everywhere. The are almost all of color . . . and they will go so far as to putting spells on fruit that they offer to you to rope you in" (Gauguin and Cucchi).[3] Gauguin plays off the legend of Potiphar's wife in the Book of Genesis, who attempts to seduce and force herself on Joseph, even pulling clothes off his body as he struggles from her grip. Humiliated, she accuses him of rape and uses the clothing he left behind as proof that he had approached her. In other words, Gauguin jokes that the Creole women's mythological charms are as treacherous as they are seductive. Any indiscretion will be doubly their fault.

Despite its exotic inscriptions and dubious distinctions, Leona anchors her clandestine genealogy in this marginalized

Afterword

and transnational history. Through it she finds a means to establish points of historic orientation for herself: her place in the abolition of slavery, her place in the travels of Western art and artists, her place in the canon of French letters and heroic adventures. Her life lies not just in the interstices and margins of colonial life, French poetic and artistic movements, and the island's political and natural history; her life is front and center in these texts and histories, even as the official authors of the latter seek to discount, dismiss, or expropriate her creative potential in them and rightful ownership of them through imperial acts of dispossession and anti-imperial acts of repossession.

Like the historic and global economies of "sweat, sugar, and blood," Leona's reconstructed, imaginary, and interstitial genealogy is one that explores the hidden narratives of the multiple that resonate within and beyond the narrative of the one inscribed and consumed in dominant discourse. From the epigraph of *Climb to the Sky,* Dracius relates the imagery of consumption to grand narratives and the movement of history, or historical processes. Here, storytelling relates story-consumption; and grand narratives of colonialism, and anticolonialism for that matter, carry within them hidden or slighted counternarratives, historical and imaginative, that Dracius's protagonists tap into to sustain themselves. Through a visceral resonance with the multiple within the dominant, they negotiate personal value in the devaluing economies of imperial world relations.

Discovering personal value despite loss comes through exploring *métisse* histories of relations, which have served as the lifeline for several generations of Leona's family history. The intimate relations of her *métisse* history were nothing other than socially taboo relationships of survival, compromise at best. Still, this history propelled its own distinct demands for freedom, for recognition, and even authentic love. For despite the violence and displacement that constitute the conditions of possibility for *métissage,* Dracius imagines the way authentic relations of love and life, authentic creations, spring forth at the very sites of these violent breaks of history, culture, and

Afterword

language. Semi-theorized as an impossibility within colonial society in Fanonist critical thought and literary history (see Roger Toumson), authentic love marches on through the treacherous patriarchal terrain of colonial, anticolonial, and postcolonial cultures of division and exclusion.

Many scholars point out the problematic colonial past of *métissage*, but when considered in Dracius's work, the term's usefulness has to do exactly with the fact that re/production—and the re/producer—of racial mixity cannot be divorced from this past. *Métissage* marks the break of the black Atlantic, a historic and cultural tear, but it also constitutes a mode of renewing and re-knotting, re-membering Creole history. Through these relations across the divide the protagonists find themselves. They are not complete, nor completely free; yet by following intuition and imagination they remain insatiably open to the world beyond their purview.

Writing in free indirect discourse, slipping into and out of autobiographical fiction, Dracius artfully takes the reader through but also just beyond the very limits her protagonists explore as they test themselves and their potential. Leona doesn't fully realize the depth of her *métissage* or the way her genealogy intertwines with more than one crucial figure in Western cultural history. She also does not arrive at a political consciousness per se. But she traces her path in history toward some measure of freedom and self-definition. Her self-affirming stance harks back to a Césairean moment of arrival, but Dracius illuminates something different: the challenges of and therefore the power within psychological and historical assumption of *marronnage* and *métissage* together.

The act of assuming comes in literally plunging into the dangerous waters of the unknown, literally challenging the limits of her body and imagination, but each protagonist breaks into the beyond at her own peril. Leona dives into the sea: "Ah, diving into the belly of the sea! Coming out of each immersion, emerging from it, triumphant. Playing with death each time, enjoying this dangerous delight, shooting out splashing from this painful happiness" (38). Emma slips away from the

Afterword

watchful eyes of family and domestics so she might discover the world of the distillery just beyond the woods she sees from her veranda. "Lacking air, she can no longer see clearly. Sweat is running into her eyes. She has never gone so far. Never has she gone so deeply into the woods, up to the extreme limits of the property. Is she going to end up getting lost?" (96).

The teacher in "Virago" finds herself in singular fascination with a violent motorcyclist. What is the sexual rush of such hazardous mobility for a woman, she wonders. "Exhilaration, a feeling of power, even superiority? An impression of independence, far from constraints, outside all barriers? I could not be sure" (120). The experience is literally breathtaking, but not without risks and limits; nevertheless, while you're speeding across the island you feel a certain power "when fresh air bites your face and you confront it laughing" (119). This high-risk mobility pushes each protagonist beyond herself—"You are not an ordinary person, with all those kilos of steel between your legs" (119–20)—while pushing the boundaries of gender as well: "I couldn't help but know the brand, displayed in gigantic letters on the scarlet curves of the machine. The model as well: Virago, in more discreet, more stylized characters. But this name made me smile: does it not evoke the Latin word that means 'man' in the male sense (*vir*, as opposed to *homo*) to refer to a specimen of male-woman pejoratively?" (120).

Motorcycles, trains, and cars cut through the erudite references to antiquity, Western mythology, foundational Caribbean travel texts, and French literature to create a writing self-space in constant motion geographically and culturally but also temporally. Why movement? Why routes over roots? Capturing the transnational back-and-forth between the *métropole* and the island, as well as the important relocations on and between islands in the Caribbean, this "stay at home nomad, an encaged adventuress," reads and writes her way out of her gender-assigned position in domestic, public, and international space. The trajectory from the beginning of the collection, when Leona descends Climb to the Sky Street and moves out into the unknown just in time to avoid the volcano's complete erasure

Afterword

of a historic Antillean site of *métisse* culture, to the end of the collection, when a more powerfully situated writing subject can now speak directly to the writer with the familiar form *tu*, the struggle over the designated place of the woman with respect to the text ends up where it begins.

Again, like the gigantic letters on the scarlet curves of the motorcycle, mobility involves taboo acts of writing and reading. Self-definition comes in no small part through relations to textuality, relations that are doubly torn given the way as women and as people of color these protagonists are doubly denied access to education and barred from the literary. Leona's struggle might never have been performed on stage at the Theater of Comedy, in fact she is denied access to the Theater even as a spectator, but she is aware that her life's drama measures up to and beyond the representation of the stage in its own way. She and other protagonists imbue their life and its meaning with texts, even when they don't fully understand them. Even though she may not know what it means, with her son deprived of title and genealogy/name, Cendrine names her son "Alexandrin," a name she snatches from a conversation about poetry she overhears as she can. In turn, Alexandrin continues the half-naïve, half-insolent practice of claiming denied relations in and to text.

Emma B.'s story in "Sweat, Sugar, and Blood" resonates with Leona's story even as the latter is a "lowly" young domestic and the former a married young *mulâtresse* occupying a high station in mixed colonial society. Emma has access to the texts and education about which Leona could only dream. Well-read, Emma can speak about the four corners of the earth, but, isolated in her designated place in Martinican bourgeois society, she remains painfully ignorant of the reality just outside her window. That her social standing puts her on a bourgeois pedestal was not exactly her choice; rather, she suffocates in this domestic isolation. While Leona was denied title and name, Emma B. bears her title and its ability to claim legitimacy in social space like a boring burden pinning her into a uninteresting place in colonial society: "The Saint-Pierre B.s

Afterword

have a square named for them right in the middle of Saint-Pierre, in honor of one of their own, who was a great man in that town (Emma forgot why)" (88). It's not the title and the confines of privilege that interest her, it's "that world that Emma brushes by every day without really comprehending it, this side of humanity to which she does not have access" (94). And this other world to which she's denied access is the Creole world.

In "The Three Musketeers Were Four," set in contemporary Fort-de-France, a woman calling herself Yich Lumina Sophie dite Surprise has been arrested by police for taking down Victor Hugo Avenue signs and replacing them with Alexandre Dumas Avenue signs. She, too, attempts to inscribe herself by reclaiming her place in history and space. Again, the question of inscription has to do with forgotten/erased genealogies. If d'Artagnan makes the Three Musketeers actually four, to the three Alexandres (grandfather, father, and son), the protagonist cites a fourth: Cessette, the enslaved black mother who gave birth to the first of the Alexandres. The protagonist's oral account ends up defying the typewritten official police report; her given name and the reappropriated name of her street are not located in the official local telephone book. Replacing street signs, this protagonist re-locates herself in a writing gesture of social space. And her writing gesture is criminal as well as nonsensical to the forces of order. It faces the violence of official discourse, its policing agents, and its mental institutions. From the turn of the twentieth century to present-day Martinique, Dracius imaginatively re-inscribes erased genealogies of imperial and local history like her protagonists do. Her explorations result in probing forays into the ways literacy, writing, and texts, function in mechanisms of patriarchal authority and legitimacy in the context of colonial and postcolonial Martinique.

This exploration of the social text turns on the question of the name, names denied or forgotten, names with secret meanings, names that comment on international events and that crisscross linguistic boundaries, names that are titles and that

Afterword

stake their claim in history and space. Naming, collecting texts, and piecing them together, tapping into structures of feeling and family stories, tracing new paths through racial oppression and male domination—taken together, these actions constitute themselves as alternate gestures of writing and forms of literacy. Colonial systems of power barred them from access to education, socially and financially banned them from the theater, and attempted to exclude them from political consciousness. Without education or letters of nobility, these protagonists avidly assemble stolen letters, devouring them, fetishizing them, offering them, passing them on to their own, wielding and wearing them, inscribing them in alternate circuits of value even without always gaining a full sense of their dominant value.

Another crucial dimension of this concern with text takes place at the level of intertextuality. While "The Three Musketeers Were Four" harks to Dracius's play *Lumina Sophie dite Surprise* (2005), a historical reference to a young woman involved in a legendary insurrection of sugarcane workers in the 1870s, "Sister Soul," at the exact center of the collection, the fifth story of nine in *Climb to the Sky*, brings this intertextuality to the forefront in its relation to *L'Autre qui danse* (The Other Who Dances), Dracius's first novel, published in 1989. Through intertextuality Dracius relates themes of lost sisters in history to ideas about erased or forgotten lineages, doubles that recall a forgotten other. The intertext reveals Caribbean symbolics of proximity and possibility at work in self-text exploration.

The short story "Sister Soul" picks up where *L'Autre qui danse* ends: with Mathildana dealing with the loss of her sister Rehvana, who was consumed in the violent essentializing and patriarchal dynamics of an ultimately misunderstood negritude. The overwhelming and oppressive longing for roots that saturates Rehvana's desperate quest for black Caribbean "authenticity" in *L'Autre qui danse* leaves her literally stuck in the mud of the mangrove where she would, if she could, submerge herself completely, "finding in [its] slippery grip infinite peace, absolute security" (283). In contrast, Mathildana finds herself by finding her body in motion. She comes to terms with herself and her plurality by giving herself over to the intensely corporeal yet transcendent experience of dancing with others. She accepts "the truth of the dance," this heady spinning of herself with others, "because there's nothing to lose in this magnificent whirling, neither oneself nor one's balance, there's nothing to lose and everything to regain" (79).

Unlike Rehvana, who "become[s] caught in a position of total dependence on a man whose initial seductive power came from an apparent ability to satisfy [her] need for concrete ties to a long-lost African culture and identity" (31), as Françoise Lionnet puts it, Mathildana, in *L'Autre,* "throw[s] off the dead weight of archaic memory" (31) to free her self and her body for acts of self-inscription in time and space. Again, names are highly significant here. While *Reh*vana's name evokes the "rêves" of negritude, illusory if seductive "dreams" of black purity and wholeness through a mythic return to origins that ends tragically, Mathildana's identarian "math" is able to "calculate" a way of balancing the different, even contradictory, facets of her being, finding a stable site for the self within power-torn relations of the multiple (Vété-Congolo).

Through this imagined genealogy of soul sisters who defiantly assume the power of their *métissage,* an autobiographical Dracius slowly appears in "Chlorophyllian Creation." Situating herself through a transnational Creole network of *métisse* women writing their way (otherwise) between the New World and the Old, Dracius clears out a path and place for her own writing self, a *locus solus,* as the writer herself puts it. The latter is not alone, strictly speaking; rather it is filled with the spiritual presence of other Caribbean writing selves who have indicated the path. It "belongs" to her, it forms the soil from which her art will grow; at the same time, this *locus* is shot through with multiple languages and creative energies that extend beyond the writing self.

For a moment, this sacred writing place seems to be an elevated mount on high, beyond any one language or place. In the original-language version of the short story, Dracius moves

Afterword

from French to English in her identification with Rastafari worldviews. Her *locus solus*, as she writes it, seems to be "a humble hut made by helping hands, deep in the tropical forest, in the shadow of a mango tree, to write there as she pleases, among the Brothers, YES I!" (154). From this perspective, a final elevated and transcendent arrival seems imminent. Rastafari phraseology seems to portend an out-of-selfness that goes far beyond the self-centered "nombrilisme" announced in the opening of the short story, and the writer seems on the verge of locating herself as a mythic *marron* on high. But ultimately the Afrocentric mythologies of roots and returns prove ill-fitting for her:

> Our writer lifted no less swiftly her overly long potential-apprentice Rasta-woman skirt that hindered her running, tearing down somehow or other, twisting her feet in her African sandals along the sides of Césaire hill, tumbled down, shook about, giving thanks to all the saints of Catholic heaven, the only ones she knew, at the time, not knowing the Rasta saints, thanking divine Providence that the return path and the path to salvation were by chance on a descending slope (contrary to what mister priest affirmed in catechisms), so well that she found herself short on benedictions when she caught sight of her car, her dear little car, quite recently doomed to contempt, appearing barely undisturbed in the evening humidity, faithful, still in the same place, and from which, Thank God, only a hubcap was missing, stolen by some unknown Brother.
> And which even started up right there.
> She blessed technology. (155)

This writing self is resolutely of her modern place and time. Instead of losing herself in a mythological past and elsewhere, she opts for the limited tools she has on hand in compromised conditions of the present. Why deny their potential for creative *élan* and expressive presence? Ultimately the *locus solus* for this *métisse* Caribbean writer is a moving site in time.

If the attempt to re-create a whole from fragments of the past has been thought of as a common theme in French Antillean

Afterword

writing, Dracius turns the assumption behind this theme on its head in "Written in Lime Juice." It is not from a situation of lack that writing comes, rather writing here results from an overfullness. Again, this explains the multiplicity of the writing *I* in Dracius's account. The writing self surges forth from and through this multiplicity too full for the singular subject to contain. This too-fullness is too much for the boundaries of gender, race, and place. The writing subject is thus an explosion (or implosion), harking back to Mount Pelée, and the volcanic eruption of 1902 that marks the turn of the century in the Antilles.

By the time Dracius ends with an interrogation of official titles and labels for (her) literature—*écriture féminine*, Antillean literature, etc.—one has a more profound sense of the stakes of such appellations as well as their deep resonance with histories of race and gender that served to devalue women and Caribbean texts in the first place. Simply put, Dracius stages her transnationalism as constitutive of an interrogation of writing and gender as much as an interrogation of race and coloniality.

As Dracius channels a transhistorical and transnational network of women writers, she opens up the meaning of writing as a mode of interrogating the strictures of official texts and traces. The challenge lies in discovering and recovering alternate modes of reading and writing one's psychological, cultural, and corporeal existence in the world and in history. In other words, the *quête d'identité* has everything to do with finding oneself among texts, those of travel writers and French colonial fiction, but also those of the everyday: newspapers, street signs, and local histories. Finding oneself is a textual act involving alternate modes of literacy; inscribing oneself is a writing gesture that involves the location of the woman's body in the past and the present. It's almost as if Dracius tells us that to be *métisse* is already to be a writer, to be an assembler of fragments from the past who inscribes herself as she gathers herself up in the multiplicity.

Afterword

Notes

1. See, for example, Tracy Sharpley-Whiting, *Negritude Women* (Minneapolis: University of Minnesota Press, 2002); Brent Hayes Edwards, *The Practice of Diaspora: Literature, Translation, and the Rise of Black Internationalism* (Cambridge: Harvard University Press, 2003); and Jennifer Boittin, *Colonial Metropolis: The Urban Grounds of Anti-Imperialism and Feminism in Interwar Paris* (Lincoln: University of Nebraska Press, 2010).

2. This interview was published in French. The English translations of the interview here are my own. The original gives "cette identité multiple, féminine d'abord. . . . C'est vrai que je me définis féminine, je me vis femme mais au pluriel."

3. My translation from the original French: "Je te promets qu'ici un blanc a du mal à conserver sa robe intacte car les dames Putiphar ne manquent pas. Presque toutes sont de couleur . . . et elles vont jusqu'à opérer des charmes sur les fruits qu'elles vous donnent pour vous enlacer."

Bibliography

Antoine, Régis. *Rayonnants écrivains de la Caraïbe.* Paris: Maisonneuve and Larose, 1998.
Condé, Maryse. "Order, Disorder, Freedom, and the West Indian Writer." *Yale French Studies* 83, no. 2 (1993): 121–35.
Dracius, Suzanne. *L'Autre qui danse.* Paris: Le Serpent à plumes, 2007.
Dracius, Suzanne, and Jean-Pierre Piriou. "Entrevue avec Suzanne Dracius." *French Review* 76, no. 6 (2003): 1216–24.
Gauguin, Paul, and Roger Cucchi. *Gauguin à la Martinique: Le musée imaginaire complet de ses peintures, dessins, scuptures, céramiques, les faux, les lettres, les catalogues d'expositions.* Vaduz: Calivran Anstalt, 1979.
Lionnet, Françoise. "Inscriptions of Exile: The Body's Knowledge and the Myth of Authenticity." *Callaloo* 15, no. 1 (Winter 1992): 30–40.
Nesbitt, Nick. "Caribbean literature in French: Origins and development." In *The Cambridge History of African and Caribbean Literature,* 643–69. Cambridge: Cambridge University Press, 2008.
Rinne, Suzanne, and Joëlle Vitiello. *Elles écrivent des Antilles (Haïti, Guadeloupe, Martinique).* Paris: L'Harmattan, 1997.
Vété-Congolo, Hanétha. "Rehvana's 'Negritudism' or Mat(h)ildana's Métissage—Marronnage in Suzanne Dracius' *L'autre qui danse* and *L'âme soeur.*" *Postcolonial Text* 3, no. 1 (2007).